Turn to Burn

Michael F. Stewart

Renaissance
Diverse Canadian Voices

PressesRenaissancePress.ca

First edition 2025

Cover design by Martin Stiff of Amazing15
Interior design by Hannah Wells.
Edited by Callia Paige, Kiri Stockwood, and Samira Aden.

Legal deposit, Library and Archives Canada, September 2025.

Paperback ISBN: 978-1-990086-93-9
Ebook ISBN: 978-1-990086-99-1

Renaissance Press - pressesrenaissancepress.ca

Renaissance acknowledges that it is hosted on the traditional, unceded land of the Anishinabek, the Kanien'kehá:ka, and the Omàmìwininìwag. We acknowledge the privileges and comforts that colonialism has granted us and vow to use this privilege to disrupt colonialism by lifting up the voices of marginalized humans who continue to suffer the effects of ongoing colonialism.

Printed in Gatineau at
Imprimerie Gauvin
Depuis 1892
gauvin.ca

The author gratefully acknowledges Ottawa City's Cultural Funding Unit.

To my daughters—shine.

Chapter One

Soon, Nike would burn.

Ahead, her father hunted through the pools of shadow that filled Kensington Market's empty produce stalls. Signs of the alien's passage hung in stringy, viscous tendrils from a bakery's awning and drooled down the edge of a fire hydrant.

A notification lit her phone. She fumbled to shield the glow, bright in the dark.

Too late.

Her dad spun, coat flaring. "Get off that thing," he hissed, thunderstorms raging behind his gray eyes. He jabbed a finger toward the fire escape. "It's up there."

She followed his arm into the alley's murk but saw nothing.

Without looking, her fingers tapped *gtg*—or so she hoped. She slid the phone away. "I want to go out tonight … after," she said.

Her father's gaze had already swept back to the alleyway.

"I know it'll be late, but can I?"

He stomped ahead. An overripe dragon fruit burst beneath his boot, the stink of sweet rot hanging thick in the air.

Nike clenched her gloved hand, pressure easing the pain of still-raw fingers but doing nothing to dampen her irritation. Her father's gray oilskin coat half-vanished into the mist. The hem of hers flickered with embroidered flames, like a witch in a bonfire.

A violet glow erupted from the ultraviolet light strapped to her father's palm, illuminating graffiti she'd painted last week. Beneath the wall, a snoring man lay stretched out on a cardboard box, his grimy socks pointed toward them.

"There," her dad said, as if she could see anything. All she made out was the sleeping man and the raitgur's snot-trail fluorescing under the ultraviolet glare, betraying the evidence of their enemy, *his* enemy.

"Light up."

He was telling her to set herself on fire. The least he could do was answer her question.

"So, can I?" Nike whispered.

"Light up?" He wasn't even looking at her.

"No. Go out with Joula, after."

Her father lifted a hand, palm aimed at the sleeping man. "It'll be too late. What are you burning tonight?"

If they finished fast, she'd have time. Joula wanted a paint-off. Graffiti was best done after dark anyway.

"My butt," Nike said.

Her dad turned sharply, eyes flint.

She stood firm, chin high. "My right butt cheek."

"Bone, Nike. I need bone."

Nike carefully tugged off her glove to reveal bandages. Her fingernail itched at the tape, catching the edge. She unwound the gauze, wincing with every orbit of her hand. Beneath, fire had carved away her pinky and most of the finger beside it, leaving behind raw, glossy skin slick with salve.

He looked away. "Your buttock would be worse. It may seem like a good idea because of size, but flesh burns too fast these days."

"So you're saying I have a fat ass?"

"Nike."

She grabbed his shoulder and slung her neck forward to squint into eyes nearly level with hers. "Trayling."

Their stares clashed.

With a warning in his tone, he corrected her, "Dad," he said, and glanced back at the alley. "Its tentacle is on his face. I need you. One more minute, and the man is gone."

Nike's fingers found the chain around her neck, drawing out a thick slab of chewed leather. She slipped the leather between her teeth and bit down, the earthy taste churning her stomach. From her coat pocket, she plucked a gold Zippo, flicked it open, and dragged the striker across her arm. Fire chased shadows.

The ruined skin of her hand caught. It fizzed, then *lit*, scabs crackling, the scent of beef on charcoal rising. She jerked her head away. Like all Burner sources, her flesh lit like cardboard.

Her father's hand glowed. Then he sucked up more power until her finger blazed like a road flare and his hand filled with a fireball.

"Good." He swept a leg back to brace himself and lifted his blazing hand toward the sleeping man in the alley. Fire rolled in his palm.

Her finger seared, its flame magnifying from orange to yellow to white. She bit hard on the leather, tears blurring her vision, a scream coiling tight in her throat. She couldn't see what her father aimed at. He always described the raitgur as a sort of deep-ocean squid, translucent and pulsing with bruised bioluminescence that only Burner fire could snuff.

Energy suckled oxygen. Air crackled. Pain built until her father's arm jerked with recoil. A spike of agony, quickly swallowed, and then relief. A fireball hurtled into the alley, sending something invisible tumbling back into the shadows, sparks fading, darkness returning.

"Did you get it?" Nike rasped. Her hand stung. She hated the pain, resenting the drugs she'd need to take later to dull it. The glow of his outstretched hand competed with the flicker of her still-burning second finger's blue pilot light.

Her father lowered his arm, started to turn—

Then *whirled*.

Agony blinded her. Magnesium-white light swallowed her vision. Heat tightened her skin, instantly drying her cheeks. Fire siphoned sound from the alley, leaving only her frothy, hard-fast breathing and the rattle of a raitgur spine on pavement. The alley reeked of ozone and charred seaweed.

"I missed, I guess." Hot fingers fell on her shoulder. She shrugged them off. "Came at me. Dead now," he said.

When her eyes cleared, her father's broad, scruffy face loomed before hers.

"I'm sorry, Nike," he added. "I'm so sorry. I'm burning more—I don't know why."

She saw it then. Her second finger was gone. Skin split and cooked. Two nubs of knucklebone.

She spat out the leather.

Her father flinched. "Go see Joula, okay, Kitten? Be home by two."

The raitgur spine smoked at his feet, but she couldn't tell if she was smelling burnt alien or burnt Nike.

She hurried away, tugging her coat tighter despite the summer heat. Two blocks later, she doubled over, vomiting Pad Thai into another alley. Her uninjured fingers pressed against a cinderblock for support.

"A little upchuck never bothered me none," a voice slurred from the darkness.

The words were followed by the slosh of liquid in a bottle, the scrape of boots.

Nike wiped her mouth and shoved off the wall. She lifted a precious, trembling middle finger.

By the time she hit a busier street, she found her voice again.

"Asshole."

But the word was quiet. Tight with anguish.

Spoken only to herself.

Chapter Two

In the narrow alleyway, metal raked stone as Trayling shoveled the remains of the raitgur into a pile, careful to scrape every last bit of ash and spine from the cracks. Behind him, the man snored on, oblivious—likely sleeping off whatever had put him there in the first place.

Alcohol had little effect on Trayling—not with a Burner's metabolism—but nights like this made him wish it did. His mind kept circling back to Nike's hand. Half a finger gone in a single burning. Far too much. When she was younger, he'd only had to take the tiniest tip of a finger, letting it heal before moving to the next. A slow rotation—ten days before coming back to the first. Back then, the hunt had been a quiet game played with her daddy, the pain readily salved by his praise and an ice cream sundae. Back then, the hunting had been good.

He scooped ash into a black plastic bag and slid the now-cool spine in along with it—Major Santana hated when melted plastic ruined a specimen. The man behind him muttered something, shifted, and settled back into sleep. He'd never know how close he'd come to infection. To the living death that followed.

A bottle of Canadian Club rolled over to clink against the brick wall. At the sound, something twitched in the shadows.

Trayling froze. His eyes, still crisp from burning, swept over the brick, his ultraviolet light picking up the faintest glimmers. There—a tendril of unnatural purple light squished into a crack in the mortar.

He might have missed it without the contrast of the garish orange flames of some melodramatic graffiti. He'd never found the right words to describe a raitgur's glow; to call it light wasn't quite right. More like if darkness could shine. If shadows could thrum.

Trayling glanced over his shoulder. "Nike," he whispered. His hand dug for his phone, thumbed a quick message—his location. She'd know what it meant. Without her, he was nothing, and the man would be lost. Trayling twitched in Nike's direction, but he'd never catch her in time.

The raitgur's tendrils dripped down the wall. If he couldn't burn it, he could at least give the man a chance.

"Hey!" he barked.

The snoring stuttered.

Alien flesh slopped onto pavement, pulling toward its target.

Trayling lunged in, kicked the man's ankle, and leapt back before the raitgur could latch on. The man only grunted. A tentacle hooked into his belt loop, slithered up his stomach. Trayling kicked him again, harder.

"Get up! Get outta here!"

The man's eyelids fluttered, but his gaze was unfocused. He sagged back, head lolling.

"No, no," Trayling hissed. The raitgur sloughed up the man's chest, eager light coruscating within its body. It lowered over his face. A tendril slithered past his lips.

Only Burner fire could save him now. And Nike was gone.

The man's body whipsawed around his head, which remained static. Raitgur flesh brightened for a moment, revealing the inner wiring of the creature. The thrashing slackened as the alien glow waned and then faded into darkness. The man's breathing deepened, and his knees curled to his chest. His head tucked into his knees.

Now nothing could help him.

Trayling swore.

The raitgur shifted, turning toward him. No eyes. No face. But Trayling felt it watching him.

He wrapped the excess plastic around the spine, slapped his skateboard to the ground, and whirred away. Guilt clung to him like a bad smell, but he was powerless.

There was already so much to be guilty for.

Two raitgurs. How could he have missed the second? How could he have missed his shot on the first? Not that he'd never missed, but a single squid had never cost Nike so much. He'd been sure he'd hit with his first blast. Could have sworn he saw the squid go rolling.

He juddered now with the same nervous energy he had after every burning, his skull full of the euphoric buzz that he'd always tried to tamp down in the face of Nike's pain.

Outside Kensington Market, pedestrians, cyclists, and cars multiplied, and he was back in the hurry of Toronto. Trayling wove through traffic, desperate for distraction. He leaned into a turn off Spadina onto Queen, barely dodged an annoyed sausage cart vendor, and shot toward

Moss Park. Headquarters was the backend of a massage parlour hidden amongst the mix of subsidized housing, discount stores, pawn shops, and his favourite skate shop. The electric longboard in the window called to him as he passed it, gleaming behind plate glass.

Men lined up outside the shelter across the street as Trayling hopped the curb and kicked his board into his hand. Skunky smoke mixed with the reek of urine, exhaust, and sodden summer heat.

A bell jangled as he entered Healing Touch. The scarred walls were the colour of the decade-old tightie-whities Trayling kept balled in the back of his drawers. Master Corporal Tyler stood behind the counter, cream-coloured shirt rolled up at the cuffs to accommodate her black, tank-barrel arms. Nearby, an old woman in a frilly silk blouse sat waiting, a skirt pooling past where her legs should have been. At her side, a table offered a fan of well-thumbed Chatelaine magazines selling "Top Relationship Fixes." The old woman was a source for the Rosedale Burner like Nike was a source for Trayling. Her fancy electric wheelchair said money. The hungry glint in her eyes said she always got what she wanted.

Trayling blanked on her name. Marnie? Margot? He saluted instead. She licked her upper lip in response.

"Room four, Trayling," Tyler said.

"Unless you're looking for a massage?" the old woman added, laughter like a snake's rattle.

A sharp bleat at Tyler's console cut the air. The soldier went rigid. Trayling stepped aside as she yanked out her sidearm and levelled it at the old woman's face.

The woman smiled up at the barrel.

The door clicked. A put-together middle-aged Burner, Sylvain, swept inside, bulbous diamonds dragging at her earlobes. They'd refract flames nicely. She barely glanced at the gun before sighing. "That really necessary, Tyler?"

"It's customary to leave your source out of range. I'm here for everyone's safety. Ma'am."

Sylvain rolled her eyes. "I'm not tying my mother up outside like a dog."

"Thanks, Corporal," Trayling said. "I feel safer."

A Burner and a source together might as well be a loaded gun. And Burners didn't play well with each other.

The old woman cackled.

"You're clear for entry, sir," Tyler said.

Trayling ducked through the door. The lock clicked behind him. Lights flickered off, then back on as he moved down the hall. The rooms on the right—'A' through 'C'—were for massage therapy. The numbered doors on the left were for military use. He only ever went to number four at the end of the hall. He leaned his face against the retinal scanner, another click was followed by a hiss, and he shouldered the door open.

"Yes, only one," he said, before the room's lone occupant could ask.

Major Santana stood over a stainless-steel slab. She laughed. "Good evening to you too, Trayling." Calipers pinched the width of a spine. Her black hair barely made it into a bun, a swoop of bangs covering her forehead. A lab coat squared off her body and hid the heat Trayling knew she packed on her hip. The room looked more like a basement lounge than an alien morgue—decorated with couches, a bean bag chair, even a lava lamp. The commercial fridge was as likely to hold beer as samples of snotties. Major Santana was as likely to laugh as give orders.

"Rough night," he muttered, attempting to relieve a sudden tightness in his chest and voice.

She stepped toward him. On the slab before her ranked a dozen spines, all close to the same length, close to the length of the one in his bag.

"Let's have a Coke." She pointed to one of the couches pushed up to the side wall.

"Not ready for therapy."

"It's a lonely job, Trayling. I know it. You know it. There's a reason I've served longer than any unit head since a certain meteor punched a hole in Toronto and brought our malignant hitchhikers in with it." Trayling struggled under the major's smirk. His wife Analia had had a smirk like hers. "And why's that, do you think?" she asked. He looked away. His mind was still in that alley. Still caught between the euphoria of burning and the sound of Nike's seething breaths. She stepped closer. "Because I know we're helping people."

His jaw tightened. "Is that enough?"

"Absolutely. But you have to believe it. And …" She smiled. "That's tricky when we're dealing in invisible aliens."

Trayling sank onto the couch, lifted his hand, and curled his last two fingers down. "I'm burning her bones right off."

Santana's mouth worked, her lips parting before she swallowed. "That's the price, right? Can't burn without a source." She opened his haversack and slid the plastic bag out with the spine inside. "Odd though, you've always had a low burn ratio. One of the lowest. What's changed?"

"I try not to burn, but tonight …" He shook his head. "Not only tonight, the last month or so. I've needed to burn way more of her."

"If you're burning bone, I recommend the index fingers first." Santana's voice was steady, matter-of-fact. Trayling could only nod. "Most Burners start with pinkies, but it's a mistake. The brain adapts to the loss of the index finger faster. The pinky's important for grip."

"We're well past pinkies," he muttered. "How do I stop it?"

"Have you spoken to Chuck? Last I heard, Charlotte still had all her fingers." Santana cleared her throat. "I'm sorry. I only mean to say, he might have ideas on how to improve the burn ratio."

Chuck ran things in the financial district. His source was his daughter, Charlotte, but she was young—maybe not even in her teens.

"Chuck's an ass."

Santana snorted. "He is that."

"What about Ambrose?"

"He's gone off the map. Haven't heard from him since his daughter …"

"Yeah. Me neither. Not since the funeral."

A silence stretched between them, heavy with everything unsaid. Then Santana turned back to her work. "How's the relationship with Nike?"

He shrugged. "Nothing to do with it."

"There's a correlation between burn efficiency and relationship closeness."

"The relationship's good." He coughed, rolled off the couch. "This is sounding a lot like therapy."

"You might need a little. Not like you can talk to a real therapist about any of this." Her laughter filled the room, unexpectedly light. Then her tone sharpened. "Nike is sixteen?"

Santana moved closer, her hips pressing against the slab.

"Seventeen," he said.

"A woman."

"Nearly."

"No," she corrected, eyes gleaming, "a woman."

She grinned. At his discomfort? At some private memory?

"Sex?"

His mind blanked. "What?"

"Is she sexually active?"

"Oh. No. I don't know. No. Maybe." He fumbled in his coat, producing several vials. "These two are snotties from Kensington Market. This is from Dundas and Bathurst."

"When am I going to convince you that snotties aren't particularly interesting, biologically speaking?"

He shook his head. "Just trying to help. Or have you found a cure already?"

Her smile faded. "I'm getting closer. We're trying."

"I know. I'm sorry."

He picked up the spine. Laid it next to the others on the slab.

"You're five off quota for the month."

"Nike wanted to go out with a friend, and after I burned her … I'll make it up." He hated to fail Santana. Hated more to burn Nike.

"There are going to be increased infections in your district."

He thought of the sleeping man, curled into himself like a dying spider. His district. His responsibility. "I can handle it."

"The Italians want more quota," she said. "It would mean less damage to your daughter."

His pulse spiked. "You can't ask that of me." He met her gaze, hard now. "I can handle it."

Any other Burner, maybe. But not Fumo.

Santana inspected the spine, its oblong length, the serrated edge.

"That's not your call." She gauged its size, tape measure clattering as it rewound. "This one was near reproductive maturity."

"It's the same length as the last two. Same as these, too. All exactly the same length? What are the chances of that?"

"Sylvain brought in two. Still waiting on three deliveries."

Which meant another Burner had brought in ten. A huge haul. Maybe the Italians were already poaching from his territory.

"I'll approve this specimen." Santana set the spine down. "You work on your daughter. We need her happy."

"We've a great relationship," he said through clenched teeth.

She smiled, almost indulgent. "Relationships with daughters can be tricky, but they can work." A pause. "My dad and I—we did everything together. I miss him every single day, and I know he's still with me. That's what you want. That level of closeness. It all comes down to love."

Her fingers found the medallion at her sternum, tracing it absently.

Trayling's jaw tensed. "Sounds unhealthy."

He slammed the door on his way out.

In reception, he stopped beside Tyler.

"Who was in before Sylvain?"

"Smoke, Ash, and Fire," she said.

Fumo, Cenere, and Fuoco.

That confirmed it. The remaining spines belonged to the Italians.

How were they tracking so many targets? Even without the lingering effects of burning sharpening his thinking, Trayling's instincts blazed with suspicion.

Chapter Three

The perc was kicking in, but Nike's hand still throbbed ten times too big, stuffed into a black leather glove. She climbed the subway station steps toward the location Joula had texted.

Nike had ignored her dad's message on the train. By then, it had been far too late. No more burning tonight. Tonight, she painted. Better—she duelled. As the drugs dulled her pain, tonight would offer distance from her problems.

Kitten—screw him.

She hooked around a sushi restaurant and slipped into an alley nearly covered with graffiti. How Joula had found a clear canvas for tonight's duel, Nike wasn't sure. Writers had rules, and number one, you didn't paint over someone else's work. Not unless it was crap. But Joula didn't always follow rules. They'd met over a duel like this a year and a half ago—though they hadn't called it that then. Nike had scouted a savage canvas, only to return with her paints to find Joula homing in on it. They'd argued until Nike had challenged Joula to a paint-off—they'd split the canvas in half, whoever won could paint over the other's workspace. They'd been friends ever since.

Joula, at twenty-two, had made it—an independent artist, earning a living. Nike knew how rare that was. If anyone could help her escape her dad cooking her, it was Joula.

Shadows shifted near the alley's end. Joula loved scaring the shit out of her, but Nike was alone, past midnight. Her oilskin was gone, replaced by ratty jeans and one of her dad's old Def Leppard t-shirts she used for painting. Grateful for the cover of darkness, she tucked her gloved hand behind her back and out of sight beneath the base of her backpack.

"You can come out now," she called to the alley walls. A gray rectangle painted on the brick caught her eye—it was a sick canvas.

A low moan drifted from the alley's depths.

Nike clutched her phone tight, wishing she'd pulled the mace from her pack. The moan heightened. As it heightened further, Nike rolled her eyes, shoulders slumping.

"Bitch," she said, switching on the phone's flashlight function and scanning for Joula, who was tucked behind a dumpster, head barely peeking over the edge. "What the hell are you doing?"

The moan broke into giggles, then roiling laughter that did more to soothe Nike's pain than any opioid.

"You made it, girl!" Joula screeched, bounding from the dumpster and yanking Nike into a hug, lifting her clear off the ground. What she lacked in height, she made up for in wiry strength.

"As if I'd let you win by forfeit." Nike sighed at Joula's outfit. The sleek black dress would catch every paint spatter her bare shoulders and cleavage didn't.

Joula's laugh cut short as she tilted her head toward Nike's hidden hand. "Show me."

Nike huffed, but Joula snatched at her elbow, pulling her arm around. Nike whined as Joula tugged off the glove. Underneath, the hand was bandaged.

"Another burn?"

"Glass-blowing accident," Nike said. Best excuse she'd come up with since leaving her dad's townhouse. She knew Joula would be triggered by the wound—ever since Joula had fled her abusive family, she assumed everyone else needed to leave theirs, too.

Joula wagged a finger under Nike's nose. "I told you—one more burn, and I'm calling protective services." Joula seemed taller when she got into Nike's face like this.

"It's not as bad as it looks."

"Your fingers look fucking gone."

"An accident. Let's paint."

"No one does that to themselves." Joula pulled out her phone.

"Don't. It's complicated." For eight years, Nike's dad had been burning her. Never enough to lose function, just enough to hurt. She'd seen the people they'd saved—believed in it. Was a piece of bone worth a life? That was the real question now. That man in the alley—he could live his life because of what they did. But Nike was starting to wonder when her own rights would kick in.

Joula leaned close, voice low. "You don't need to take this shit."

"It's not what you think. I'd tell you."

"You'll tell me what really happened?"

Nike wanted to. She'd been explaining away burns ever since she'd met Joula in that wintry alley and fought over the space to tag. But she'd sworn to her father she'd never tell anyone about the raitgur. "Yes. But not now. I'm here to forget this shit."

Joula stared hard at her.

"You don't want cops showing up." Nike forced a grin, unshouldering her backpack and pulling out a sweating beer. "They'll bust me for underage drinking, and I'll tell them you're my supplier."

Joula hesitated, then reached for the beer. "Fine. But you're sleeping on my couch tonight, so I know you're safe," she said, snapping the cap off the bottle. Nike saluted her. "Let's do this. I had to chase off two other writers already."

They stood before the fragment of gray wall. A faded swastika peeked through the fresh paint—painting over hate was always fair game.

"What's your plan?" Joula asked.

"Not telling."

"You pick sides."

A crack ran through the left side, screwing with Nike's idea. Tonight, she planned on exploring pain. She pointed to the right side. "Two hours."

"One hour," Joula countered. "You were late and I've work in the Joula-cave tomorrow."

The Joula-cave, her workshop … an invitation into her secret lair would mean something to Nike, a shift in their relationship to artistic equals. Nike couldn't create a refined piece in an hour, but she wanted to prove to Joula that she was worthy of being called an artist. Maybe if she beat her tonight, Joula would finally invite Nike into the workspace she jealously guarded.

With a beep, Joula started the timer. Nike dropped her pack and fished out her supplies, including more beer and a mask. All thoughts of aliens, infections, and burning faded into the shadows. Three times, Joula told her to stop humming before Nike realized Joula hadn't painted in half an hour.

"What're you doing?" Nike asked.

"Thinking." Joula winked. "I like yours. Gonna be real hard to beat that."

Nike squinted at her. "You're messing with me."

A scuff of a boot froze them both. Nike calculated the distance to her mace. A man stood at the alley entrance—broad-shouldered, Black, that was all she could tell even with the light of two phones on him.

"Sahle!" Joula ran to hug him. Nike sagged in relief, tugging her mask down around her neck.

Closer now, she took him in—an inch shorter than her, which was unfortunate but not a dealbreaker. Gorgeous cheekbones. A chest built for cats to nap on. A smile she wanted to smother.

"Nike, meet Sahle," Joula said. She had him by the wrist. "Sahle's a friend of Martinez—the jewellery maker. Filigree like you wouldn't believe." Nike just nodded. She could never keep track of Joula's entourage. "Nike's a fellow artist." Joula grinned. "Tell her about yourself, Sahle."

She had a way of putting everyone on their heels.

"Uh… okay," he said. "I'm at university, studying philosophy, working part time. What else … I don't know … sunsets, walks on the beach? Is this my Tinder profile?" Nike laughed. Swiped right in her mind as his warm gaze fell on her. "What about you?"

What could Nike say? That she was seventeen, starting senior year in a couple months, counting down to prom, not really an artist—even though it was the only thing she'd ever loved—not old enough for Tinder? That the last people who promised to pay for her painting refused when they saw it?

"I prefer dawns," she said. "The beach is shit for walking on. Sand gets everywhere. What brings you to a dark alley? Serial killing?"

He blinked, then let out a deep, warm laugh.

Joula cut in, "Um, Sahle forgot to mention that he works at homeless shelters and connects hookers with community services."

"Sex trade workers," Sahle corrected, still smiling. "You paint?"

Nike hesitated, then instinctively stepped in front of her half-finished piece. "Yeah, but I'm not done."

Joula tapped her wrist. "In fact, Nike has fifteen minutes left before I'm proclaimed the winner."

"What? No way, this was a time-out," Nike protested.

"I only have fifteen minutes to do mine. Same rules."

"Is he here to—"

"No better distraction than a hot, single man," Joula teased.

"You used him, conniving—"

"Actually," Sahle said, cheeks flushing, "I was in the area anyway. There's a guy I'm worried about. I want to find him. I'll see you later?"

His eyes met Nike's. She nodded, torn between the burning witch on the wall and the man walking away. "Nice to meet you."

With her own face smouldering, she turned back to work.

A minute later, Joula joined her, shaking a can of black spray paint.

"Can't believe you," Nike muttered.

"You mad?"

"Yes … shit." She botched a contour. The cap was too fat. "Omigod, he's fit."

Joula laughed. "Yes, he is that." Then, all was fumes and bursts of black and red.

Nike focused, blocking out everything but the art. She barely glanced at Joula, though she'd heard her heaving plywood from behind the dumpster.

Nike's witch took shape—sensual, powerful, half-clothed. A seductress, and she burned the worse for it, wreathed in flames, vengeful fire licking up from the bones of conquered men. Anguish twisted her features. It was rushed, but good.

She grabbed a can of yellow to add the tagline.

"Can I use that after you?" Joula asked.

"Sure." Nike frowned at Joula's painting. Nearby, the plywood had cutouts. "You used a stencil? That's cheating."

"No one said we couldn't."

Nike studied Joula's piece. A little boy stood on a pedestal, a statue in silhouette, leaning back, holding his dick.

"What the hell?"

Joula snatched the yellow spray paint and drew an arc from the boy's penis to Nike's burning witch.

The kid was pissing on the fire.

"Water beats fire, every time."

"That's not …"

"You're predictable, Nike. Stop it. Art is ninety percent idea, ten percent execution. And the idea can't be predictable."

Nike stared at the wall. Despite the careful shading, the vibrant colour, Joula's stark black-and-white and *yellow* work killed hers.

The tagline she'd planned now felt ridiculous, but she wrote it anyway: *She was asking for it.*

"Asking for a golden shower," Joula said, fists at her sides.

"You're gross."

"You're good, sister. Really good. You deserve more than abuse. Ever think you should start listening to your art?"

Nike's paintings always came back to this—women burning for their choices. She'd perfected them.

But deep down, she knew what her father did wasn't abuse. Or at least it wasn't meant to be. It was the family business—but she didn't want it anymore. She didn't want more of the pain. Joula was out of her parents' house, a few years older than her, but still, could Nike leave? At seventeen, her dad wouldn't stop her. She'd need a job, but she'd been working on that for a week and had sent resumes out to art galleries and stores. Unfortunately, minimum wage might be enough to cover rent on a squalid room. Joula was right. Nike needed to change tactics, to grow.

"I'm moving out," Nike blurted.

Joula high-fived her so hard it stung. "Good girl. Get out of the fire."

Nike grinned, glancing at the wall. Her eyes flicked to Joula's stencils.

"How long did those take? More than an hour?"

Joula hesitated.

"Bam!" Nike jabbed a thumb into her chest. "Winner, by way of disqualification—Nike Highspire!"

CHAPTER FOUR

Trayling waited up for Nike, slouched in a ragged leather chair, a Coke bottle balanced on the arm. His phone sat cold in his palm, no new messages, no replies. He tried to slow the bezoar of fear, anger, and shame calcifying in his gut. Hours ago, he'd tracked her phone to Joula's apartment. It hadn't moved since.

He stopped waiting for her, but not worrying. His fingernails drummed across the wooden armrest as the seconds ticked by on his wristwatch.

3:32 AM.

He forced a smile, his voice lonely in the cold, empty living room. "Happy birthday, baby girl. See you soon."

Twenty years ago, at that exact minute, his eldest daughter, Sabra, had been born. The doctor had pressed her floppy, angry-red helplessness to his bare chest, and he'd drawn in a deep breath of afterbirth, transmuting it with the magic of fatherhood into the sweet smell of new baby glory. He'd cut her umbilical cord. He'd cut both his girls' cords. It felt as though Nike strained at an invisible one now, a cord he wasn't sure he had the strength to sever. Twenty years.

After flipping the phone over, Trayling fell asleep and dreamed of being buried alive. He woke choking on air as if something heavy tamped the dirt above his coffin. Coke glugged from the fallen bottle, pooling at his feet.

Four hours of sleep, four cups of coffee, and a slice of last night's pizza later, he grabbed his backpack and skateboard.

Their townhouse sat in the heart of Little Italy's Burner district, wedged between immaculate homes with wrought iron fences, white concrete lions, pruned, gushing rose bushes, and porches with steps washed and swept with sanctimony. Their house, in contrast, was a blistered, peeling rebellion. Long strips of paint curled from the clapboard. Gravel choked the garden. A raven statuette perched on the gable, watching.

He knew what he was doing. The locals hated his house. No one more than Fumo, the Italian Burner who had sought the Little Italy licence for years, only to watch Trayling be handed it. That pissed Fumo off, and Trayling thrived on pissing people off.

Living in Little Italy would've been better if Nike weren't gluten intolerant.

Trayling's wife and eldest daughter lived a mile away, in a private long-term care unit for psychiatric patients. Except Analia and Sabra weren't psychiatric patients—but he couldn't tell the doctors what they really had. Part of Santana's role was to use samples of snotties, ashes, and spine to discover a cure for their infections. That was the deal.

Trayling burned the enemy, kept the infestation contained—if not eradicated—and in return, the government protected him from those who weren't in the know. Paid him per spine. Worked on a cure. They wouldn't pay for the private care, though. No dice.

The facility specialized in chronic illness and catatonic patients. A quiet place. Rooms circling a central rec area and a nurse's station attended by quiet nursing staff and a doctor doing rounds. Despite the building's cold, government-gray exterior, the nurses waved him onto the ward with glowing smiles. He spared a moment to conjure a daisy from behind a nurse's ear and presented it gallantly.

"Good morning, Trayling." Nurse Chui offered him a bowl of thick, unappetizing goo. "You look …" Chui coughed into his fist. "Good."

"I look like shit," Trayling corrected, taking the bowl. "Part of the job. Buskers work night shifts." Analia and Sabra's room was a double, each bed ringed by a privacy curtain.

"I've known you for eight years, and in all that time you didn't age. If you think I'm just being nice, ask half the nurses in here—Jenefer over there once called you an immortal Clooney in his prime. Thought you were aging backwards for a while. Until lately."

Trayling scoffed. "Forty-five's like flipping a switch. Suddenly I need glasses and more than two hours of sleep."

"Two hours?"

"Not anymore."

"That's what I mean." Chui snapped his fingers. "You've been lowered down to the rest of us mortals."

"Really appreciate the pep talk."

"Just worried. Cancer can do things like this. You have a family doc?"

"I'll get right on it." Trayling waved the nurse away, holding back snarkier remarks. He might not appreciate Chui's attention, but it was what he wanted for his family.

He pulled back Analia's privacy curtain and set down his haversack, keeping Sabra's side closed. Chui had already raised the bed, propped her up with pillows, and cleared yesterday's wilted flowers from the vase on the bedside table. Trayling pulled three daisies from his bag and slipped them into the vase. One for Sabra, too.

"One minute, honey," he murmured. "I have to talk to Mom."

Analia's mouth hung open.

Trayling dropped to his knees beside her. Whispered the prayer his mentor, Ambrose, had passed down.

"The Burner burns. The source giveth of her body. Where evil goes, the flames shall shine …" He looked up at her blank face. "And the broken will rise again, cleansed by fire."

Slowly, Trayling rose and sat back in the chair, then took her limp, cool fingers in his own. "Love." He worked the joints gently. "Our baby's twenty today. All grown up. Remember when she fit in the crook of my arm?" He cradled the ghost of her. "I do. But …" His voice faltered. He needed Analia. He needed absolution. "I'm no good at this, Kitten. I hurt Nike. I'm losing her. Lost her, maybe. I need you."

He squeezed Analia's fingers, but they reminded him of Nike's burned hand. "Santana says the worse the relationship, the worse the burn," he whispered. "Vicious cycle, right? The more I hurt her, the more she hates me, the worse I hurt her." He swallowed hard, searching Analia's face for judgment. For an answer. She stared on. "Something's wrong with me."

Chui was right about that much.

Trayling had sent a message to Ambrose. He hadn't spoken to the old source since the funeral of his Burner daughter. Maybe he'd have insight into how to reduce the burns—or maybe Trayling just needed someone to talk to. He had no one else. His relationship with the other five Burners—Chuck, Lena, Sylvain, Farhan, and Fumo—wasn't exactly cozy.

"You're right," he said, watching Analia's vacant expression. "I'll keep trying. Try harder. A father never gives up."

He spooned the thick goo into her mouth. Waited for her to swallow. "Go ahead, eat up." When she didn't, he stroked her throat until she did. Another spoonful. "We got one last night. Tricky bastard—took two burns." Another bite. "No, it wasn't any bigger than usual. Weird that it was the exact same size as the last ones."

His voice dropped to a whisper. "Nothing like the one that got you."

He fed her again, voice quiet, thoughtful. "They were bigger back then. But they're getting harder to burn. I'm seeing patterns. Once I explain them to Nike, she'll understand why we need to keep going."

Chui's shadow interrupted as Trayling scraped the last of the bowl. "Yummy," Trayling said, covering the silence. The nurse held another bowl of slurry. "Won't be needing that today." Trayling dug back into his haversack and pulled out a chocolate cupcake stacked with icing.

"I'll blend it," the nurse said.

"Not yet." Trayling shifted in his chair and pulled Sabra's curtain back. Though three years older than Nike, Sabra was smaller, younger-looking, in a rainbow t-shirt that read: "It's my birthday! Fuck you!" Even at twelve, she'd been dark, impulsive, and rebellious. Trayling had always tried to respect that.

"Her favourite shirt, thanks," he murmured, placing a stuffed bear beside her and tucking it beneath the sheet. He set a novel—*Pride and Prejudice*—on her lap. "We can read that later."

From his bag, he pulled a lighter and a birthday candle, stabbing it into the cupcake before striking the flame. "Happy birthday," he whispered, then held the cupcake out. "Make a wish, Sabra."

He gave her a second, then brought the flame closer to her lips. Silently making his own wish. After a moment, he leaned in and helped blow it out, sending wisps of smoke curling skyward. "Good girl."

Chui held out his hand for the cupcake. "I'll take care of it."

"First, we sing."

Chui flushed. "You really don't want that."

"For me."

"I'm not paid enough for this."

"For Sabra, then."

When Chui didn't answer, Trayling started. His rocky baritone filled the space. Chui sang like his testes were being run through a meat grinder.

"That was awful," Trayling said, as faint applause drifted from the hallway.

"I warned you. My daughter doesn't let me sing. Says I ruin it."

"So yours hates you too?"

Chui smirked. "Might, if I existed to her. She does these dances and sells advertising on some app. Bought herself a laptop yesterday with her own cash."

"Maybe we both can learn something from our kids," Trayling said.

"You don't want to see me dance. If you thought my singing was bad …"

Trayling's gaze lingered on Sabra. He smiled, remembering the bear-hug tackles she used to give him. "Any new treatments coming down the pipe?"

The creases on Chui's face deepened.

Trayling plowed on. He always plowed on. "We could try transcranial magnetic stimulation again? More ECT?"

"Trayling, you're a good caregiver. One of the best I've seen. Every day we learn more about depression, but Analia's and Sabra's cases are exceptionally treatment-resistant."

Trayling nodded. It was up to him and Santana. He pulled headphones from his bag and connected them to his phone.

"New death metal playlist?" Chui asked.

"Gotta give her something to work out to." Trayling flashed what he thought was the hand signal for devil's horns.

Chui laughed. "Yeah, that means 'I love you.' But I know what you were going for. Back in a jiffy."

Trayling manually shaped the acid-mauled fingers of his left hand into the "I love you" sign, then lifted both hands toward his wife and daughter. If they couldn't hear, maybe they could see.

After their hour of physio, he trimmed Sabra's bangs, then spent the rest of the day with her reading *Pride and Prejudice* until Chui nudged him awake.

"I'm off shift."

Trayling ignored the amused glances from staff as he packed up, kissed his wife and daughter, then skateboarded home toward an empty house. But Chui's expression had been tight with worry. Trayling wondered what would happen to his wife and daughter if he were gone. Would Nike be able to afford their private care? He'd prepared for the eventuality, but not enough. Not nearly enough.

For the first time in forty-eight hours, he crashed in an actual bed.

After what seemed a moment, he jolted awake to movement below.

Scarred fingers wiped drool. Old keloid scars, which ran from hand-to-shoulder, rasped over his lips. More clanking brought him fully awake. He grabbed the baseball bat stowed beside his bed and padded to the doorframe.

In the hall, he listened. Footsteps.

"Nike?" he hissed.

No reply. No end to the furtive noises.

He took the stairs hard and fast, leaping the last few, bat raised—

"Oh, hiya, Pops."

Nike stood in the kitchen, earbuds in, holding a beer and a pizza box. The relief at seeing her, safe, quickly turned to annoyance.

"Hi. Ya?" He left the bat on a step and entered the galley kitchen.

"What? Sorry?" She plucked out an earbud.

"You didn't come home."

She shrugged. "Stayed at Joula's. Sleepover."

"I want you to text me next time."

"You're always telling me to get off my phone."

"It's disrespectful to not reply to my texts."

Nike sipped her beer. "Sorry, Daddy."

Normally, "Daddy" would end the argument. Not tonight. He sat at the Ikea kitchen table. "Sabra's birthday was today. Did you visit?"

"Are you looking for a fight?"

Maybe. "I want you to consider your responsibilities."

"I made you pizza." She set the beer down and opened the box. Gluten-free. Ham and pineapple. Passive-aggressive as hell.

"We can't afford takeout if we're not on quota." He shut the box.

"So it's about money. Why is it all the other Burners have money except us?"

"Because we need to think about our future."

"My future? Or Mom's and Sabra's?"

"You don't want to care for your family?" The question hung dangerously. He feared her answer. "Nike, I'm just trying to understand you. Beer isn't gluten free and it's not a good breakfast."

"Um … I'm only intolerant, and … it's 8 p.m.?"

"Which is breakfast if you sleep all day."

"I wouldn't have to sleep all day if I didn't have to work all—"

"You were at a party." When she went back to the fridge, he held it shut. "No more beer."

As a Burner, alcohol and drugs may have no effect on him, but that wasn't true of a source. Nike had started keeping beer in the fridge a few months ago. When the burns worsened.

"I'm getting hot sauce. Or is that a crime now?"

He swallowed, unconvinced. She wouldn't look him in the eye.

"It wasn't a party," she continued. "I've been … looking for a job."

"We have a job."

"YOU have a job. I'm something to burn."

"I can't do it without you."

"That's not my problem!"

"It's all of our problems, Kitten." His tone softened. "Your mother and sister—"

"Mom and Sabra are *gone*. They have been gone for eight years and I have been a tag-along ever since. Am I supposed to be dragged around every night, single because of—" She lifted her burned hand. "Until I'm ash?"

Trayling shut his eyes. He wouldn't win this fight.

"I don't know what's wrong with you, but last night cost me a finger," she said. "This has to stop while I can still hold a can of spray paint."

Trayling thought back to his promise to Analia: that he'd try.

"If we don't do our job, more people will be infected. People like your mom and sister."

Nike tensed, lips parting as if to argue, but he was already moving—crossing the room to a map that hung beside the table. On the map, roads and green spaces were spattered with red dots. On each dot, a number.

"I want to show you something." His finger jabbed at a cluster of dots blooming on the west side of their district, Little Italy. "Look—this spread of raitgur is younger. All about the same age."

The numbers on the dots weren't random; they corresponded to spine length, measured in inches. Santana wasn't the only one keeping track. The data didn't lie.

Trayling's hand swept east across the district, to Chinatown. "Over here, it's scattered. Some young, some old—what we'd expect. But here—" His fist thumped the southeastern area of the map. "Nothing. Not a single one this year. The distribution doesn't make sense. Why the cluster of similarly aged raitgur?"

Nike exhaled sharply. "Let other Burners deal with it. I can't even see the frigging things."

Trayling's jaw slackened. "You can see their spines. Their snotties. The statistics." His arm flung toward the map. "You can see the people in the hospital. Your infected family."

She shrugged, noncommittal.

His voice softened. "You don't believe …?"

"Dad! I believe! You shoot fire from your hands! Acid burns suddenly appear on your skin! I see the scars! I'm *flammable*." She splayed her fingers. "I lose pieces of myself. And for what? I don't want this to cost me my life. I feel like the guy in the trolley problem."

"Trolley?"

"Yeah, do you kill one person to save five?"

It wasn't the same. It wasn't.

"My burns and scars are an honor."

Nike snorted. "I want to go to college."

"For what? Art?" The words left him before he could stop.

Her eyes narrowed to slits. "That so wrong?"

"I just want you to feel like you're doing something important."

"You were in mutual fund sales." Her voice turned razor-sharp. "You went to college. Had a normal job. You travelled."

"Exactly! And I wasn't fulfilled. What we do—it matters."

"Like me and my art." Her eyes challenged him, and he knew it wasn't worth engaging further.

Trayling inhaled, steadied. "Hunt with me tonight. Help me figure this out. I'm close."

She probed the inside of her mouth with her tongue. "Can't. Going for a walk."

"With …?"

She looked away.

"If you can't tell me, ask yourself why not."

"Because you'll react like this."

Trayling didn't mean to, but his neck cracked when he turned. Loudly.

"And," she added, "because you don't want me to do anything but follow you around, burning me down piece by piece."

"No—" His hands gripped the table edge until his knuckles whitened. He forced himself to breathe. Calm. "Can I meet him? . . . Her? Them?"

"Him." She hesitated. "But maybe this isn't the best time. Give me some space."

"You've lost weight." His voice softened. "You need more than pizza. You need protein. Burns eat through calories."

"Jesus, Dad—why? So there's more of me to burn?" She grabbed her backpack and headed for the door.

"Not what I meant." The door opened. "Hunting later!" It slammed.

Trayling grabbed what was left of her beer, took a swig, and spat it out. The bottle shattered in the sink.

He stared at the shards.

Then, without another thought, he grabbed his board. He might not be able to burn what he found tonight, but he could still hunt. Still scout. Still solve the mystery of the alien cluster.

Chapter Five

For the third time, Nike caught her fingers drifting to the hidden pocket she'd sewn into her dress for easy access to her phone. "Concealed carry," Joula called it. She forced Nike to sew holsters into every one of her own outfits.

Nike itched to text Joula about how hot Sahle looked in his ripped jeans and tight shirt that—praise be—revealed abs she could lose nails on. The world of Queen West looked hot too, shimmered around them—clubbers in leather and bare skin.

Sahle grinned. "You're smiling. Covered in fireflies."

"This?" She twirled, her dress flaring up her thighs, facets of sewn crystals sparking under streetlights. "Thanks, I made it. I'm happy. It's my sister's birthday." *As if* she'd forget.

His face softened. "You should be with her."

"I am." Her voice didn't break. "In a way. I celebrate for her. She's sick—in a coma. Has been for years. So I party for her."

"That's ... sad."

"Yeah." Nike darted through a cluster of guys, laughing as she emerged.

"But you're laughing."

"Remembering." She exhaled. "We had a clubhouse in our apartment's boiler room. Part of it had been bricked off, but if you were small enough, you could squeeze through a gap between two missing cinderblocks and step into this ... fairyland of discarded things."

She could still see it—pillows, abandoned stuffed animals, old clothes left behind by renters. Their kingdom of found things.

Truthfully, it had been Sabra's.

Light from a single murky window turned dust motes into pixie dust. Trinkets and religious icons crowded the space—a bric-a-brac sanctuary. One piece, gold gilt and renaissance, always caught Nike's eye. Bobble-headed children painted on wood. Abraham, about to sacrifice his son. Not unlike her father now.

"One person's trash is another kid's treasure, right?" Sahle mused.

Nike smirked. "I think some of the bronzes and paintings came from a retired priest's storage locker, not the garbage." She bit her lip. "But he probably shouldn't have had them either. Sabra was a free spirit. I was just happy to tag along." It had been their lair. In it, they had been truly free.

An image came to mind of her sister, twirling until she fell on a fuzzy chair made of stitched-together teddy bears. Nike hadn't felt as free since. Had stopped looking forward to the future. Tonight was how Nike celebrated her sister—not by visiting the desiccated husk of what she'd become, but by being her. Living for her. "Probably where I got my eclectic style from." She smoothed her dress.

"You majoring in fashion?"

"At college?" Until now she'd managed to keep the conversation out of dangerous territory, like her age, her burnt hand, her high school.

"… What else?"

"College of Art and Design, yup." Compared to the lies Nike usually told about why she had burns or couldn't keep her eyes open in class, saying she was in college seemed pretty tame. She'd tell Sahle her age eventually, once he was ready for it, but for now she didn't think a relationship comprised of a few texts pushed by Joula and half an hour's walk would survive the age difference.

"You make this too?" He tugged at her leather backpack.

"I like textiles."

"It's cool. I couldn't sew a sock, but I bet my mom would love it."

Nike frowned, but not at him—at the snotties hanging from an air conditioner. Fresh. Snotties disintegrated in hours, which meant—

A raitgur was close. Large, judging by the slime trails.

She swallowed hard. Not her district. Not her problem. Which was one of the reasons she'd wanted to meet Sahle here, far from where her father might be doing reconnaissance. She hated that she was automatically scouting for raitgur trails.

"What is it?" Sahle asked.

"What?" She forced a smile.

"You see something?" He shifted, feet light. A fighter's stance.

Nike's pulse kicked up. A lick of movement disappeared into the AC unit. Her body went rigid.

Sahle took a step toward the heap of blankets stuffed beneath it.

"Don't," Nike said. A raitgur could be on them and she'd never know.

Too late. Sahle wasn't listening.

A pair of hot pink running shoes poked out.

Sahle chuckled. "Dan. I'd know those shoes anywhere."

"You know him?"

"Yeah. Was looking for him last night," he said. "Dan, you okay in there?"

"Looks out of it."

"Sleeping rough. You ever try it?"

She shook her head.

"Not recommended."

Nike didn't move as Sahle knelt, slipped a rolled ten into Dan's shoe, then patted his shoulder. "Sleep well, friend."

He turned toward Nike, relaxed and smiling, but she was farther down the sidewalk, hoping Sahle would follow. "You don't need to be afraid of him."

She shook her head, not wanting him to think she was elitist. "That wasn't it …"

"What, then?" he asked, catching up.

"Nothing …" *Alien slime.* The truth would end the date faster than her age. "Just a sense of something. Can't explain it. Nothing we can see."

"Ah, Gorgias."

"Say what?"

"Gorgias. The philosopher. Nothing exists. Even if it did, we couldn't explain it."

"That's checks out."

Next to him, Nike felt small. Not short—small. Sahle was lean, muscular, radiating an energy that crackled in the space between them. And his brain? Way too hot.

"Don't mind me," he said. "Philosophy major, remember?"

"What can you do with that?" His face reddened, and she blurted, "Sorry! That sounded like my dad. I didn't mean it that way."

"It's okay, my mom's always talking about turning learning into action."

"Great. So I sound like your mom, who also likes to sew."

He grinned. "No, she's right. You're right. How will what I learn change what I do? I've been going to protests. Trying to help people like Dan back there. It's hard, though—finding something that really matters." He held her gaze a second too long, then jerked a thumb back in the homeless guy's direction. "You going to the protests with Joula?"

Nike shook her head, heat rising to her face. Joula had asked, but Nike had actively avoided City Hall because of those protests.

"We need to get people off the streets," Sahle said. "That's where they get sick. Where they can't get help. The new fentanyl? It's laced with something bad—turns people into vegetables."

"Shit," she murmured. "That's—awful."

"Oh my god, I'm sorry. Is that what happened to your sister?"

Nike stiffened, shook her head. He didn't push.

"I want to be an artist," she admitted. "But I know it's not enough. It won't change anything."

"Is that your dad talking again?" He shrugged. "Why wouldn't art be enough? Sewing is a serious skill. Just because it's not valued by the establishment because it's deemed feminine, doesn't make it less important."

"Okay, woke dude." She laughed. "But sewing isn't my art." Her fingers found his and when his hand closed on hers, energy ripped through her arm and into her chest. He'd seen what she could do in a rushed forty minutes—but he hadn't seen something she was proud of.

A flicker of doubt crossed his face. Was the date bombing? Of course it was. She'd spent the whole time telling him what she wasn't.

"Come on." She pulled. "Let me show you what I actually do."

Chapter Six

Wind whipped through Trayling's hair, a brief respite from the day's heat, which was still radiating from the asphalt. Moonlight filtered through cell towers, glazing the upper floors of condos and office buildings as he hurtled down the street on his skateboard. Within minutes, he was back in Kensington Market, nearing his last raitgur sighting.

At the first flash of lights ahead, he leaned back, slowing his board. Not cops—an ambulance. A small crowd had gathered, letting him blend in without standing out.

"Heard it was tainted fentanyl," a woman whispered to the person next to her.

The other nodded. "Did the Jitterbug."

Two paramedics rolled a man onto a gurney, then collapsed its legs and slid him into the ambulance. Trayling caught a glimpse of him before the doors closed: the homeless man, eyes vacant, jaw slack. It reminded him too much of Analia. The spectators trickled away, but he stayed. As the ambulance pulled out, the driver's gaze locked briefly onto Trayling, until a building cut off their line of sight and they were gone. Another infection. Another lost soul.

"Know that the Burner sees you. Know that I am coming," he murmured after the retreating vehicle. "The broken will rise again, cleansed by fire."

He texted Nike his location, along with a message: *Meet me in the field. Scouting.*

Nothing moved here but the rats. Trayling lifted his fingers, triggered the ultraviolet light in his palm, and swept the ground for raitgur trails. In the alley, he toed the man's abandoned belongings—a blanket, a gym bag of clothes. Even under blacklight, the whites were so soiled that they didn't brighten. He stepped back. The graffiti-witch on the wall seemed to follow him with her painted eyes.

Her orange flames burned under his UV light. Even without the caption—*'She spoke at the meeting'*—melodramatic or not, the meaning was clear: women were demonized. Maybe witches were just women who refused to conform, and the grain they went against was men. But the artist had used a UV-reactive pigment—an invisible layer meant for those who knew where to look. A message not just about oppression, but about *him*. About the Burner. About Trayling.

One of Nike's?

He studied the tag: HT2B. He couldn't place it, but it *could* be hers.

Even if he was oppressing her, what choice did he have? Raitgur infection caused catatonia—a living death until they found a cure. He was saving lives. Controlling a population of aliens that could explode without their work. Until recently, the cost to Nike had been some bad burns on her hands—not ideal, but they'd always healed well, with no permanent damage. It wasn't until a few months ago that it hadn't been enough, that he'd needed to burn deeper. To the bone.

Maybe Santana was right. Maybe their partnership needed fixing. But without help, Trayling knew exactly how this would end for Nike. Other sources were losing more than fingers. Limbs.

If a little angsty for his taste, the mural was beautiful, but was Nike even *this* good? He didn't have a problem with her pursuing art as a hobby; everyone needed something to escape from pain. But—

A thin strip of mortar between the bricks glowed under his light. He switched it to white. The mortar was missing. It wasn't mortar at all. A snotty smear trailed down the wall.

Trayling drew a hunting blade and probed inside the crack.

Something moved. A translucent tentacle flinched, curling tighter into the space.

"There's the little shit."

The tentacle snapped out. Fast. Razor-sharp.

Agony lanced across Trayling's forehead.

He gasped, hand flying to his bag, yanking out a squirt bottle. Water was his only defense against the acid. He flushed out the burn, feeling a sharp sting as the water dripped down his face.

Hands trembling as he fumbled for his phone, he texted: *Have one.*

Then: *Small. Hurry.*

The alien assholes punched way above their weight. Reversing the phone's camera, he took in the burn, angling the screen to check the damage—a thin red line across his forehead. It would spread, but maybe he'd flushed it fast enough to avoid scarring.

"Damn," he muttered.

He focused, stretched his palm, willed the fire to come.

Nothing.

Nothing would without Nike.

The raitgur launched from the crack. He dodged, slashed with the knife, nicking a tentacle, but the creature barely changed course as it sailed over his shoulder to cling to the far wall. Its tentacles reached for purchase as it climbed.

The raitgur could hurt him. But without Nike, he couldn't kill it.

His fingers gripped the edge of his board. He flipped it onto its wheels, switched the UV light back on, and leaned in to follow.

Chapter Seven

Nike ignored her buzzing phone. This moment was perfect, and she was staying in it. Besides, she didn't want Sahle thinking she was one of those girls who couldn't keep her head out of her screen.

As she pulled him along the sidewalk, a smile touched his lips and suddenly they were fast-walking, jogging, laughing. "Down here," she said, darting into an alley.

"Another alleyway, of course," he said. "Nothing good can come of this."

They held onto each other by fingertips, and Nike felt on the verge of losing her grip. Around her, graffiti swirled over walls, windows, dumpsters—even painted recycling bins studded the area like colourful monsters.

"You're a serial killer, aren't you?" Sahle mused. "You pose your victims artistically."

Nike giggled, then immediately regretted it—too young. She doubled down. "Yep. It's performance art. Then I stuff their balls in their mouths and arrange them like roast pigs."

Sahle's mouth opened, but no sound came out.

Might've overdone it.

She steamrolled forward. "You really should stalk your dates on social before following them into dark alleys without protection."

"You're savage."

Nike swallowed another laugh, surprised her grin alone wasn't brightening the alley.

They stopped before a mural. It had been up for months, practically ancient in alley years. The piece worked with the architecture—an alley within an alley, two buildings pinching closer until they crushed together in shadow. A dead end, except for the thin wedge of the next street, just barely visible.

Nike stood alone, in the dark, with a guy she definitely couldn't over-power. She hated that she had to think that way.

"We're here," she said. Sahle let go of her fingertips, and she felt the loss of his touch.

"What am I looking at?" He cocked his head, and Nike pulled out her phone, flicking on the flashlight.

Across the alley's gap, a witch blasted lightning from her hands, eyes, and mouth, zapping the enormous, bulbous head of a pale guy. Beneath it, the caption: *Licenced to Shrill.*

The tag: HT2B.

Other artists had encroached on the space, but none had dared cover it.

"This is you." Sahle stepped forward, fingers tracing the cinderblock. "You painted this? We share some politics, girl. What's the tag mean?"

"I'll let you in on it one day." She swung off her backpack, pulled out a can of red spray paint. "Why don't you make a tag of your own? Find a bare spot." Easier said than done.

Sahle turned, saw the can in her hand, and laughed. "Always locked and loaded, huh?"

She let the bag drop and stepped into him, arm wrapping around his neck. Resisting the urge to graze his abs with her bandaged hand was an act of pure discipline.

"This is amazing," he murmured.

Nike couldn't tell whether he was talking about the art or her, but she agreed, pulling his chin closer. He tasted of coffee and cinnamon. Silently, she thanked Sabra, felt her urging Nike on. She pulled him into the narrowest part of the alley.

"I'd have to think about my tag," he said. "Feels like a big decision."

Nike held his gaze. "One of the best things about graffiti? It's not permanent."

"Change, the only constant."

He spun, and suddenly her back was against the cool brick, his knee nudging between her legs. He kissed her, and she melted into him. Finally, he pulled away, and she opened her eyes, startled by movement in the alley behind him.

Something had landed. Something big.

"What?" He frowned. "What is it? Shit, I'm scaring you. I'm so sorry. I thought … I thought …"

"No." Her hand scrabbled for her phone.

A bruised liminal light illuminated the garbage cans. No, *not* the cans—the *thing* behind them.

"Holy shit … I can't believe … I can see …" She found her phone and blurted, "Text Dad, Daddy—help."

Sahle jerked back. "Help? Your dad? What'd I do? I didn't do anything. *Did I?*"

He lifted his hands. Backed up.

Backed *toward* the thing she could somehow see.

The alley's light dimmed, sharply outlining the nightmare shape. At the same time, the alien core flared, a furnace of hungry light.

Four purple-black tentacles rose into the air.

Nike shoved Sahle sideways. "Run!"

He grabbed her wrist instead, yanking her behind him, foot planted, arm up. Ready to fight.

"Get your stuff," he said, eyes scanning for the enemy.

"No, run!"

"Is this a joke? What are you running from? There's nothing here." His hands were on his hips as he stared up through the massive, pulsing raitgur right in front of him, taking up the whole damn alley.

Sahle scowled at her. "If that was a get-out-of-this-date text, just say so."

CHAPTER EIGHT

Trayling lost the alien in a thicket of shoppers. Damn thing was slippery. From the stoop of a vacant store, he scanned the garbage piles, alleyways, and crevices raitgur favoured. Nothing.

He leaned forward on his board, triggering its gyroscope. The electric engine hummed. He rode down the sidewalk, wheels snapping over the cracks, until he spotted a fire escape. Turning, he caught the ladder with one hand and yanked it down, hoping to climb to a better vantage point. The heavy treads of his boots clanged up the rungs, rising above the clamour of the street.

Gotcha.

From his new perch, Trayling could see a raitgur loping across the Golden Goose Restaurant's awning. Same size as the last one. Was it the same one? Maybe. Probably not. But what he'd said to Santana and Nike was true—why the hell were they all the same size? Why a cluster? And why now, after all these years?

Only taking his eyes off of the extraterrestrial slimeball long enough to ensure he wouldn't land on his board, Trayling dropped from the fire escape to the pavement, rolling forward as the squid-thing slingshotted across storefronts.

"Out of the way!" He dodged pedestrians on instinct, the powerful headlight on his board clearing most of them.

Not all.

A shopkeeper yelled at him, distracting Trayling enough that he sideswiped a stand of starfruit that rattled over the ground in his wake.

"Sorry!" He wasn't. He was grinning. The hunt felt good—almost as good as burning. He accelerated, driving through the thickening crowd.

The raitgur flung itself onto a lamppost, swung to a streetlight and then into traffic.

Traffic.

Trayling leaned back—hard. His board nearly shot out from under him. He bailed, stumbling at the curb just as a cyclist zipped past.

"Watch it, ass!"

His heart pounded. The raitgur slunk through the intersection, weaving between cars, sliding through a car's grille. Nothing physical could stop these things. A thick slime marked its path—snotties. So many snotties. It darkened the pavement ahead and behind, a stream of it, as the alien passed over to the other side of the road, out of Trayling's district and into that of the Italians.

Fumo, the Italian Burner, glowered across the six-lane thoroughfare. A third of his face was melted from alien acid, but he still managed to look like a boss in a pinstripe suit, sharp as a blade.

Beside him, Cenere, Fumo's mother, sat in a wheelchair—armless, legless, yet somehow the most intimidating person on the block. She puffed furiously on a cigarette that wouldn't survive the next thirty seconds.

And then there was Fuoco, Fumo's daughter. Nice kid. Unfortunate name. In her frilly Sunday dress, she was nudging her father and pointing at Trayling. She appeared to have all her fingers, which pissed him off.

Trayling waggled his hand in greeting.

Fuoco pointed harder.

Fumo ignored him. Cenere ignored him. They ignored the raitgur too. His mood darkened.

Trayling wanted to camp out near the trail of snotties to see if more raitgur crossed. Was it a coincidence that they crossed at the same point, or something more?

Trayling pulled a silver coin from his pocket, flashed it at Fuoco. Then he slipped it into his palm light, triggering a red glow so it looked like it melted. That got Fumo's attention. Cenere lifted the stump of an arm to her cigarette. After a dramatic pause, Trayling opened his hand, switched off the light, and revealed the now bent coin.

A few onlookers clapped. He bowed.

His wife had loved his magic tricks. He saw the same light in these strangers' eyes as he had seen in hers. God, he missed that light. Performing a few tricks would give him a chance to reclaim it. Also, if he was lucky, he might make a few bucks. After all, 'busker' was literally what was on his tax forms.

Fuoco's expression shone with curiosity. Fumo's could cut steel.

Trayling popped the bent coin into his mouth. Swallowed. Heaved.

Regurgitated the original round coin. This part of the trick was real and a crowd favourite—he'd taken a couple of months to master regurgitating both coins, palming the bent one.

A small crowd formed. Still, no new aliens.

Trayling flipped his board over, letting it double as a tip tray.

"My name is Montague, and my trade is magic." His voice boomed over traffic. "Beware! To acquire my powers, I descended into the very depths, deeper than any human should. Through eight planes of Hell, into the ninth, where the greater demons dwell!"

He peeled back his collar, revealing acid burns.

"There, I paid a harsh price to learn the dark arts. So shall you."

He winked and dropped the coin onto the skateboard for effect.

Then, with a dramatic swirl of his cloak, he crouched. His palm light filled the fabric with a deep purple glow. Hidden, he slipped in yellow contact lenses. Lights off.

Then—BAM.

He burst upright, eyes glowing gold.

A collective gasp.

Another raitgur slipped across the street, this time toward him.

Trayling caught a notification ping. He glanced at the contact's name: Nike. A half dozen missed texts.

Swearing, he flipped his board—scattering his few meager coins—and took off.

No goodbyes. No dramatic monologue. Just pure, uncut panic as he rocketed the wrong way down Bathurst, weaving between cyclists, cars, and pedestrians.

Move or get run over.

Faster, faster—

***

The raitgur lunged for Sahle. Nike tackled him, and they slammed against the alley wall, limbs tangled.

"Back to thinking you're a serial killer," Sahle said, flashing a luminous grin.

She tracked the alien, struggling between the part of her mind that wanted this to be an illusion and the logical part that explained that the glowing, tentacled creature was exactly what her father had been describing for the last eight years. "Real, real, real," she said to herself.

"*What* is real?"

"Do you want to keep your balls?" she shot back, eyes locked on the creature.

His grin flickered. "Yes?"

"Do what I say." She knew that her father could be hit by the thing. Burners could be *killed*. Sources were the only people who were immune to both infection and acid—everyone else could be infected, including Sahle.

The raitgur compressed against the brick, tentacles coiling like springs. "It's jumping. Go!"

Sahle hesitated. "What's jumping—"

She yanked him, and they bolted. The alien launched, slammed into the alley's corner, then dropped to block their escape. Nike shoved Sahle off course as a tentacle lashed out, missing his throat by inches.

"I felt that! What was that? I didn't see anything."

Nike barely heard him. How do you tell a guy you just met that aliens are real and one is actively trying to eat him?

"I'll explain later."

"I'm not moving unless you give me something."

What lie could she tell him? There was a sniper? The only thing he might believe was that she was hallucinating, and that would probably get him infected.

"Wait—is this what Joula meant by your needing my help?" he asked.

"*I* need help?" But Nike didn't need an answer. It was clear now that this was a setup. The texts. The date. Sahle's job was to help street youth. With her burns and her decision to leave her home, she wasn't a date— she was a case. The kiss just made him a dick.

The creature blocked the alley, but it hadn't moved.

"Don't get me wrong, I—"

"Raitgur," she said finally, not caring anymore.

Sahle blinked. "Rat-grr?"

"Close enough." A quirk to his lips suggested he thought it might all be a joke, but the raitgur tentacles slithered across the alley before them, forming bars to a cage. The thing was huge. "Back up!"

The alley ran the length of the block, giving them room to retreat. But the alien was also *fast*. "If I'm about to die, I should at least know why, right?" he suggested, still not taking it seriously.

Nike dragged him away just as the raitgur vaulted overhead, like a cat playing with its food.

"Can't I get more than 'rat-grr'?" he panted.

Nike shot him a hard look. She'd seen what happened to people who got infected—her mother, her sister. If Sahle caught this, he wouldn't die. He'd be better off dead.

"Aliens," she said. "First time I've seen them. Only a few people can. It's aliens that make the goo we saw earlier, above Dan—*Dive!*"

They dropped to the gravel. The raitgur flashed overtop. "They use people. Infect them. Leech off their nervous system," she said. "Roll!"

They rolled as the raitgur shot past again. Nike landed hard, shredding her dress, stones biting into her shoulder. Sahle hauled her up, eyes scanning her bloody arm.

"This is crazy. You're bleeding. You need help."

"I am not a hooker—sex trade worker, whatever—"

"I didn't mean—"

"They cause depression."

"Aliens," Sahle scoffed. "Depression is scientifically—"

"Never said it wasn't. This just works like it. And there's no treatment."

He stopped, giving her an exasperated look—which, honestly, was better than having a raitgur planted on his face, but not how she'd imagined the night going.

"So something is here. Right now. Trying to infect us."

"Yes."

"And it wants me specifically?"

"Yes."

Sahle turned on his heel and marched toward it. "Okay, see, this is where your logic fails—"

Nike whirled. The raitgur loomed above, tentacles stretched across the alley walls, sparking with dark lightning.

It dropped.

Her dad hit them like a human wrecking ball, skateboard screaming underfoot. He caught both Nike and Sahle, barreling them backward until they smacked into the alley walls.

The raitgur landed where they'd been standing and then slowly rose.

"This the boy?" her dad asked, eyes glowing—busking, then. Not hunting.

"Boy?" Sahle sputtered.

"Really, Dad?"

"This is your dad?"

Her dad folded his arms. "You wanna tell me why you're in a dark alley with my daughter?"

Sahle's hands shot up. "She was showing me her art!"

Nike groaned.

"You know better. He shouldn't be here—" Her dad stopped as he turned, taking in the raitgur fully for the first time. "What the … big fucker."

"This a family thing?" Sahle asked.

No one answered him.

"Kill it!" Nike yanked off her glove and fumbled for her lighter.

Sahle's eyes locked on her mangled hand. "What happened to—"

"Not our district," her dad muttered.

"The raitgur doesn't care!" Nike snapped.

It lunged.

Trayling yanked Nike. Nike yanked Sahle. They tumbled. Sahle slammed into the wall and landed on top of her.

"Get off my daughter!" her dad bellowed.

"Yes, sir."

"Dad!"

The raitgur hovered, tentacles pulsing. Nike's gold lighter gleamed on the far side of the alley.

Her dad turned to Sahle. "You smoke?"

Sahle blinked. "Weed? Not like, every day—?"

Nike shrieked, "We need a lighter!"

Sahle fumbled in his pocket, pulled out a pack of matches. Nike snatched them. Hands shaking, she spilled half the sticks before managing to grip one.

"You shouldn't smoke," her dad said.

Nike held her middle finger up to her father, struck the match against the cinderblock and lit the fingertip.

"Holy shit, no!" Sahle lunged for her wrist.

Her dad shoved them aside as the raitgur slammed into him, pinning him against the alley's jagged dead end. The match was out and so was her fingertip.

"Daddy!" Nike screamed, scooping up several matches from the ground, lighting them all and then her finger.

The alien loomed over him, its bulk pressing him tighter into the wall. His breathing sputtered, ragged with pain, muffled by alien flesh. He cried out, "Don't. Touch. Her!"

A gust roared down the alley, and flames burst from his hand. Nike shrieked, clutching her searing finger. The raitgur swallowed the fire, then detonated, flesh puffing into fine ash, whisked away. Its spine wobbled upright for a moment and toppled. Sahle danced out of its path, yanking off his shirt to smother the flames still guttering on Nike's hand. She bit down on a cry, tasting blood.

"Is it clear? Are you okay? What blew up?!" Sahle's words came out in a rush as he scanned the alley, tugging at the strap of her dress like it might hold answers.

The alien's charred spine lay smouldering on the ground, embers glowing faintly along its serrated edge. Nike's dad poured water over his reddened skin, then peeled off his scorched oilskin jacket. Yellow fumes twisted off the leather in sickening tendrils. "You okay?" he asked.

"Yeah, no," Sahle muttered.

Nike would've laughed if her hand weren't screaming in pain.

"Are you okay?" her dad asked again.

Nike peeled her fingers back, wincing as she exposed the wound. Her middle finger was burned down to the knuckle.

"What did you *do* to her?" Sahle demanded, his wide eyes darting between the alley's exit and the spine like he couldn't decide whether to run or faint. His gaze landed on Nike, searching.

I help people, like you do, she wanted to say. But she didn't.

"Just go, Dad. Let me explain to Sahle."

"Do you have your kit?" her dad asked.

She shook her head. "Didn't think I'd need burn ointment for a walk."

"We need to get you home. You need treatment."

"Sahle will take me," she said. "You take the spine."

Her dad knelt by the spine, his blistered cheeks grimacing as he inspected it.

"What is that?" Sahle asked.

Her dad's eyes flicked to Sahle's muscular torso. "How old are you?"

Sahle looked at Nike. "How old are *you*?"

"Please, Dad. Go."

With an oven mitt pulled from his backpack, her dad hefted the spine onto his shoulder. "I'll drop this off. Meet me at Dundas and Bathurst in two hours. There's something you need to see." He winced, either from the weight of the spine or his wounds. "We can't let them grow this big."

"Okay, Dad. Fine." Anything to get him out of here.

At the alley's mouth, he turned. "You could see it this time?"

She nodded. "I saw it."

He dropped his board and rolled off.

Sahle helped her to her feet, his eyes on her burned hand. "What the hell was *that*? Your dad—he threw a fireball! And your hand ... your hand, Nike." He gestured helplessly, his gaze flicking to her art supplies like her paintings might somehow explain things.

"My dad's a Burner. I'm his source. He can't burn aliens without burning part of me."

"That's ..." He rubbed his temples. "That's so *sick*. And not in the good way."

"Some people who get infected turn into Burners or their sources. They're always in the same family. It's a genetic link, they think. But most just ... stop. Eating, breathing, existing, but not living. Like my mom and sister."

"I'm sorry," Sahle said.

Nike sighed. "It's been like this since I was nine. Ever since the meteor brought the aliens here."

He blinked. "Wait, *what*?"

"It's a government secret," she said.

"Secrecy is strongly correlated with corruption," he replied. "So, let me get this straight—fire-wielding government wizards are fighting invisible aliens that cause zombie-like symptoms?"

Nike flinched. "They're not zombies. More like awake coma patients."

"And burning you is the only way to make this fire?" He frowned. "Regular fire doesn't work? Bullets? Lasers? Missiles? *Anything* else?"

"Not sure anyone's tried missiles," she muttered. The pain gave way to chills, and she stumbled toward the street.

Sahle picked up her backpack, the red paint, the lighter, and then took her by the elbow, steadying her. "This is insane," he said. "Like, conspiracy-theory insane. But it's been happening for years?"

"Yeah. People either don't believe it or freak out."

On Queen Street, her reflection in a store window caught her eye. Haggard, thin, wan, rough. Not someone who could be Sahle's girlfriend. Someone who needed help.

"If I hadn't seen it, I'd think you were crazy," he admitted. "But fireballs ..." He gave a nervous laugh. "Aliens. Gorgias would have a field day."

She sidled closer, gripping her wrist. "I need drugs."

He patted his pockets like some might magically appear. "I'll take you home."

As they waited for a rideshare, Sahle turned to her. "So … you're a Burner too?"

Her breath hitched. "No, I'm not like my dad. I can't cast fireballs—I'm just something he uses."

They stood in silence at the curb as chill crept deeper into her bones. "When I'm not in high school, that is."

As if her age could possibly matter to him now.

Chapter Nine

The spine barely fit through the door. Santana rushed to help.

"It's okay," Trayling said. "Just awkward."

"Can't you accept help instead of scratching my paint?"

He glanced back, realizing too late that the spine's tip had gouged the drywall. "Sorry." He took a deep breath, catching a hint of her perfume and breathing deeper. The spine scraped against the concrete floor, loud enough to set his teeth on edge. He didn't need help now, but with Santana so close, her hand brushing his, he kept quiet.

The spine clanged onto the steel slab. They both stepped back. She pulled off her latex gloves before running her fingers through her hair, brushing a shock of it over her forehead, covering scarring he hadn't noticed before.

"Big one," he said, a flicker of pride slipping through.

"Trayling, it's years old. You have to do better."

The words stung. He nearly snapped that it wasn't his district, but hunting outside his own would cost him his licence.

"It almost killed me. Almost killed my daughter's friend. You think I should've left it?"

"I worry you're letting them mature to this point. Number of specimens and spine length, the shorter the better—those are the metrics."

"Boundaries aren't fixed for raitgur. I can't stop them crossing into my district. They follow trails—deer runs, preferred routes."

"Raitgur have preferred territories too. If it was in your district tonight, it's been there a hundred times. Your district, your responsibility. Other Burners meet quotas with immature specimens—learn from them. This counts for half."

"Half? It's huge! Should count for double."

"And I want them small. How many lives did this monster ruin? Look at you!"

Her gaze drilled into him, taking in the acid-scored jeans, the flecks of red on his hands. His face felt cracked, tight as old leather. His favourite cloak was ruined.

"I'm giving Trinity Bellwoods access to your district," she said.

"You're handing my district to the Italians?"

"You're not listening. Your district stays yours. They'll just help until spine lengths drop to non-infectious levels. Once the numbers stabilize, it's yours alone again."

Trayling started to protest, but she simply pointed a finger at the massive spine. He hadn't realized they could grow so large.

"Raitgur don't get this mature without something being wrong," she said. "You need help. Rest. Have you even looked in a mirror?"

He avoided mirrors with the diligence of a vampire. His tongue ran over parched lips. "What if it wasn't my district?"

Queen West was Chuck's, along with the financial district. Throwing him under the bus was tempting. The last time he'd seen Chuck, the man had accused him of killing the Burner from Chinatown. She'd been found torched in Little Italy. A Burner meeting had been called shortly after the murder and took place in High Park, with the Burners in the middle of a large field and their sources separated by a football field to avoid a fight. That hadn't stopped Trayling from punching Chuck in the head for the accusation.

Santana's eyes narrowed, sharp as flaying blades. "If it wasn't your district, you're in a bind. Either take the spine and the help or admit you were poaching. You'd lose your licence."

Trayling swallowed hard, looking away. "Nike saw it."

Santana's scolding softened into curiosity. "A source who can see?"

He nodded.

"All of it?"

Trayling hadn't thought to ask, but Santana was the scientist. "Not sure."

"Could it touch her?"

"Don't know that either."

"How bad was the burn?"

"Worse than before. You think there's a connection between her seeing them and the burns?"

"I don't know. There's too much we don't know. That's why I need you to understand. I'm not blaming you, but you need help. Fumo has two sources. The Italians stay."

He nodded, bile rising at the thought of Fumo scouting his territory. Still, it gave him something: the excuse he needed to search theirs.

Chapter Ten

Nike waited for her father at the McDonald's, leaning against the sloppily tagged wall. She almost didn't recognize him in his ragged white t-shirt and jeans with his acid clawed skin. He skateboarded through the pedestrians. The sag of his shoulders broadcasted his bad mood, but he straightened when he spotted her and grinned.

She hated his skateboard. *How old does he think he is?* His smile did little to ease the throb of her hand, or give her back the time she'd spent with Sahle, which had left her only half an hour to return home and chew meds on an empty stomach.

"Why are we here?" she asked, as the whirr of his board's electric motor died.

"Do you think your friend will go to the cops?" he asked.

"I don't think so."

"Santana won't like that answer."

"Don't tell her."

"You planning on seeing him again?"

"Dad." They'd been attacked by a monster of an alien, Nike could *see* them now, and her dad was all in her face about *Sahle?*

"How'd he take it?"

"For a guy who just learned about an alien invasion?" She shrugged. "Pretty well. *You,* however, scared him shitless."

Her dad chuckled, bobbing his head. "Shooting fireballs out of my hand must be worse than showing up to meet him with a shotgun."

"The glowing eyes didn't help," she said. "He called you buff, by the way."

"Promise not to steal him," he teased.

She scowled.

"Santana says to reduce the burn we need to work on improving our relationship. The worse our relationship, the worse the burn." He paused, taking a moment to gather himself. "Things have been different between us lately. I'm sorry."

"I'm not going to counselling."

He started to laugh, tried to stop fast, and ended up coughing. "Me neither."

Nike stared at him, a knot in her chest loosening. It had been a while since she'd last heard him laugh.

"No counselling," he said. "But we need an open line, you and me. Not only as a safety thing. It's important for all of us."

Nike rolled her eyes, knowing what he was really talking about and not wanting a lecture—again. "Dad."

"Like it or not, Kitten, whoever you start a relationship with also joins the team."

There is no team. The knot returned, tighter than before. Her father glanced away, unable to hold her stare. So he wasn't sorry about burning her. He was telling her he needed to approve of her boyfriend choice. She was too drugged and tired for this. All she wanted was to be home in bed, with her hand on ice.

"Let's get this over with," she said. "What do I *need* to see?"

Her father's expression darkened, but he pointed toward a trail of wetness crossing Bathurst. "See that?"

"Snotties. Yeah."

"A river of snotties. I think the raitgur are hunting in one district and nesting in another."

"Don't crap where you eat. Makes sense."

"Exactly. It means when we're hunting them, we're losing them to boundaries. Can't trace them to their nest. And they know it."

"*Know* it?" Nike struggled to keep up in the slurry of pain meds. "Raitgur aren't supposed to be smart. They're rats that arrived on a meteor— they don't *know* boundaries."

"We don't know much about them. Real scientists can't see them to study them, and the half-dozen Burners are a mishmash: a truck driver, a chef, a real estate agent. Rumour is Fumo was a leg breaker with the 'Ndrangheta family. Not exactly known for their expertise on extra-terrestrials. Besides, rats are smarter than people give them credit for."

The light changed to red, and her father started to weave through pedestrians.

"Where you going?" she shouted.

"Grab my board," he called back.

This was a different kind of danger. Nike could leave now. Head home. With the drugs, she'd sleep regardless of how angry her father made her. This wasn't just another hunt. This was an incursion into another Burner's territory.

She'd cross the road with him and then leave.

He crouched in the middle of the intersection, boots straddling the snotties. "Santana let the Italians into my district. I say that means I can poke through theirs."

"You just said Fumo's a 'Ndrangheta. That's mafia, right?"

Her father didn't reply, only stuck his knife into a pothole.

"Dad, you can't be pulling knives in the middle of the fucking road."

A couple of girls stared at her and her father in disgust as he lifted a long tendril of snottie with his blade. "Don't swear." In his other hand was one of the vials he kept for samples.

"We're scientists," Nike told the girls. "Whatever you do, don't eat this stuff," she said, and the girls took photos of them. The walk signal flashed. "Dad, the light."

Her father worked on the vial's lid. The light changed. A truck honked. He slow-walked the rest of the way across, like it was his goal to piss off everyone.

"How long have you known Sahle?" he asked.

"Dad. I'm not seeing him again. Turns out, I was set up with him because someone thought he could get me out of an abusive relationship."

He had the decency to blanch. "Nike—"

"I don't want to talk about it. You can scout alone. I'm not like you—I need more than two hours of sleep every night. Let me go to bed and wake up to burn kits and high protein diets."

Trayling stared at his daughter. "Last night, after you left, another rait-gur arrived. Infected the man we'd saved ten minutes earlier. I couldn't do anything. I tried to wake the guy, but … somewhere out there someone lost a son, maybe a sibling or a parent. If I hadn't shown up tonight, what would have happened to Sahle? Our not being a team has consequences."

"I don't want the weight of that, Dad. I don't. Our *being* a team has consequences, if you haven't noticed your face? And—?" She held up her half-destroyed hand.

"Santana wants to hear more about how much of the raitgur you can see. She seemed really interested. Scout with me a bit. We won't burn."

"Promise?"

"Promise."

She hesitated. "One hour."

They swung south of Dundas Street, the crowds thinning with every block. The quiet thickened as the distance between islands of streetlight grew. The longer the silence stretched, the more she knew her father wanted to ask her something.

"Spit it out," she said.

"Is it so wrong for a father to ask his daughter about the ... *man* she's dating?"

"I don't believe this."

"How long has this been going on?"

Nike knew her dad wasn't about to stop hounding her. "Not for very long."

"What does he do?" he asked.

"Takes philosophy."

"University age." It was an accusation. "What's he going to do with that degree?"

Nike stopped in a puddle of streetlight. "Have you met a seventeen-year-old boy?"

"I'm only saying it can be dangerous."

"Philosophy? Really? He's going to knife me with Socrates or maybe shoot me with Seneca?"

Someone opened their front door, saw them arguing in the street, and went back inside.

"Not knowing a man," her dad said, lowering his voice. "Going out on dates. Late at night. Alone."

"What am I supposed to do? FaceTime him?" He turned away and started to walk on; she hurried after, feeling like she'd gained the upper hand in the argument. "Is it really more dangerous than my life right now? And what's it to you, anyway? My dating is not your business."

They stood at the edge of a dark park. The late-night traffic was gone. A strange mist found hollows in the park lawn.

"Until you are on your own, out of the house and paying your way, I get a say, that's how this works."

"Typical my-way or the highway shit."

"I know what guys want."

They entered the park. Nike had been so fixated on their fight that she'd missed that they were following a trail of snotties ablaze under her father's sporadic flashes of ultraviolet. Bruised light flitted amongst the trees. More than one.

"And if a girl wants the same thing? Dad? What about that?"

The shadows had already enveloped him, a ghost skirting the skeleton of the playground. She rushed after, snotties glittering in tree branches. "You should be more sex positive. Or are you trying to burn me so no one will want me?" *Was he even listening?*

"Light up," he said, when she reached him. "Be ready."

"Oh, I'm ready, Dad."

He stopped and grabbed her by both shoulders. "Enough drama. Focus on your job."

Her body quaked with anger. "You promised, no burning tonight." At that moment, she wanted to burn, wanted to burn so he would see what he was doing to her. But he didn't see—he turned away, hand up, ready for battle.

"You promised," she hissed.

"People walk through here. People who we can help."

"Tell the Italians."

He nodded, eyes darting from movement to movement. "We need to provide proof of a nest."

"What nest? No poaching, that's the rule."

"Look around! There's got to be a nest. I won't take the money—the Italians can take the money, for all I care. I want to stop the goddamn aliens, so no one else loses a wife and daughter to them! Don't you?"

She shook her head.

"The Italians must already know about this," he continued. "Which means they're doing nothing to stop it. We need proof."

The raitgur gathered closer. Nike could feel their pulses in her skull as her father murmured, "We have to. We have to."

"Look what you've already done to me!" She pulled off the glove, unwound the bandages, and shoved her mangled hand in his face.

His gaze lingered on the damage. "What choice do we have?" The pulse of the creatures buffeted them. Nike felt them all around her. "We're close to ending this, I swear."

She trusted that look. It was the look of pride he'd given her after every burn. When they would share an ice cream and ice her finger. When he'd tell her stories of all the things the people they'd saved would go on to do. Because of her.

Truth was, she too sensed this was almost over. Years ago, they'd bring down two dozen raitgur a month. Now, they were lucky to take six spines.

"Okay, Daddy." She hesitated over whether to ignite the last finger and decided instead to burn more of the knuckles to the left of it. But the flesh and bone didn't immediately catch. It sizzled.

He waved his hand for her to hurry.

Nike usually lit like paper and had needed to be careful around open flame. "I'm trying," she said.

There. The lighter's flame singed her intact right hand, and she shook it out, leaving a low-burning pilot light wobbling on the ruined portion of her left. It kindled yellow.

Her dad strode into the innards of the park, sinuous mist threading his legs and waist, his glowing hand a torch.

She hesitated, and the pilot flame dipped to a guttering blue.

"Don't do that," he said, and waved her on.

Had she done that? Made the flame lower?

Beyond the playground, the first tents of a homeless encampment choked tree trunks, the path between them muddy with snotties. She'd never seen so much in one place. It shone molten under the ultraviolet light. At the periphery of the park, abandoned and boarded-up rowhouses looked on, shuttered, blank, empty. A sign welcomed them to *Promise Complex.*

Raitgur followed them in the shadows, purple wraiths. "Shit, Dad. You seeing this ...?"

"Nice to share it with you, finally."

"Yeah, beautiful father-daughter moment."

He chuckled. "It's one thing to tell you what we do is important, another for you to see it."

"My hand is baking while you talk." That's what was important.

"We need to find the nest. Destroy them all at once. Bring back the spines to prove the Italians are up to no good."

Nike didn't care about the Italians, but judging by all the movement in the trees, her father was on to something. "You didn't say anything about destroying a nest. We only need the proof. We should wait." They should come back, but he held up a glowing warning hand. Her flame simmered steadily. People in the tents slept on, breathing, snoring, muttering—how many infected? There was no question that the poor bore a disproportionately high infection rate.

Nike slogged through the mud toward the rowhouses. A chain link fence divided the park from the development. Old plywood hung askew, revealing cavities where windows and doors had been. *Not* empty. In the depths of the cavities lurked raitgur.

Many, many raitgur.

"Jackpot," her father said.

The raitgur that had been following them closed in at their sides. Nike sidled closer to her father. "Too many, Dad."

Dad lifted both his arms; he never used both, but they'd never faced so many, seldom more than one. Flame swirled in his palms. His eyes were ablaze. Rivulets of fire ran up over his bare arms and danced down his back.

Nike fumbled for the leather bite guard, biting down on it so that it caught her scream.

Chapter Eleven

Fire roared from Trayling's hands. Sweat swept down his face and back as power exploded from him. Flames scythed through tentacles, engulfing the aliens.

The burn sharpened his mind, his eyesight, his hearing, even his smell. The weight of the task lifted, leaving him light and terrible. He saw the raitgur clearly now—so many of them, roaming freely and no doubt feeding on the encampment. With clarity came fury. These raitgur were infecting untold numbers of wives and daughters. Out of the corner of his eye, he watched Nike drop to her knees.

"Analia!" he screamed, a cry of triumphant rage—for her, for their daughter, for the toll this took on Nike. "Sabra!"

A half-dozen spines fell. Each of his hands worked independently, picking off one creature, then another, never letting up. Still, the raitgur rushed in, offering a glorious abundance of targets. One, larger than the rest, skidded from the impact of a fireball but recovered and surged forward, swelling angrily as it attacked. Like the one in the alley before, it took both of Trayling's hands and all his concentration to torch it.

"More, Nike! Open her up!" he shouted, moving toward the fence where larger raitgur lurked. Between fireballs, his shadow danced, cast by his daughter burning brightly behind him. Pride filled his chest. They were a team. A duo.

"We're doing great!" he called, bringing his hands together to send a sheet of flame over the fence. The fire splashed against the rowhouses, flooding orifices and flushing out the creatures.

Suddenly, the flame was gone.

His eyes hadn't adjusted yet to the darkness. His ears felt stuffed. "Nike?"

She sobbed.

Something chittered.

Violent alien light wove between tree trunks—small ones, a score of them. The chittering heightened. "Nike, they're communicating," he whispered. He'd rarely encountered more than one at a time. He tried to remember the sound for Santana. Wonder-touched terror mounted in his chest as the chittering grew raucous, like a colony of birds.

Nike stayed silent, save for her hitching breaths. Trayling pumped his hand, willing a fireball into being, but without a source, it was futile. The raitgur regrouped, their ticking and growls growing more animated. Were they planning an attack? Could they even plan?

"Nike!"

He heard her spit out the leather bite guard.

"No, Daddy."

He spun to look at her, then reeled from the hatred in her eyes. She turned and began to hobble away.

"You're right—we need to prepare," he conceded, calling after her. "We'll go. But back me up while I collect the spines." Without the spines, he couldn't prove what was happening here. Scattered before the fence, amongst the long grass and burrs, lay enough spines to ensure Santana couldn't ignore him.

As he reached for one, a raitgur curled onto it. A tentacle flashed, laying open a gash in his hand. He jerked back. Without his oilskin, even small raitgur posed a serious threat. A dozen more clambered onto the fence, chittering hungrily.

"You've got to be shitting me," he muttered, as they lined up two deep. Others roamed to outflank him. "Nike!"

She'd made it only a hundred feet, trailed by a half-dozen good-sized aliens. Abandoning the spines, he sprinted after her. Fear clamped his throat as he caught up, grabbed her good hand, and pulled her along.

"Fire, Kitten—they're coming. Coordinating. Light up. So many."

Her pace quickened, but she didn't light up. Around them raitgur pulled themselves into the treetops, swinging and catapulting between branches. *Slop-pop, slop-pop*—they slung themselves along, keeping pace. Closing in. The bones of the playground loomed ahead, free of the raitgur's eerie light and mist, nearer to the lights of the city. His boots dug into the playground's woodchips. Nike ducked under the slide, then stopped so abruptly he nearly collided with her.

The playground wasn't deserted.

Fumo and Fuoco stood on the far side. The ember of Cenere's cigarette pulsed from her chair.

"What's the punishment for poaching, Fumo?" Cenere asked.

"Maybe a warning?" Fuoco suggested.

"Warnings are for children," Fumo replied. "You still a child, Nike?"

Cenere leaned down and touched her cigarette to the stump of her leg. Flames licked at her ruined thigh as Fumo's fingers shone like hot iron. Fuoco struck a lighter, but Fumo placed a hand on her shoulder to stop her.

"Nonna burns well enough," he said, turning his attention to Trayling.

"Light up!" Trayling shouted to Nike.

Cenere's legs flared like jets. Fumo grunted, sending a fireball wide through the playground bars, taking out several raitgur. A warning. There wouldn't be a second.

"Get out of our district!" Fumo ordered.

"We didn't poach!" Trayling yelled. "Now, Nike. I need you!"

"You promised." Nike clutched her head. "Never!"

He saw it then, at the side of her skull. What he'd done. Her hand. Gone. Her face a rictus of pain.

"Never again," she screamed.

And she ran.

Chapter Twelve

Nike grabbed first-aid items from the medicine cabinet—ointments, gauze, antiseptic, anything for burns—and dropped them into the haversack gaping in the sink. Her life went into the bag, a life of wound care.

She knocked a pack of bandages off the shelf and tried to catch it, but it only hit her stump. Pain narrowed her vision. She gripped the porcelain and breathed through the nausea. When it subsided, she thumbed off the cap of her painkillers and dry-swallowed two pills.

Her father knocked. She ignored him. Trayling could wait.

Her phone buzzed. A message from Sahle: *Time to hang? Discuss the meaninglessness of most of my philosophy books in light of proof of alien existence?*

Nike couldn't muster a smile. She swiped the message away, wondering what his game was now, and texted Joula instead: *I need a bed and no questions.*

Joula replied: *You have a couch.*

Nike nodded at her pale, pain-lined face in the mirror. Maybe it was time Joula knew. She'd told Sahle. Joula should have known long ago. Did it matter anymore? Her father would never burn her again.

She slipped the phone into her jeans, mourning the fact that she'd need to buy looser ones. One-handed, these would take her twenty minutes to pull on. Into the bag, she swept half the shelf's contents, then went to zip it. Her eyes fell on her stump.

The sight of it turned her stomach. She gagged, heaved, her empty stomach trying to empty further. Spittle and crushed pills drooled into the sink. She clenched her eyes, taking deep, steadying breaths. Finally, she shouldered the bag and opened the door.

Her father blocked her, but she was ready.

"No, Trayling."

Before he could respond, she held up her red-blackened wrist.

The effect was immediate. He jerked back, hitting the drywall hard enough to dent it. She ran down the stairs, bile rising in her throat, and out of the house.

On the sidewalk, she turned. Her father stood at the second-story window. She knew he'd see her looking back as a sign, a search for a bridge to return. But for her, it was the last look before she jumped off the cliff.

The rideshare's door opened. She didn't glance back a second time—she didn't need to. He was there. Always there. And she hated him for that, too.

Within minutes, she arrived at Joula's apartment and collapsed into her friend's arms.

"It's okay. It's okay. Joula's got you."

Too short for shoulders, Joula wrapped her arms around Nike's neck, and Nike buried her face in her hair. Without another word, Joula towed her inside and sat her at a kitchen table nearly covered in printed circuit boards. The apartment was a chaos of tech and art—robotics, laser-etched glass, 3D-printed bobbleheads, one of which looked suspiciously like Nike.

Joula steeped cinnamon tea in silence while Nike tended to her wrist—her stump—spreading burn ointment over it to cool the pain. The routine of first aid steadied her.

"Got any cling wrap?" Nike asked.

"Serious?"

"Doesn't stick. Sterile. Handy stuff."

"Learn something new every day." Joula opened a drawer and pulled out a long box. She went to hand it to Nike, then hesitated.

"How much do you need?" Joula asked.

"Couple feet."

Joula pulled and tore a length.

Nike was careful to discard the outer wrap, which might not be sterile. She laid the rest over the stump, leaving slack to account for swelling. It was hard to be so close to it. She didn't want to see it, but when she shut her eyes, it was still there, the injury a lighthouse of pain and a constant reminder of her relationship with her father. "Help me with the gauze and tape? I need a hand."

Joula stared at the stump, visible beneath the transparent film. "You need a doctor."

"Doctors ask questions. I know what to do about burns."

Joula pressed a hand to her mouth, muttering something in Spanish about friendship. "Sometimes talking is a good idea."

Nike shook her head, the painkillers making the movement feel slow and heavy.

"Fine. No questions tonight. But, Nike, your hand … dude."

"Can I stay here for a bit?"

Joula's lips pursed. The longer she paused, the more the bobbleheads jiggled, as though mocking them. Nike thought of Sabra. If she'd been well, Nike would have run to her. If she had Sabra, she wouldn't be here.

Joula said, "My super already hates me. My parties. Thinks I'm running a business with all this gear. Which, I guess, I am." Joula seemed to read the desperation in Nike's expression. "I'll have to give him something more if I have a roommate."

"Thanks, sister."

Nike's phone buzzed on the table. A text from her dad: *Come home.*

Not in a million years, she replied.

Smeared with ointment, the phone continued to vibrate, but Nike ignored it.

"I have questions," Joula blurted. "I know this shit is wrong."

"Not tonight," Nike said. "Please …"

"I'm literally watching my friend burn through her chances at a good life."

The bobbleheads nodded in agreement.

"It's over, Joula. It'll never happen again." Nike paused, struggling to focus. "Ever."

"It's not supposed to work like this," Joula sighed. "What can I do?"

"I need a job." Nike grinned faintly. "I've been looking, but I haven't had a single callback."

Joula swore in Spanish. "I know a place hiring."

Nike leaned forward. "I'll do anything."

"Stop saying that shit." Joula sighed again. "But it's not great."

"I'll take it."

"Manager's a misogynist."

"I'll take it."

Joula shook her head. "I'll share the contact."

Nike shut her eyes. "I also need ten pitchers of ice water and a steak."

Chapter Thirteen

Trayling, bouquet of flowers in hand, caught the young nurse's sidelong wink at the aide and the knowing smile the aide returned. They pitied him—thought the flowers and devotion were sweet, but assumed his wife and daughter were gone. They knew nothing about raitgur infections. Analia and Sabra were still locked in their own minds. To not spend time with them would be cruel—it would be evil. He might be losing Nike, but he would never lose Sabra and Analia.

He slid his bag beside his wife's bed and replaced the daisies in both vases.

"How are you today?" he asked, then nodded, imagining her response. *Good, honey. You?*

"Not so great, actually." He swallowed, gathering himself for the admission. "Nike's left. I burned her really bad." His voice broke.

Is she okay? Is she safe? How are you doing?

He leaned forward to take both Analia's and Sabra's hands, his head bowed between his shoulders.

"I don't know what to do—yes, she's safe, but … but you should've seen the way she looked at me. It was horrible. She looked at me as if I had burnt off her hand on purpose, for fun, and without her being part of it." It was the same way he'd looked at himself in the mirror.

He lifted his head, looking from one to the other, their flat expressions, their staring eyes. Better than the look Nike had given him. "I can't let this be the end. I can't let those bastards get away with what they've done to us."

The familiar scuff of Chui's flats alerted Trayling to the nurse's presence.

"Everything okay over here?" Chui asked.

Trayling unzipped his haversack and pulled out a bottle of lotion. "Today's the best day—it's foot-spa day. Who wants a pedicure?"

Chui lifted his hand. "Love me some glitter on my nails."

Over Chui's shoulder, around the ward, several nurses and aides raised their hands too.

Trayling flushed. "Sorry, only time for my two girls. You know how long it takes me to paint nails."

Chui looked as though he wanted to say something.

"Go ahead," Trayling said.

"It's been, what? Eight years since Analia's and Sabra's diagnoses?"

"Eight years, two months, fourteen days since Analia's. Sabra's came a few months later."

"Right. And I've been working here for fourteen years. I've seen a lot of committed caregivers like you."

"Like me."

"Actually, none quite like you. They were committed, sure, but they also had other lives." Chui stared at Trayling as though he should understand the significance of the difference.

"I don't understand."

"I'm the nurse for Analia and Sabra, but that also means caring for their families. You've lost weight. You're not sleeping. You used to look like some superhero; now you're … injured. Graying. I haven't seen your other daughter in ages. You spend a lot of time here."

Trayling nodded. Chui continued.

"See over there?" Chui nudged his head toward a nurse—a fit Black woman, smartly dressed with a broad smile. "Nurse Jenefer. She's amazing." Chui raised his eyebrows meaningfully. "She's also single."

Air hissed through Trayling's teeth, holding back what he wanted to say. He reached behind and jerked the curtains closed around Analia's bed. Glowering, he turned to Chui, who raised both palms.

"Okay, okay," Chui said.

"I have a wife," Trayling whispered. "And she can hear every word you say."

Chui backed up, eyes darting to Trayling's fists. "Hey, I'm sorry. Maybe I was out of line."

Trayling clenched his jaw, then deflated. "Yeah, you were."

The nurse left. Trayling took a moment to settle himself. He trimmed Analia's nails, massaged and moisturized her hands, then approached the ward sink and filled a basin with warm water. The staff gave him a wide berth—the tension in the room was as heavy as it had been with Nike. With Analia's and Sabra's hands soaking, he relaxed into the routine of his family's care. Chui returned.

"Sorry, brother," he muttered while checking Sabra's vitals. Trayling recognized the gesture as an olive branch and appreciated it.

"Don't you ever wonder why Toronto has such a high rate of depression?" Trayling asked.

Chui kept his gaze on the blood pressure gauge. "Some say it's because we're better at diagnosing it. I say it's our fricking winters, right? Keeps me working anyway."

"Yeah. We've all got jobs to do, don't we?"

Chui seemed to agree and wandered off to do his.

Trayling shifted his chair until he was close enough to smell the detergent on his wife's sheets.

You going to do your job?

"You're right, honey. Just because I can't destroy them doesn't mean I can't flush the extraterrestrial snots out. I may need a source to snuff a squid, but I don't need one to destroy a nest."

From his sack, he took out nail polish in red, orange, yellow, white, and blue. On Analia's and Sabra's toenails, he painted flames.

***

This wouldn't be Nike's first job. She'd babysat, house-sat, cat-sat, dog-sat, old-person companioned—all the other shit-paying jobs girls typically got. Once—just once—she'd been commissioned to paint a mural on a wall near a community garden, but they refused to pay her, complaining that too many of the flowers looked like vaginas. Had they seen the graffiti painted by men? Had they looked at a flower lately?

A nightclub job, though—that would be different. Real. Joula had told her not to take any shit from Oscar, but Nike didn't have much choice. She'd applied to art studios and galleries, put out an offer for private graffiti lessons (the only dude who signed up no-showed), and even tried the local paint store, despite knowing minimum wage wouldn't cover her needs. But the manager lost interest as soon as she spotted Nike's hand.

So here she was, at a nightclub. For a hostess job. A woman's job. But with it, she could be like Joula—on her own. An adult in control of when she slept, what she ate, and who she dated. She wouldn't be wrapped up in her father's crazy plans. That morning, he'd texted: *"Gathering data on the Promise Complex nest. Will keep you posted on eradication plan."* Who the hell else had a dad like this?

But she didn't have the job yet.

A leather sleeve covered her entire left arm. Even with the swelling, it fit comfortably. Joula had designed it, adding a zipper for easy removal. Nike planned to embroider some leather flames to match her oilskin, but for now, the sleeve was cool on its own, complementing her black top, silver skirt, and long glove.

A man greeted her at the door to the club, Knocked Back. "Hey, hey, how ya doing? Joula's friend?" he asked. "I'm Oscar, the manager. Come on in."

The leather pants and gold chains draped over his hairy chest didn't help Nike's first impression. But even in daylight, the club was sick, all chrome and black lacquer, with reggae playing softly in the background.

Oscar sat her at the bar, behind which the bartender was slicing limes. Sprits of citrus masked stale beer.

Oscar's gaze kept roving from her stump to her breasts and back. "Hey, I'm guessing you're not looking to bartend. Or waitress, right?" He chuckled, clearly a bit uncomfortable.

"Right, because I'm not of age," Nike replied, "not because I *can't* physically do those things." She wanted to add, *and saying so would be ableist and discriminatory,* but her stomach sank at the thought of sending out more résumés.

"Hey, yeah, yeah, didn't mean anything by it. It's okay. You don't have to be nineteen to host." His eyes lingered too long on her stump. "Sorry, honey, but I'm trying to decide if that's super sexy or terrifying. What the fuck happened?"

Nike shrugged. She and Joula had agreed on the simplest story. "Born without it."

"No shit, huh. And no prosthetic? You can do sweet things with those—like shoot bullets and shit."

"That shit costs money ..."

"Right. So, a job, huh? We've got a culture here—look around, see if you fit." He gestured vaguely, directing Nike's gaze toward a waitress whose skirt barely covered her butt as she swept the floor.

The waitstaff were all midriff-baring, low-cut-top-wearing, and tiny-skirted. She hated herself for already dressing to match. But she hadn't expected the snotties hanging from a ceiling fixture.

"You get better tips," Oscar concluded.

"I can fit in," Nike said.

"Good. And you're right, you'll help with diversity around here. We'll start you on a couple shifts, see how it goes."

Nike stood, wanting to be out of there, but knowing she needed the job—a decently paying job, which meant tips, which meant bullshit. She shook Oscar's hand, and he held on longer than she liked. Even so, a lightness spread through her, smoothing her brow. It wasn't drugs; it was independence. Here was a paycheck. A start. *Her* start.

"Training tonight? Ten o'clock," Oscar said.

"Thanks, Oscar. I appreciate it. I'll do a good job."

Oscar winked. "Training's unpaid, of course."

Six hours later, Nike returned, her feet wedged into two-inch heels and her ass into Joula's leather skirt. A long glove ran up her right arm to the elbow, and her left arm's leather sheath was now trimmed with red and orange flames.

She adjusted the sheath higher as she approached the club. Her gaze traced the path of a raitgur as it slopped across the wall of an apartment—it seemed to be racing toward something.

Top 40s pop played over Knocked Back's patio speakers, the autotuned rhapsody punctuated by the clink of glasses. She checked a notification on her phone.

Sahle: *You can't ghost me. Not after what happened. You just can't.*

He could text Joula for updates on their lost cause.

Nike turned toward the bar, walking past a line of mostly men, likely held up by the hostess to attract more clubbers prowling Queen Street West.

"Nike?" The hostess's eyes widened, doe-like, as she tossed chemical-white hair. She tiny-stepped her heels around the podium and hugged Nike. "I'm Sophie! Your hostess mentor!"

"Uh, hi," Nike said, tense in the embrace of Sophie's skinny arms.

"Come on, silly." Sophie hustled back around the podium, tugging her tube top up and her skirt down. Nike followed.

"This is the best time to talk. It gets real crazy later. You've got the phone, the line, the boys. Stay out of their way when they're workin'."

One of the "boys" was a hulking bouncer Joula would love. He winked at Sophie before lifting an appraising eyebrow to Nike.

Nike raised her stump in reply.

"You got to learn the regulars," Sophie yammered on. "They don't have to wait if they just wanna hit the bar. But reservations are required for food." She laughed. "Not like anyone comes here for the food."

"Crazy."

"I know. It's okay, you'll get the hang of it. It's a good job. I love mentoring new girls." Sophie winked back at the bouncer with heavy fake lashes.

Up close, Sophie looked older than Nike had first thought. Heavy foundation masked wrinkles and blemishes dusted with glitter. Her lashes drew attention away from tired eyes, and her forehead hadn't moved once. Sophie had clearly been training new girls for years.

"Any slimeballs?" Nike asked, more to fill the silence than out of curiosity.

The bouncer blew air from his cheeks, his gaze fixed on the line.

Sophie squeaked. "Oh, yeah. It's kinda them against us."

As if on cue, a thirty-something hipster with a trim beard and sleeveless lumberjack jacket swaggered up, bypassing the line. Sophie nodded toward Nike.

"Reservations?" Nike asked.

"I'm good, sweetie," he said.

Sophie's lashes fluttered as she waved him through. As he passed, he brushed close to Nike, running a thumbnail along her thigh. She gasped and slapped his hand away. He sidestepped inside, chuckling.

The bouncer's gaze stayed on the line, but he smirked.

"It's okay, it's a good job," Sophie said. "We all split tips."

"Fucking men," Nike muttered.

"Oh, no, it's not the men who tip. You'd think so, right? Men trying to impress hot chicks? But it's actually the girls who tip more 'cause we're looking hot. Weird, huh? But science."

"Internalized misogyny."

"So you know science?" Sophie asked.

Another guy approached, this one dancing a little left and a little right, shit-eating-grin dead center.

"Hey, hey, ladies," he said to Sophie. "We have a new Knocked-Up virgin?"

Nike blinked. Sophie placed a hand on Nike's clenched fist as she leaned in to whisper, "It's the club's nickname—Knocked Up, Knocked Out—you'll hear it all pretty quick."

"Hilarious," Nike hissed.

"Hi, Wally, regular table?" Sophie asked.

"Yeah, baby, set up my blind. On the prowl to-NIGHT!"

He sauntered past. Nike kept an eye on his hands, watching how Sophie preened.

Nike's feet already ached in the heels, her stump throbbed, her painkiller was wearing off and her patience thin. Sophie was showing asshole to his hunting blind, leaving Nike alone with the boys and the next guy in line—a man clearly desperate to enter the almost-empty club and pay for an overpriced beer.

The hours fled faster than Nike had expected. Sophie's constant chatter was a balm against the worry and weight of alien hunting. As the night wore on and the crowd thickened and sweated, the waiters and bartenders welcomed her to the crew. She'd met more people in a few hours than she had all summer.

Finally, the phone stopped ringing, and the only line was for last call at the bar. Wally left with a woman who needed to lean on him to walk.

Oscar approached Nike, his eyes glassy with booze. "Good job tonight, honey."

He pressed fifty dollars onto the host podium.

"I thought I was training. No pay," she said.

"The bartenders treat the ones they like well. They like you."

She nodded. She could tolerate the "dears" and "honeys" if she was being paid. She wasn't so sure about the hands on thighs, though.

"See you tomorrow night. Start at ten. You need a walk to your car?"

She shook her head, and he disappeared inside, where most of the staff were either clearing out the place or having after-work drinks.

She fed the fifty into her phone case. On the screen, she saw a series of missed texts from her father. She swiped them away without reading them and stepped out into the emptying streets.

Chapter Fourteen

A nursing home and a retirement home flanked the Legion Hall. Its sentry, an old soldier slouched on a stool, looked like he'd be stumbling to one or the other after his shift. The door to the red brick hall was cracked open, and the reek of stale beer spilled onto the sidewalk.

Trayling snapped the soldier a salute, just in case he was more alert than he appeared—he wasn't—and stepped inside to the clamor. The man he'd come to meet was easy to spot under the bright fluorescents: Ambrose sat in an electric wheelchair, his broad face frowning down at his cards before peering over them and catching sight of Trayling.

"Give me a moment, boys." Ambrose dismissed the three men at the table, leaning down to show his hand. Bad cards.

"Always throwing in the towel when he's winning and about to lose," one of the men complained.

"A good general knows when to sound the retreat," Ambrose replied.

Another man laughed, adjusting some kind of naval cap. "No one's flag rank in this joint."

The others collected their drinks and money before leaving.

"Didn't know you served," Trayling said, taking a still-warm chair.

"We serve, old friend. Besides, the beer's cheap, and no one's gonna question the guy with one limb left. They know better than to ask for war stories."

They clasped hands.

"How are you doing, Ambrose?"

"How does it look?" Ambrose leaned forward to grab his beer. The last time Trayling had seen him, Ambrose had been leaner, his long hair less streaked with silver. He'd only had one arm then too, but it had been enough. Now, he looked flaccid, though his eyes hadn't changed: hard and full of yearning.

"You look like you've got three more friends than I do."

Ambrose seemed to chew on the response. "I've made peace with my uselessness, and that's made all the difference."

"Don't know how you stayed sane."

"Who says I did? After Emily died, I spent the first year trying to figure out if I could still do the job. Tried everything, but if you can't see the things, it's pointless."

"I still say the prayers you taught me. *The Burner burns, the source giveth—*"

"Utter bullshit. I gaveth, and look what I gotteth." The silence stretched a moment too long. "Santana taught me that."

"Last time we—"

"Emily's funeral. It's okay. You weren't the only one to disappear. How's Nike?" Ambrose seemed eager to change the subject. "I remember her in pigtails when I was showing you the ropes."

It had been two days now. Trayling knew she was at Joula's, but beyond that, she wasn't responding to texts.

"Pigtails are long gone." He sighed. "She's doing okay, but I'm burning more of her than I like. Than she'd like. She doesn't want this anymore."

"Can't say I blame her. You Burners can be a smug bunch."

"You remember with Emily—how you simultaneously wanted to protect her and watch her fly, all at once? It's like that. Feels like I'm losing her, but I know she needs more freedom."

Ambrose lifted his beer. "To shared pain." He grimaced and took a swig.

"You miss it?" Trayling asked. "Being burned. It never seemed to bother you."

"All this?" Ambrose gestured to his missing arm and legs. "Yeah, I miss it. And them. But being burned did bother me. That's why I call it service."

"Had a rough relationship with your daughter, I take it?"

Ambrose cocked his head, suspicion flickering. "Why would you think that?"

"Santana has a theory: the better the relationship with the source, the easier the burn."

No surprise registered on Ambrose's face. "It's a good feeling to burn, isn't it?"

Trayling didn't like the look in his eyes. "It's like lightning in my veins."

"Lightning in my veins," Ambrose repeated. "Makes it hard to stop."

Trayling nodded. He'd never learned how Emily had died, only that it involved Burner fire. The memory clearly haunted Ambrose.

Ambrose grunted. "That relationship theory would've been nice to know back then. But it's not like our benefits extended to family therapy. Now, you didn't ask to meet me for cheap beer. What's really up?"

Trayling hesitated. "You ever keep data from your hunts? Locations? Spine size? Numbers?"

Ambrose squinted. "What for?"

"I have a theory too. I'm hoping if it pans out, I won't have to burn Nike for much longer."

"My data's old, from before the districts."

"But you still have it?"

"Somewhere on the boat with my old burn kit. What's your theory?"

"Can you get it for me?" Trayling asked.

"What are you hiding from your old mentor?" Ambrose's stare dug into him. "Just because I made peace with losing my job doesn't mean I want to be useless, Trayling."

"Missing a few limbs doesn't—"

Ambrose slammed his fist on the table, cutting him off. "I used to burn to kill aliens. I was more of a soldier than anyone in this place. I don't want to write a memoir—I want to burn again. Give me something."

Trayling considered the quavering in Ambrose's eyes. "Why'd they create the districts?"

Ambrose shrugged. "Burners turned on each other. They were following each other, stealing spines, staking out territory. The Major formalized territories after … Emily …" Ambrose fell silent. Trayling had heard Ambrose killed the offending Burner and her source; all that had been left was pulp. He'd done it with one arm. Ambrose cleared his throat. "After Emily, Santana set up the quota system, the rules against poaching, and it cut down violence to a fraction."

Fumo had tried to kill Trayling since—and had nearly gotten Nike too—but saying so wouldn't help. "Okay, but why did we start fighting in the first place?"

"The raitgur were being hunted out. And a Burner needs to eat."

"Wasn't that our job? To hunt them out?" Trayling watched Ambrose, waiting for him to connect the dots. He didn't. "What if we were close, and the district system is now preventing eradication? What if we could've cleared out the aliens years ago?"

Ambrose's brow knitted. "Before I lost my …"

"Exactly. And Nike never needed to burn," Trayling said.

"Santana—"

"Santana's intentions were good. Like you said, no more Burner deaths. But she's not going to like being told she made a mistake. I'm going to need data to prove it."

The thought had come to him while he itched at his new burn. What if the infighting among Burners had happened because their battle against the enemy was actually successful?

Ambrose's eyes shone, and a half-smile tugged at one corner of his mouth, deepening his crow's feet.

"We can end this, Ambrose. Kill every last piece of alien crud. But we need enough data to figure out where the nests are. Individually, we don't have it—but together, we might."

"I don't see how my data can help, old as it is. But I'll get you what I have. You need to call a Burner meeting."

"Can't. I've got Nike to think about. Some Burners aren't going to like me poking around, taking away their payday. Other Burners are taking advantage of the system. I've gotta do this on my own."

Burner meetings could come at a high cost. Ambrose had escorted Trayling to his first. Back then, there wasn't the protective vault that now kept Burners from accessing their sources. But the Burners-only rule had been in place, and sources were kept well away—including Ambrose. He'd been pleased that Trayling was supposed to have Emily's back despite her being nearly twenty-five at the time, while Ambrose had watched over Nike alongside the other sources. Sylvain, Chuck, Farhan, Su—who would later die by Burner fire—and Lena had all been there, but Trayling's focus had been locked on the man in the pin-striped suit.

The meeting had been intended to discuss a Burner attack that had left one Burner in a coma and a source dead, but that conversation had never happened.

It took Trayling five minutes to connect the slick man—three-quarters handsome, with the rest of his face corrugated with scars—to the man he'd once pleaded with for help as Analia lay seizing beneath a highway bridge. One more minute to realize the man must have seen the raitgur and could have stopped it.

With a roar, Trayling had tackled Fumo, pummeling him until Chuck yanked him away, just as Fumo's blade sliced through the air where Trayling's throat had been.

The Burners hadn't met again until after Santana created the districts.

"Some Burners will want to help," Ambrose said. "They're not all like Fumo. Maybe this is our chance to figure out who's on our side. Let me call the meeting. Not like they can do much else to me. I'll pitch it as a way for me to get back into the business, to help out. Make it *my* idea to improve efficiency."

Ambrose had always been good to Trayling and Nike, and it was sure nice to feel part of a team again.

"Could work. You'd do that?"

"Fits in my schedule. Give me a week."

Trayling shook Ambrose's hand, and Ambrose gripped it tight. "Trayling, I'm not done yet. Nowhere near."

CHAPTER FIFTEEN

Nightly tips allowed Nike to cover her share of the apartment, food, and drinks. She had enough painkillers to keep her going. But living with Joula wasn't quite what Nike had hoped. Joula would leave in the morning for her secret "workshop" and sometimes not return until Nike was heading out for work. It was boring, and boredom led to Nike spending most afternoons cracking open a beer while streaming a show. Her tolerance had grown rapidly—she could easily throw back a six-pack without much effect.

Work didn't hold any real challenge—in fact, Jud the bouncer told her she was friendlier and better looking when she'd had a few drinks. So she drank, endured the groping and innuendos ("Knocked-up—wow, that's a good one!"), smiled pleasantly, and left most nights a little stoned with cash in her pocket.

Due to her late shifts, Nike never made it out to paint. Sometimes, when she got home, Joula would be up with a friend, and they'd drink together until dawn—those were the best nights. On those nights, she forgot she was missing a hand. On the bad nights, she scrolled through her father's texts: *"Here's the zoning map of the Promise Complex."* Or: *"Sweet-talked the building plans for the rowhouses. It identifies supporting walls. Sanitation network is next."* And: *"I should have all we need within a few more days."*

Nike didn't miss being burned. The only acknowledgement she gave her father was that longboarding was fun. Borrowing Joula's electric longboard cut her commute time to a third of what the subway took. The balance had been tricky at first, but it wasn't as hard as she'd anticipated—especially if she skipped post-work drinks. She usually didn't. Within days of starting, the bar staff had become a weird little family, and Nike was the baby sister. She wanted to be the baby sister again.

Tonight, she wobbled out of the bar as the last of the clubbers milled around on the sidewalk, sorting through rideshares. She dropped the board onto the pavement and sped off.

Another text from her dad lit her screen: *"Why do you think that homeless encampment hasn't been big news if so many infections are there?"*

At first, the question barely registered. Then she remembered Sahle saying something about a new type of fentanyl. Maybe the cops thought it was overdoses—and overdoses didn't sell papers.

"I miss you too," she muttered to her phone, while leaning into a turn. "Thanks for taking an interest in how I'm doing on my own."

She couldn't work all day and save the city. No one could do both. It was consuming her father, and it would consume the rest of her too if she let it.

Ten minutes later, she reached Joula's apartment. She hurried inside, hoping her friend was still awake so they could talk. Joula would definitely tell her to stop talking to her dad.

Nike smiled at the sound of hushed voices and intermittent kissing. A muscle-clad man filled the doorway, shuffling sideways as he left. Nike pressed against the wall to let him pass, nodding.

"Why do you only date big guys?" Nike asked, after shutting the door and grabbing a beer from the fridge. The night's earlier drinks had already worn off.

"How do you know I only like big guys?"

Some mornings, when Joula stuck around long enough for Nike to roll off the couch, it felt like Joula was judging her—as if everything was a test.

"I dunno," Nike said. "Every guy I've seen you with is all muscly."

Joula squinted at the beer in Nike's hand. "No girl should outweigh their boyfriend. Gives me some room to breathe." She laughed.

Nike nodded briefly, then realized what she'd agreed to, and shook her head. "Why the fuck not? Why can't the girl be huge and the guy a skinny twig?"

Joula rolled her eyes. "It's not the way, dude."

"Seriously, that's stupid. Okay, so you don't want to be unhealthy, but that's messed up. Wait. I know the problem ..." Nike waggled a finger as she collected her point. "You don't want him to feel threatened. Poor baby, thinks his girlfriend could body slam him. Can't have that, right?"

"No, all right." Annoyance flashed across Joula's face. "It's hard enough to find the right guy as it is. For me, it is." Her shoulders rose to her ears. "It's not me trying to protect anyone. It's men who don't want to feel threatened—it's just a fact—and I like being with guys who are into me.

It happens that guys who like short, strong girls are big. So … is that so bad?"

By the sheen in Joula's eyes, Nike realized she was treading on sensitive ground.

Nike glanced down at her stump. "Guys don't notice my arm at first. They're checking out my chest or legs. But eventually, they see it, and this light winks out in their eyes."

At work, her missing hand had become a party trick. *"What do you call a one-armed girl?" Drum roll ... "Nike!"* Then the big stump reveal. *"She'd clap, but..."*

How many choices in her life were because guys wanted it that way? Even Joula couldn't see it—and Joula was brilliant.

"No one's gonna feel threatened by me," Nike said. "I'm just something to be used."

She moved to open the fridge for another beer, but Joula barred her.

"Save it for later. And as for your arm, you better move past self-pity. It's hard for me to hear it when you've got one of the finest men I know interested in you."

But he hasn't seen my arm. "The one you told I needed help?"

"Sometimes we all need a little help," Joula said. "Listen, I'm your friend, not your mom, so I'm not going to tell you what to do. You've got to decide." She stood, grabbing her bag. "Besides, I gotta hit the Joula-cave."

"Now?"

"New commission. Prototyping a massage chair that moves to your music selection."

"Peak consumerism?"

"Not even close."

"Joula." Nike stopped her. Something in Joula's expression frightened her—it was boredom.

"Can I come see your workshop sometime?"

Joula opened her mouth, then closed it.

"All I want to do is become an artist, Joula. I want to see how you're doing it."

"Artist? What are you working on now? What have you done since leaving your dad?" Joula's jaw tightened. "You're going through some shit. Get it together, figure out where you want to go, then we'll talk."

She shut the door.

***

In the dead of night, Trayling staked out the park near the Promise Complex, assessing foot traffic and charting routine police patrols in preparation for burning it to the ground. He hung back, nervous he might attract the attention of raitgur, and pressed his back against a thick black oak. With his eyes this scratchy with fatigue, he almost missed the figure slinking toward the gates—but he'd recognize the silhouette of the man's crisp suit anywhere. Fumo.

Yesterday, Trayling had shadowed him from a coffee shop on College. But Fumo had detoured to Trayling's home, seemingly for no reason other than to glare up at the red-eyed raven decoration Trayling had placed on the roof one Halloween and never bothered to take down. Trayling knew his bias against Fumo would make Santana skeptical of any accusation, so proof that Fumo was the worst kind of gutter sludge would be necessary. Maybe tonight, Trayling would discover just how filthy he was.

Trayling abandoned the oak, pausing at the complex gate before slipping inside once Fumo turned down a side street. A narrow path ran parallel to the park fence, bordered by the backyards of townhomes, allowing Trayling to move alongside Fumo, catching glimpses of him through sliding glass doors. No raitgur attacked. The few Trayling spotted were focused on the street.

Moving closer to the rear door of a rowhouse, Trayling pressed his face against the glass to eliminate the reflection of the low-slung moon. Despite the vacancy of the complex, the streets were well-lit, and Trayling could see through the gloomy living room to the bay window at the front of the house and beyond. Fumo was greeting someone out of sight.

Trayling moved down a house, climbed a cracked concrete step, and squinted inside, dismissing visions of raitgur leaping at him from the other side of the thin glass. But the raitgur were on the street, throbbing purple and clustered before Fumo's two sources.

"What the hell?" Trayling muttered, struggling to believe what he was seeing. Fumo kept his distance from the raitgur, pacing back and forth like a platoon captain inspecting troops. The raitgur, however, didn't keep ranks—they tumbled over one another to stay close to Fuoco and Cenere. They clung more to the younger one, though she didn't seem to notice she was bathed in the creatures.

At her son's nod, Cenere lit one of her thigh stumps with the tip of her cigarette. Fumo's hand glowed. Trayling reached for his phone, held it up to the window, and hit record. On the screen, the image was blurred by the glass. Raitgur wouldn't show on video anyways, so he put the phone away.

One after another, short bursts of Fumo's fire torched the raitgur casting the street in red flashes of light. They scattered like frightened chickens, only to race back and form a cluster for slaughter. Fumo incinerated another.

Ten times Cenere's leg flared before Fumo stopped, clenched his fist, and signaled for Fuoco to extinguish her grandmother's flame. Trayling ducked as Fumo's gaze seemed to rest on him, though surely he couldn't see through two panes of glass and the streetlight reflections.

When Trayling looked again, Fumo was bundling the spines. Fuoco clutched her necklace, and Cenere pinched a fresh cigarette between her lips. The nest. The spines. The Italians were making a fortune.

They're farming them, Trayling realized, gasping as he typed the words into a text to Nike, his spine cold against the glass.

When he turned back, the Italians were gone, and the raitgur were freed from whatever had lured them. A squid toppled through the mail slot into the foyer of the rowhouse. Trayling bolted, sprinted along the path, then hopped a fence into the park, where he paused amidst the tents and tarps of the homeless encampment.

If the Promise Complex was the farm, the encampment was the pasture.

***

Nike shielded her phone from the late-morning sunlight spearing through the window as she opened last night's text from her dad.

They're farming them. They're farming them.

He'd sounded desperate. Nike, meanwhile, had never felt better. She shouldn't feel this good. She had no right to—last night, she'd drunk Jud under the table. Only her arm still ached.

Nike had pocketed over a hundred dollars in tips, and if things kept up, she wouldn't need to burn half a finger every time her father wanted to earn a thousand dollars. She thumbed the message to the left, deleting it.

"Joula?" she called, shifting on the couch until she propped herself on an elbow.

No one answered—the only sound in the apartment was the whir of the large-bed 3D printer from where it sat consuming the kitchen counter, surrounded by Nike's dirty dishes. Joula's lectures flooded back, and Nike swallowed her annoyance.

It took five painkillers to dull the throbbing in her arm. Joula was still off at her mystery cave, so Nike decided to go shopping for paints, feeling the urge to do something creative—or maybe it was Joula's push.

Painting in daylight was always risky, but old warehouses and parts of the trainyard were better explored when sunlight streamed through broken glass, dispersing shadows.

One building near the lake had been an old sock factory, slated to be refurbished into lofts or a tech hub, but mothballed in the meantime. A fire escape led to a second-floor window, providing entry. Nike wasn't the first to trespass. Discarded sleeping bags, takeout containers, and soda bottles littered the place, but the weather had been good, and she found the space empty.

Pigeons burst out, startled from their perches. Nike passed through the feathers as they drifted, aflame in the sunlight. Walls near the entry were heavily tagged, but a few floors up or down offered blank spaces for her to work.

Nike climbed to the third floor, scanning for a fresh canvas. These walls were covered with throw-ups and wildstyle tags so convoluted she couldn't even decipher the writer's names. Among them were grander works: detailed scenes of dragons, starships, and a stunning 3D illusion of a medieval hearth that seemed to pull the wall into another world.

But her focus snagged on a wall she and Joula had once shared. Joula's vibrant, anime-inspired cityscape, a riot of primary colours and whimsical characters, had been defaced with a crude, squat black baseball bat scrawled over the top.

Nike frowned. She never painted over another artist's work, even if her own piece would be better. Not everyone held the same creed.

Her section of the wall, thankfully, was mostly untouched. The centerpiece was a hauntingly realistic depiction of her recurring nightmare: a young girl trapped in a dark room, loomed over by a ghoulish figure draped in a black cloak, standing before a mysterious, blanket-draped object. In her dreams, whenever she reached to lift the edge of the blanket, she woke in a cold sweat.

She had painted the scene in hopes of uncovering more details from her subconscious, but the figure and the object remained shrouded in mystery.

Nike shook her head, climbing higher to the fourth floor. She planned something different today: a witch with arms outstretched, lightning arcing from her eyes, power coursing into the ground around her. If Joula was right, and Nike poured herself into her paintings, this was the witch she wanted to be: a Burner—not burning.

Clearing rubble, Nike prepared the space. The effects of the painkillers began to fade, her arm throbbing anew. Another dose later, her mood darkened as the sun shifted from window to window and beyond.

But she painted.

The witch never emerged. Instead, her mind insisted on something else: a raitgur, its tentacles splayed, suckling the face of a woman crumpled on the floor, her body starting where her neck met the wall. Even without a face, the body resembled Joula.

Nike stared at the finished piece, unsettled. She tagged the wall: *HT2B. Men.*

"Predictable," she muttered.

When Nike returned to the apartment, Joula was home. Still self conscious, Nike sat at the counter and chased a beer with a shot of vodka under Joula's reproachful eye.

"What?" Nike asked.

"You're looking in the wrong direction," Joula said, flipping through her sketchbook.

"What're you talking about?"

"If it's not drugs or alcohol, you keep looking to your dad to care about what you're doing. Even your new bar friends."

"They care."

"Why would they?" Joula asked, raising her eyebrows.

"Not like you do."

Joula swallowed and tapped her chest. "You need to look in the only place that counts. Right—"

"Right, thanks!" Nike hopped off the stool, grabbed the rest of the vodka, and snatched up her skateboard. "I gotta go. Don't wanna be late for work."

She drank a full twenty-six-ounce bottle on the way—an impossible amount, enough to put most people in a hospital bed. But by the time Nike arrived at Knocked-Back, it only left her staggering.

Jud rolled his eyes as she steadied herself at the podium.

"Who's up?" she shouted to the line. Her drunkenness didn't seem to bother the clubbers. "I can take any of you single-handedly."

Oscar found her half an hour later, her buzz already wearing off.

"I can find a dozen hot, two-armed hosts who aren't slammed half the time," he hissed, grabbing her bicep and pulling her aside. She blew air into his face, and he cringed. "Get yourself together." His eyes scanned down her top to the paint flecked there.

"I'm dead sober. I swear." To make her point, she strutted down a crack in the sidewalk, ground her heel as the whirled, strutted back.

Oscar's eyes narrowed, his nostrils flaring as if testing the air for alcohol. Without another word, he disappeared into the thumping bass of the club.

Nike would have brushed off Oscar's scolding, but when she returned to the podium, Sahle was next in line. Her stomach tightened. She instinctively hid her arm behind her back.

"Joula said you worked here," he said, his eyes downcast—maybe sheepish and uncertain, or maybe staring at her legs, like everyone else.

"Joula." Nike huffed, rolling her eyes. "I moved out from my dad's, only to find a mother."

"Listen, I've thought about what happened, you know. I can see why you might want to keep it to yourself. We don't know each other that well and—"

"Yeah, we don't know each other that well," she cut him off, nodding toward Jud.

"Right, but … the stuff that happened … I can't let that go either. We need to talk."

Nike sighed, her irritation bubbling over. This wasn't about her; it was about the aliens. He couldn't get past their existence. *I'm just secondary.*

"Maybe don't try to tell me what I think or what I should do," she snapped.

Sahle's expression darkened, disappointment flickering in his eyes.

Nike glanced around, noticing the interest of a few women in too-tight black dresses and Jud, who looked like he was suppressing laughter. She let the women into the club, ignoring Sahle.

"Fire blasted from your dad's hand. Aliens," Sahle said, leaning closer.

"Shut it. You promised."

"You promised to see me again," he countered. "And these infections? I think I've seen one—"

She groaned inwardly. Her dad had been right: Anyone who knew would want to join the team. *There is no team.*

Nike gave Jud another small nod. He took the hint.

"Doesn't sound like she wants to talk to you, buddy," Jud said, stepping forward.

The last three guys Jud called "buddy" had their skulls bounced off the curb.

"It's okay. He was just leaving," she said.

Sahle hesitated, his face a mix of frustration and resignation. Then he melted into the crowd, disappearing into the night.

"Thanks, Jud," Nike said.

Jud flashed a proud smile. "Literally what I'm here for—protecting chicks like you from conspiracy theorists."

Nike finished her shift, numb and struggling to clear her head. The line came and went, and she hung at the podium, slack-jawed and unresponsive, imagining her life as it was now—adding layer after layer of foundation to her face, day in and day out.

This wasn't what she'd wanted. Not what she'd imagined at all.

The alarm woke her the next morning. She hadn't set it, and its grating bleats made her burst into tears. She sobbed into her blanket until the hem was soaked.

Her arm throbbed, and she ignored the painkillers, inspecting the wound. It was still angry red, but it looked a month healed instead of a week, heavily scabbed and itchy. Something was happening to her, and she needed someone to talk to.

She drew a deep breath, then released it slowly. Joula had said Nike needed to look elsewhere, and there was only one place left to go for help.

Joula's electric longboard was fast and stable. If Nike stayed low, her balance improved. She carved wide turns around slowing rideshares as she hurtled through late-morning traffic, skirting the edge of another housing protest clogging Nathan Phillips Square and City Hall.

A Starbucks sat kitty-corner to the long-term care facility. Nike staked out the entrance, sipping a hot chocolate, waiting for her father to leave. She didn't want to see him. The man who eventually stepped out of the glass doors was smiling, despite his pallid skin and tired face. He'd even shaved—a rare occurrence. His board dropped to the pavement and he sped away, weaving easily through pedestrians.

Nike had expected him to look disheveled, maybe even broken. Maybe she'd wanted that. She only needed a glance at her arm to know why. But he had only seemed older.

Taking the stairwell instead of the elevator, she peered through the wire-mesh reinforced glass of the ward door. No patients were visible from the outside—just a nursing station and a lounge area. Her hand hovered on the cool steel door handle. With a deep breath, she pushed it open. She didn't really want to see her mom and sister, but they were all she had left.

The nurses were gossiping about the affordable housing protesters clashing with police at city hall.

"I'm here to see Analia and Sabra Highspire," Nike interrupted. "I'm family."

"Aren't you pretty," the nurse said, examining Nike's ID, then cutting her gaze away to her screen when Nike placed her stump on the counter. "Go ahead. You just missed their facials. I swear, sometimes I'm so jealous."

"Yeah, me too," Nike muttered, already regretting coming. She'd rather be at the warehouse breathing in the pigeon shit and urine that painted the walls than smelling the covert reek of illness that permeated the air here. All was white and stainless steel, quiet and clinical, punctuated by the grunts of what substituted for communication from some of the patients. Even so, the grunts were more fluent than the slack jaws of her family. As she approached their room, a nurse was assisting Sabra into a chair.

Nike hated this place. She'd lost her mother eight years ago, her memories of her vague and hazy—snuggles on a couch, being read to. *In French?* She'd dropped the course last year; she'd probably speak it fluently if her mom hadn't succumbed to the infection. She'd have a sister too. This was a mausoleum of animatronic cadavers, a house of loss.

"Is this Nike?" the burly nurse asked, beaming. "I'm Chui, Analia and Sabra's nurse. Remember me?"

She didn't but nodded anyway.

His eyes took in her arm, but he didn't say anything, only holding up a bowl of cereal. "Your dad rushed off before chow time—a first in forever—so it's nice to have a fresh face," Chui said. "You up to feeding them?"

Reluctantly taking the bowl, Nike shifted to her sister. Sabra's arms stretched outward as though reaching for a hug, but her eyes were silent.

"Creepy," Nike said, pressing Sabra's arms down into her lap. "Why are her arms like that?"

"Catatonia," the nurse explained. "Leaving them extended keeps her muscles toned."

In case she wakes up and wants to walk around, Nike thought bitterly.

Nike tried not to think about the implication that all of this was temporary. It wasn't. And until her father accepted that, it would never be over.

Then why are you here, Nike?

Sabra's features were finer than her own, closer to their mother's—delicate cheekbones, soft lips. Nike had her father's jawline, strong and angular, a feature she'd always been self-conscious about. They both shared their mother's deep brown eyes and warm, dusky skin tone. Sabra's hair wasn't quite as curly black but looked as crazy to manage as Nike's own. There the similarities ended.

Sabra's eyes were empty, unblinking. There was no life behind them.

Nike handed the bowl of cereal she'd been given back to the nurse. "Actually, maybe another time. Can I have a moment, though?"

The nurse nodded, setting the bowl on a side table before stepping out of the room.

Nike lingered by her sister's chair, but her mind was somewhere else. It was a fuzzy memory, one Nike wasn't sure if she'd dreamed up or not. The last time she'd seen Sabra conscious was in another white room, though the door had been steel, sealed shut. And in that room had been the figure: hooded, shadowed, holding a staff topped with a wavering torch.

A Burner.

The figure's other hand had emanated a strange, sultry light. Nike remembered the light so vividly, the way it gestured as though beckoning her forward. She'd stumbled toward the beacon, desperate to reach Sabra, who had been lying motionless beneath a blanket in the center of the room.

But then a rush of fire enveloped something nearby, leaving a charred, smoking stick in its wake. The blast had sent Nike staggering backward, her shoulders pressing against the cold steel door.

She had only wanted to see Sabra again, to confirm that her sister was safe beneath that blanket. But when the figure's hood shifted as though tracking something unseen, Nike felt it: whatever it was, it was coming for her.

The thing under the blanket wasn't Sabra.

It was utter blackness.

And the blackness had swallowed her whole.

The call for a *Code Blue* brought Nike crashing back to reality.

The nurse was at Nike's head, lifting it. "Easy now, easy."

Her legs were against the cool linoleum floor. "What—"

"You fainted," Chui said gently, waving off the other staff who had crowded into the room. "It's okay. You Highspires aren't exactly known for taking care of yourselves, are you?"

He helped her sit on the edge of Sabra's bed. "Wait here. I'll grab you some water, and we'll chat."

Nike nodded, but didn't wait. As soon as his back was turned, she pulled herself upright, still shaking, and hustled out of the ward with the skateboard tucked under her arm.

She woke on Joula's couch, unable to remember the ride home. The blanket draped over her smelled faintly of lavender, and dusk softened the light through the window. Her alarm was buzzing, but it wasn't her phone—it was the clock on the counter.

A note was pinned beside it: *It's not working. Sorry.* Beneath was an arrow. She flipped it over.

You're still my best friend.

Nike stared at it, bleary-eyed, trying not to cry. It was time to go.

Arriving at work, Nike's mood soured further at the sight of a bob-cut blonde standing beside Sophie at the host podium. Sophie was chatting animatedly while the blonde nodded along, disinterested.

"The tips are good," Nike said dryly as she approached them.

"Oh, hi, Nike!" Sophie chirped. "This is Trixie. Oscar's got you inside tonight."

Jud wore his usual smirk.

Nike shot Sophie a look, then glanced back at Trixie. The new girl was sizing her up with a bored expression, clearly unimpressed.

Inside, Oscar shoved a bucket and mop into Nike's hand. "Women's washroom. Bachelorette party got started early."

"Me?" Nike asked, staring at the mop.

"I'm paying you, aren't I?" Oscar replied, his eyes flicking briefly to her stump.

"Yes, I can clean a washroom," she said.

"Good. Afterward, you're on coat check."

"Coat check?" she repeated. It was late July—not exactly jacket weather.

"Just opened it. I've got floats to do," Oscar said, hustling into the club to count money.

Vomit flooded the bathroom floor. Nike winced as she stepped inside, setting to work.

What do you call a one-handed coat-check girl? she mused bitterly. *Nike? No, Peg.*

Luckily, the night didn't bring many jackets, or she might have been in trouble for holding up the line.

"Cover me?" Sophie asked, two hours later. "Make sure Trixie's good."

Trixie regarded Nike with the same disinterested expression.

"You overwhelmed yet?" Nike asked with a chuckle.

Trixie snorted but said nothing.

Nike leaned closer. "Here's some advice." Trixie turned away but, by the tilt of her head, was still listening. "Pad your bra so they're not touching you. And wear tight yoga shorts. Guys will put their fingers anywhere if you let them."

Trixie's face flushed red as she swallowed hard. "But the tips are great, right?"

"Yeah," Nike replied flatly. "Pretty great."

Trixie hesitated, then mumbled, "Because this guy just—"

"Yeah, I know. We all get it. But hey … tips."

Chapter Sixteen

After Fumo's slaughter of raitgur in the Promise Complex, Trayling had spotted him in Little Italy, strutting around as if he owned the place, dropping spines in various locations, taking photos, and writing in a black journal. Trayling knew exactly what he was doing: proving Trayling hadn't been doing his job. If Nike's lack of response was any indication, Trayling would have to stop him alone.

Trayling knew what to do. For the past eight years, he had burned raitgur out of alleys, rooftops, abandoned buildings, and the grottos of parks. They liked shelter, shadows, and solitude—more like him than he cared to admit. They didn't like open spaces or crowds. Without the secrecy and dark refuge provided by the abandoned houses, Trayling hoped the aliens would be forced into other territories, exposing the breeders for other Burners to eliminate. Anything to disrupt the little farm Fumo had going on.

Ambrose's call for a Burner meeting had gone out, and Chuck was quick to set it in his territory. Chuck was an asshole, but at least he was predictable, and he owned the vault. If it was good for Chuck, Chuck would do it. He would want control. Trayling would have done the same.

Before heading home, Trayling texted Nike again. One text was all he allowed himself per day. Today's read: *I love you. Tonight at one. I'm burning out the nest. With or without you. No judgment. I have to do this. For Mom. For Sabra.* For Nike. He added the location.

On his kitchen table lay the original plans for the Promise Complex. He'd marked the supporting walls, identified which were concrete and which were wood, which would burn. Interpreting the city's utility maps had been straightforward enough, and he'd used them to pinpoint the sewer within his district that provided access to a manhole cover inside the rowhouse complex. At night, he'd scouted the sewers to ensure limited traffic and memorized the routes. The sewers were a necessary complication, allowing him to reach the complex's center without being flayed alive by raitgur.

Earlier that day, Trayling had said his goodbyes to Analia and Sabra after an hour of sticky honey, wax strips, facial hair removal, and charcoal facials. Now, at 1:00 a.m., he waited in a parking lot beside a manhole cover, hoping Nike would show.

A fuel canister sat at his feet, topped up with gasoline. A bat was slung across his back. The weapon wasn't for the raitgur—fighting one with a bat was like hitting a rubber band; they absorbed physical blows. The fuel was for the houses; the weapon was for anyone who might get in his way. With enough of a delay before the fire department arrived, the fuel should collapse the rowhouse nest.

Trayling's challenge was to penetrate close enough to find the dwellings with the largest clusters of aliens and burn them to the ground—all without being shredded by the creatures. Raitgur acid ate through Burner skin like baking soda fizzing in vinegar. His new oilskin coat didn't feel thick enough.

The sewer entry was tucked away in an office parking lot. A car engine turned over, and one of the few remaining vehicles drove off. No one else was around, including Nike. After a final check for witnesses—and his phone for a message from his daughter—Trayling levered the manhole cover off. Iron scraped against iron. He shone his palm light into the opening, scanning the ladder, the puddle below, and the lack of aliens. He swung onto the rungs and lowered himself down, carrying the fuel canister in one hand. The ladder's corrugated rungs bit into his fingers as he descended, finally landing with a splash at the bottom.

The glow from his light revealed a low, misty tunnel. The map indicated this narrow stretch connected to a major artery a hundred yards ahead, but the tight space forced him onto his knees. He dragged himself through the muck, hauling the fuel canister forward every few feet.

When the tunnel opened into a taller east-west corridor, he straightened, tucking the canister under his arm. Red-eyed rats scurried ahead, claws scratching at the concrete. Trayling tracked his progress on his phone, which lost signal in the tunnels only to regain it under manhole covers and sewer grates.

The stench worsened. Rats suddenly stopped fifty yards past Bathurst, as if halted by an invisible barrier. Trayling slowed, inspecting the tunnel walls. Snotties hung in places, but it was difficult to identify in the sludgy mess. Something moved in the murk, something larger than a rat.

He freed the baseball bat, choking the grip in the tunnel confines as a diamond pattern of scales slithered through the sewage. Not a raitgur—a snake, its skin glinting faintly. At least twelve feet long. A python? Boa constrictor? Trayling didn't know his snakes. Didn't want to know his snakes.

It explained the disappearing rats.

The snake turned down another pipe, and Trayling released a shuddering breath. The rats resumed their advance. Soon, a faint light caught his eye. Switching his palm light to ultraviolet, he noticed a field of snotties coating the ceiling, their mucus swirling in the sewage. At the edge of his light, a young raitgur paused, half its tentacles oddly frozen, stretched out in the direction of the nest. It lingered until Trayling turned his light upon it, then scrambled into darkness. He followed, briefly losing it to a bend in the tunnel, but again, farther down, it waited. Then a hundred yards on, the raitgur stopped at a small pipe, folded itself inside, and disappeared. He couldn't shake the feeling of being lured.

Above Trayling, a manhole seeped gummy slime. He pulled out his knife and sliced a path through the curtain of snotties, then pulled out his phone to check if his hunch was right. His phone's GPS confirmed he was beneath the nest.

With the bat re-slung across his back, he checked his pocket for the lighter and then pulled on the heavy leather gloves designed to protect against raitgur acid. Braced with his boots dug into the ladder rungs and one hand on the fuel canister, he shoved the cover open with his free hand, pushing up on one side to flip it, nearly losing his balance.

The manhole cover clanged. Wincing, he counted to three before climbing into the cool, raitgur-brightened night.

He emerged into the middle of the abandoned complex.

The night glowed, the air hazy with luminescent raitgur. From the center of the fog slipped one, pulsing hotly, larger than the rest and squatting alone. If he didn't know better, he'd have sworn it was their selected champion.

"Jesus fucking Christ." Trayling backed toward the sewer. Had they led him here, to destroy him, for sport? For years, he'd thought raitgur were mindless pests. Now, he wasn't so sure. Something chittered at his calves. Dozens of raitgur cut off his escape.

The champion shot forward. Trayling swung his bat, knowing it was futile. That he'd failed. He'd never pass through an army of them. The tentacle flickered and disappeared, then they all did, and for a moment he was plunged into darkness. He felt a rush of air as something flashed close by him. The monstrous alien coalesced to his right.

Trayling swung again. A tentacle tip caught his face. He cried out, stumbling dangerously close to the sewer lip. Cursing as more hits landed against his side, he swung wildly.

"C'mon!"

Another desperate whistle of the bat. Trayling dropped the weapon and dashed for the fuel canister instead. Raitgur appeared and disappeared as if having gained the power to teleport, making them impossible to avoid. Lashes snapped across his back, shoulders, thighs, gloves. Even with the oilskin, he should be melting. But he wasn't. The bulky gloves were useless against the fuel cap, and he shook free of them, wrenching off the top of the canister, running to splash fuel on the nearest clapboard wall, a door, a ragged fir tree.

A Burner burns. *Any way he can.*

"Say bye-bye to your nest."

Another tentacle flashed down, caught him across the forehead where the last strike had only just begun to heal. He felt it curl about his head and haul backward, but then it vanished, sending him staggering. Trayling screamed as he sloshed fuel in the direction of the disappeared raitgur and then over the next house. He didn't want to start the fire until he'd used all the gasoline. Even isolated as the complex was, someone would see the flames and call the fire department.

With a row of houses drenched, he hobbled across the road, taking hits, dozens of them. He should be dead, he knew it, but the hits he had taken only scrambled his thoughts. He reached the other side of the road. The canister seemed heavier despite it glugging half empty.

He heard the chug of a fireball before it caught him in the back, sending him slamming against the wall, the reek of sulfur waking him from his blackout. The fuel canister lay on its side, dousing the cracked concrete walkway. His coat had taken the majority of the blow, but his hand, his bare hand, was on fire. It burned a cool blue. He jerked it away from the gasoline and stared at it, wondering if fuel had splashed onto it, but he knew that wasn't true. It was lit with a wobbly pilot flame. The pain set in, and he smothered the hand in his armpit.

In the distance, Cenere, Fumo, and Fuoco appeared. All lit up.

The raitgur had disappeared. But Trayling knew they weren't gone, not at all, not if his hand was burning. They hadn't changed.

He had.

Chapter Seventeen

Nike squinted at her father's text: *Light up. Just try. Please.* She'd already received his earlier message about loving her, waiting for her, and razing the nest—the usual father-daughter drama. It was why she'd thrown back two extra bottles of tequila, to ensure she wouldn't be useful to him. Yet an hour later, the effects of the alcohol had already worn off.

Feeling nervous and a little guilty, she'd switched her phone off silent mode, even though Oscar hated that. The most recent text came with a map. She was fairly certain her father was standing near the spot where she'd lost her hand. Why should she light up? He couldn't burn even if she were in the next room, and the greater the distance, the greater the pain. Hard pass.

"Trixie? Really?" a new customer laughed, evidently a regular Nike hadn't met yet, judging by the way his expression suggested he owned the place rather than just rented a bar stool. She hated these types. "And what's your name?" he asked.

"Nike."

He took her hand and didn't let go after she shook his and waved him inside.

"Like the goddess?"

To his credit, ninety-nine times out of a hundred it was "like the shoes?"

"Sure."

"That's better than Trixie. Trixie—"

Nike placed her hand on his lips. "Don't say it." She didn't want to hear what rhymed with Trixie, what puns could be made with it, or how Trixie could be the butt of his joke. His eyes widened, and then he kissed her palm. She let him, wishing Jud would call him "buddy" and sit on his head. When she felt his tongue, she snatched her hand back, unable to hide her revulsion.

She didn't stop him as he entered the club, grumbling, "I had a dog named Trixie."

"Thanks," Trixie said after he was gone. "I hate my name."

"Short for Beatrice?" Nike ignored her phone's persistent bleating and tried to focus on Trixie instead.

"Hate that more. Don't know what my mothers were thinking."

Another text. *Just try.*

"Why the hell should I burn myself for nothing?" Nike mumbled.

Trixie gave her an odd look. "Burn yourself?"

"Just thinking aloud," Nike said, waving her off as she let another guy in. Did her dad need help?

A new conversationalist approached. "A Knocked Back knock-out?" His close-shaven beard, perfectly styled hair, and deep V-neck shirt suggested the rest of him was likewise manicured.

"I.D., please?" Nike asked.

"He's good," Jud said.

"Nah, I get it." The man pulled his phone and tugged out his I.D. from a clip. "She wants my address. Okay, knock-out, here you are. That's the penthouse, by the way."

The man's grin withered under Nike's gaze, though she wasn't really focused on him. Her thoughts were with her dad's attempts to stop alien infections; with Joula's judgmental stares; and with the painting of the raitgur sucking Joula's face off. But here she was, trying and failing to get drunk, checking I.D.s for men who had something to prove, and training Trixie to wear tight shorts just to fend off the horror show of unwanted fingers.

If her dad needed her, and she didn't even *try* to help, could she live with that? What if Joula became infected?

Another text arrived. Nike didn't need to look—she knew. He needed her.

Nike held out her stump to Conversationalist. "Knock-out, huh? Really?" She stripped the leather sheath, unwound the bandage, and revealed the oozy mess beneath. In truth, it was healing incredibly fast, but it was hard to tell due to the slick ointment. Conversationalist stepped back. Jud looked like he might hurl. "Still seeing a knock-out?" she asked, disgusted with these men, disgusted with herself for pandering to them in order to earn tips from insecure women. She couldn't help but enjoy the reactions. They made her feel dangerous.

Trixie fainted.

Nike's phone flickered. Turning her arm into a torch would take the sideshow to the next level. She dug into her pocket and pulled out her Zippo.

It had been a gift—the birthday after she got her period, when she'd missed her mother and sister the most. She'd woken to find it on her bed, a tiny box propped up by a brown fuzzy koala with Velcro paws. The glossy white box had been tied with a thin blood-red silk ribbon and a tiny bell. Nike had sat in bed imagining what could be inside—a ring of her mother's, a mood stone, or a miniature journal for her secrets.

The box and her imagination had been the best part.

Inside, set in black velvet, already smelling of lighter fluid, was a polished Zippo. The inscription read: *May it light your way. Love always, Dad.*

It had lit her way ever since. She'd never questioned the way—or the love. Until now.

She held the flame beneath the stump, waiting for it to catch.

"What the fuck?" Conversationalist shouted.

Wait for it ...

Her skin sizzled. Sophie appeared beside her, spotted the flame, the stump, and Trixie on the floor, then ran off crying.

Nike waited for the flesh to ignite. But it didn't. It blistered and burned, hurting like hell, but it wouldn't light. She snapped the Zippo shut, snuffing the flame, and stared at the angry wound. "No shit."

She texted her dad: *I don't burn.*

To Conversationalist, she said, "I don't burn. Why don't I burn?"

Her inability to get drunk or stoned. The speed at which her body healed. It all started at ... *never.*

Her phone buzzed again. *I do,* the text read. Then a map appeared with her father's location and a final message: *HELP.*

In eight years, he'd never called for help. In eight years, she'd never really been able to.

Oscar jogged up, Sophie tucked behind him. "What are you doing?"

"Freaking out the customers," Jud said. "Masochistic bullshit."

"I have to go," Nike replied distantly, packing her phone and Zippo into her handbag.

"Yeah, go," Conversationalist sneered. "Freak."

Her fingers balled into a fist before she realized what she was doing. She twisted, swinging wildly. Conversationalist dropped back, blocked her arm, and kicked her hard in the stomach, sending her sprawling to the ground.

A few people in line stared at him, their gazes hard.

"You saw that!" he exclaimed. "The psycho attacked me. Time to work on your hiring skills there, Oscar."

Nike climbed to her feet, nauseous from the kick, and ran for her longboard.

***

Trayling dodged the second fireball. It exploded against the siding, igniting the gasoline in a sudden *whump*. He landed in a weedy garden and used the pulpy sill of a window to pull himself up. Beyond the grimy pane, in the light of the flames, a shape lay on the floor of the house. A person.

"Hey!" he shouted, knocking on the glass. "Get out!"

The figure didn't move. Anyone inside would likely be infected, like Analia or Sabra. Without nurses and doctors, they'd be dying slowly and alone. In the fire, they'd die for certain.

"Shit."

Trayling yanked at a loose corner of plywood covering the door, but the fire was raging, heat billowing over him. Another fireball hammered the building's side.

"There's someone in there!" he yelled toward the Italians. If they heard, they didn't show it. Or care. Even as Trayling tugged at the plywood, he realized the fire wasn't enough to destroy the nest. At best, only a few units were burning. He needed more fuel. He needed Nike.

Tentacles flashed around him, carving at his coat and whipping his skin, but the debilitating pain was gone.

Stubborn nails clung to the doorframe, even as violet wisps of light danced and disappeared in the periphery. The strikes against Trayling's body were relentless—he felt buried under raitgur. And yet, he was impervious.

Into his guts wormed an unnerving blend of loss, hope, and terror for what would happen when Nike arrived. Mostly, he felt expectant pride.

Noxious fumes pumped through the doorframe and sent him sprawling and coughing.

Whatever had changed him hadn't made him immune to smoke or fire.

***

The sweet smell of the fire spurred Nike onward. She arrived on the outskirts of the rowhouses, breathless and aching from the kick to her stomach. The punch had been stupid—an impulsive act born of frustration and from watching too much television. She was no fighter. An underfed, underweight, one-handed seventeen-year-old wasn't going to take down a grown man twice her size.

But her self-recrimination ended when the orange glow of flames bubbled out over the rooftops. The longboard accelerated.

Raitgur were everywhere, loping alongside her, tracking her movements. How stupid she'd been to stop bringing her burn kit and oilskin to work. She was exposed. All she had was her leather bite guard tucked into her top.

Nothing attacked her, though. She didn't have time to wonder why.

In the distance, her father roared, followed by the crack of splintering wood. Jets of flame shot up near the park. A comet of fire disappeared from sight but was followed by her father's cry and another puff of flame.

"Daddy!" she screamed.

"Nike!" he shouted back. "Over here!"

She found him lying beside a charred hunk of plywood that had once covered an open doorway. He was crawling with raitgur.

"Daddy—"

He flipped, rolling on top of an alien, putting his hand right out to another.

"Dad, you …"

"They're on me, aren't they?"

She nodded, horrified. The raitgur swarmed him, but he barely seemed to notice. More terrifyingly, his face had changed—slack and pale, even in the flush of fire and heat. "We have to get out of here."

He pointed inside. "There's someone in there."

The roof of the house was ablaze, flames licking up its sides. Her dad clambered slowly to his feet, his coat smoking. Yellow-black smoke roiled beneath the ceiling in the home's front hall. He shoved the board aside.

"Dad! You can't go in there."

But her father wouldn't leave someone to die, even at the cost of his life. Shielding his face with his coat, he barreled through the doorway.

Raitgur lined the sidewalk, watching her. "They're everywhere," she whispered, gripping a wheel of her skateboard to swing it like a weapon.

The Italians stood beyond the park fence, arms and stumps crossed, watching impassively. Fumo incinerated any alien that ventured too close. A scattering of spines littered the yard where her father had been lying. Sirens joined the sparks whirling in the night sky.

"Hurry, Dad!"

From inside, he called, "I have him." She heard grunting and heavy stomps.

A tiny raitgur hopped onto the cracked concrete step. She resisted the urge to kick it away.

A wispy tentacle tested the air, then licked across her big toe.

Pain spiked up her leg, radiating into her chest and bursting into white-hot agony. She gasped, the raitgur leaping back as if startled, then skittering to rejoin its kind.

"Dad, I can feel them! They can touch me. And—" Another spasm of pain shot up her leg. She groaned. *They hurt.*

From the doorway of the home, her father dragged a man by his armpits. His head lolled to one side. Her father coughed.

"Is that—"

It was the man from the alley. Many days dead.

"Jesus," her father said, noticing it too. "How? I saw the paramedics pick him up."

"We'll figure it out later," Nike said. Her father resumed dragging the man toward the road.

As one, the raitgur surged forward flogging her dad with tentacles, swarming him. Ranked along the sidewalk, they blocked passage. Or tried to. They couldn't hurt her father any longer.

"The raitgur are there," she said, feeling danger prickling at the base of her skull for the first time on a hunt.

"Just want the fire department to find his body, not ashes."

"Dad—" She stared at him, feeling the heat of the fire licking at her skin, the raitgur acid burn still sending twinges up her hip. "They're going to rip me to shreds."

Concern twisted his features, then gave way to understanding.

"Dad … what if …" She faced him, and in his eyes, she saw not just understanding and resignation, but something more. A yearning. "The acid. The fact that I can see them now …"

Her voice faltered. He'd already guessed. He'd known when he texted her—perhaps she had too.

"It's your turn to burn, Nike."

Her father hauled the body through the raitgur. They clambered over him, whipped at him. If they hurt him, he didn't show it. Only darkened splotches of wet marred his coat. Slowly, purposefully, he strode up the steps and raised his index finger—the one already scarred by acid.

"Santana says it's the finger to burn first." He thrust it into the fire crackling along a windowsill and cringed as the flames licked his skin. "You can't light up anymore. But I can. Maybe because I can."

When he pulled his finger out, it flickered blue-green-orange. The sight seemed to clear Nike's mind. Sounds sharpened, and the lines of her father's craggy face grew vivid.

"Ever since I did that to your hand," he said, "things have started changing."

"I'm the Burner," she whispered. Beneath her glove, her hand prickled insistently. With her teeth, she pulled the glove off, revealing her glowing palm. She glanced at her father, his flame-sheathed finger wagging.

"Hurry. This hurts," he said, his laugh strained.

"Uh, yeah!" she replied, but movement from the Italians caught her eye, snuffing out any humour. The young daughter, Fuoco, lit her pinky. Cenere bent low, igniting her arm stumps on her already smouldering leg stumps. Fumo raised his hands, fire sparking between them.

"We have to destroy the nest," her father said.

"No, Dad," she said. "I don't wa—"

He shoved her aside. His coat was engulfed by flames as a blast slammed him against the siding. She yanked him from the fire, and he was soon back on his feet. That one had been meant for her.

"Stop it!" she screeched at the Italians. "Just let us go!"

The raitgur approached. She had never felt so vulnerable and so alive.

"They're everywhere, Daddy!"

"Use it! Burn!" her father shouted.

Flames leapt unbidden from her hand, running over her fingers. She stared at them—their cool blaze, the power creeping up her arm and into her skull, obliterating fear and worry, leaving only the desire to burn. The aliens shied away.

"Christ, that hurts," her father gasped.

She pushed past the intoxicating power. "Sorry." She clenched her fist, extinguishing the flames.

"No, no, it's the only way. We can do this if we do it together."

"This isn't me learning to ride a bike—it's burning off my dad's finger. I don't want to. I won't."

"Do you have a choice?"

Not really. Her father had dragged her into the raitgur nest and forced her hand. "This is a setup," she whispered, realization clearing her tears. "You played me. You knew I'd come."

"I did what I had to do," he said, feverish eyes pleading. "If I couldn't kill the raitgur, I could at least burn their nest. I didn't know if you'd be with me." His voice softened. "But you came. You're here. We can destroy the nest. Maybe Santana will see for herself when she cleans up this mess."

As he blathered on, Nike had never felt more alone. Her dad wanted nothing to change.

"I have a way out," he added. "After. The sewer. We just have to reach the street."

The Italians lobbed a fireball, scattering a small group of raitgur, their spines clattering on the pavement.

"Are you crazy?" Nike shouted at them.

"Poachers!" Cenere yelled.

Sirens drew closer.

"Nike …" Her father nodded toward the fire blazing in her fist. The burn cleared her head. It didn't bring pain, but energy. Clarity of thought. A feeling of invincibility. His finger flared brighter as he dropped to one knee.

She tried to care. This was what her father had felt every time he lit up. If she did this, she wouldn't be able to stop—just like him.

"No!" Nike snuffed the flames again. "I'm not you. I don't want this life. We'll run for it."

He couldn't see the raitgur horde tightening their circle. Maybe it wouldn't be as bad as she feared. But the angry welts on his face, hands, scalp told her otherwise. Still, she led him toward the waiting raitgur.

At first, they parted for her, even as they crawled over her oblivious father. They seemed to recognize him as the dangerous one. Like crows recognizing someone who had once stolen an egg from their nest. His gaze stayed fixed on the ground as he reached for a spine.

"Leave them, Dad. We're getting out of here."

He didn't. He grabbed greedily. Cenere's indignant screech split the night. The raitgur closed off the path to the manhole and the house.

"They're proof of the nest!" her father insisted. "If we can't burn it, we can bring Santana proof."

A tentacle whipped around her waist, tearing at her skin. She screamed, and fire burst from her hand, engulfing the alien. The surge of strength made her whoop.

As one, the raitgur rolled back, stunned and silent. Nike stared at them, not breathing, ashamed of her shout but unable to suppress the lightness in her chest.

A chitter broke the silence. The swarm surged forward. Nike met them, burning everything that closed in.

Behind her, her father's breathing was ragged. "You're doing good, Nike. Doing good. A little farther."

Good? All she felt was power. She reveled in it. She no longer had to make herself small or vulnerable. Never again.

"Poachers!" Fuoco shouted. Fumo hurled another attack. Nike's father yanked her down, shielding them both with his coat as heat slammed into them.

Nike leapt free, a marble of lightning rolling in her palm. She hurled it at the Italians. The energy burst against Cenere's wheelchair, snaking over her flesh, toppling her.

Nike burned a path to the sewer. At its lip, she extinguished her flames and descended into the cool darkness. Spines showered after her, followed by her father, who landed heavily. His elbow braced against her shoulder as he switched on his palm light.

His finger was gone.

"We're really going to have to work on our relationship," he said.

His joke echoed hollowly in the dark.

CHAPTER EIGHTEEN

Standing before headquarters, Trayling leaned on his daughter's shoulder, amazed not only by her strength tonight but by her ability to hold herself together in the past. He tried to take more of his own weight, tried to straighten, tried to ignore the burning-powered grin on her face, but he couldn't stop shaking.

"Chills," Nike said. "Those are bad. You should have your feet up."

The slog through the sewer had been long but uneventful. No raitgur. No python. Just the stench and the rats. Nike had refused to make the trek to Trayling's entry point, leading them instead to a quieter street a few blocks from the rowhouses. She'd hauled her father out, glaring at the spines clutched under his arm. Still, it was what he'd come for. If not to burn down the rowhouse complex, then to return to Santana with proof of Fumo's duplicity. But what truly buoyed him was the power within his daughter—the chance to burn again, if not himself, then through her.

Santana would know what to do. In hindsight, Nike's refusal to raze the nest had been smart. She wasn't ready. He wasn't ready. The major would need to bring in a team of Burners. And what about the breeding pair—or however the bastards procreated? What the hell would they even be like? The creature in the alleyway had taken everything in Trayling's arsenal. He didn't want to face anything bigger, and he'd been an experienced Burner. Had been.

"And, Dad, protein. You were always saying it, but you were right. I needed meat to heal."

He managed a smile. "Finally won't have you on my case about eating too much steak."

She bit her lip, smoothing her skirt and inching it down. "And now I see why you had trouble holding back some nights. Holy crap, the rush—"

Jealousy stirred in his gut. He'd craved that rush lately, but he forced the envy away—this was what he wanted. On the slog back, he'd caught her staring at her hand, her back rigid with newfound confidence. She'd been oblivious to the lingering gazes of night folk on the barbecued old man and the scantily clad young woman.

"I'll be back in ten," he said, steadying himself as Nike disengaged. Fuck, his missing finger hurt. How the hell had she done this night after night and still gone to classes the next day?

He shoved open the massage parlour door with his burned hand, pausing for a moment to catch his breath. Inside, he waved to Corporal Tyler and headed straight to the back, too pained to ask for permission.

Santana sat at a workbench on the far side of the room, back to the door, testing something. Grids of tubes filled the space in front of her. Trayling tossed the spines onto the steel table beside him, where they clattered.

"I have proof Fumo is farming raitgur," he said.

Santana froze mid-pipette. "You what?"

"The nest we found—it's in their district. A hundred raitgur, easy. Most of them young, like they're culling them before they get too big. It explains why so many of the spines we're giving you are so close in age. It's not a nest; it's a farm. They're farming them. And they range into my district to feed, increasing my infection rates."

"Fumo is farming raitgur," she repeated. Her gaze was steady.

"I know I have every reason to want to see him burn, but I swear to you, Major, I've seen this. He's farming them."

The pipette snapped in Santana's fist. Finally, she shot to her feet, strode to the table, and leaned in over the scattered spines, lining them up one after the other. "Fuck!" She swept the spines to the floor, where they skittered across the concrete. Her fingers balled into fists at her sides and then slowly unfurled as she came back into control. "You're right, I'm going to need independent proof."

"I have charts that suggested it," he said, going to wring his hands but stopping with a grunt of pain. "Farming would sure make it easy to hit quota, I'd bet. I don't like cheaters."

Her gaze absorbed the destroyed coat, missing finger, and the spines.

"Nor do I." Santana's fury had turned grim. "But we do need to be very careful. Your feelings about Fumo are well known—this can't come from you alone."

He understood her dilemma. Fumo was her best Burner. Her superiors would come down on her too. He swallowed hard, the memory of eight years ago flashing back. Holding Analia as she convulsed, calling for help, and seeing only Fumo and Cenere standing there, watching.

"Fumo watched while an alien attacked my wife. Watched and did nothing. He could have stopped it."

"I know. I'm sorry. Be patient with me," Santana said. "You've done a good job, now I need to do mine."

It had been his word against Fumo's then, too. He nodded. "But you believe me."

"I believe you," she admitted with a long sigh. "Today was supposed to be a happy day. I have something for you."

He nodded, fierce and sharp. Santana pointed to his burned hand. "Where's Nike?"

"Outside. Safe. Why?"

"Nike did that?" He swung his arm behind his back but didn't answer.

"Fascinating. I'd wondered. Bring her in. Nike's the Burner."

"She's not—"

"New Burner. New contract. Bring her in."

"She's not some science experiment. She's seventeen. I'm still her guardian." He swayed, hand throbbing.

"You're the source now. She's the Burner. We pay the Burner."

***

With his skin pallid and his eyes exhausted, her dad looked more pissed than usual as he led her inside. A small part of Nike wanted to smile when he clenched his eyes and breathed through a spasm, or when he shoved open the door to the massage parlour and had to brace against it because he'd used his injured hand—how many times had she done that? Schaden-something, Sahle would have called it.

Sahle. Tonight changed everything. She desperately wanted someone to talk to about this—someone who wasn't her father but who believed in alien conspiracies. But it wasn't like Sahle would want to talk to her after she'd sicced a bouncer on him.

Her father shouldered open the door to the lab.

"Come in," he told her, gesturing impatiently.

Nike had met Major Santana a handful of times, none of them recent. Her hair bun and lab coat weren't doing her any favours, but that piercing gaze and toothy smile hadn't changed in eight years. Not that Nike was in any state to criticize appearances.

"Wow!" the major gushed, more like an aunt than the leader of a military unit dedicated to destroying a hostile alien species. "I remember when you were at my shoulder, and now …"

Now Nike was six inches taller than Santana, even with the filthy soles of her feet pressed to the polished concrete.

"What happened to your shoes?" Santana asked.

"Long story," Nike said. "But my footwear wasn't compatible with … well, anything. Definitely not with cooking aliens."

"You look all grown up. Congratulations on making this change."

Nike really hoped she wasn't about to pinch her cheeks.

"Yeah, my dad said you wanted to see me? This about what the Italians are doing?"

"No, no, leave that to me. I have a contract for you. All Burners sign a contract, and now you're the Burner."

"I don't want …"

Santana's smile flickered. "A Burner's piece rate is a thousand dollars a spine."

Nike forgot what she'd been about to say. "My money? It's mine to keep?"

"I've been putting money aside for you," her dad whispered, avoiding her gaze. She didn't want to hear it.

"Better than sharing tips, huh?" Santana said.

"Wha—? How'd you—?" Nike started.

"To receive your piece rate for the spines, you have to sign. We offer money and protection."

"Protection?" Nike laughed.

"I've quashed ten complaints about someone wielding a flamethrower in your district this year alone. The dealer you buy painkillers from? We provide the supply and the safe space."

"You're my dealer?"

"We take care of both our Burners and sources."

"And a cure," Trayling added. "You're researching a cure too."

"Right," Santana said, with a wink. "Hold that thought."

A contract. It felt too real to Nike. Too fast. She looked to her dad, but he had a crazed smile on his face, taking way too much pleasure with her induction. She wouldn't have to find a new job.

"Okay, I'll read it."

Santana rolled her eyes but bounced back. "As suspicious as your father. One minute."

She disappeared through a door and returned with a slim sheaf of pages. "It's the same one your father signed, updated for territories."

"When I signed, we didn't have districts," her father explained. "We hunted on our own reconnaissance."

"Led to some altercations," Santana said.

"Bad ones," he agreed.

"That's why it's important to stick to your districts," Santana said, narrowing her eyes at Trayling.

"The district model works only as long as Burners do their job and don't cheat the system," he replied.

Nike half-listened; they weren't really talking to her anyway. Most of the contract was legalese—limitations on liability, the government denying involvement if Burners caused civilian damage, and no payments beyond spines or a $50,000-per-limb-lost bonus for sources. Payment was in untraceable digital currency. There was nothing about protection, just secrecy, and a clause stating burning outside a licenced district meant military tribunal and imprisonment.

Hell. Nike glanced up from the contract to take a hard look at Santana. Who else knew about this place? How was it funded? To discredit a Burner or a source was easy. Just separate them and let them talk—they'd sound psychotic. Nike and her father had never talked about it, and she'd never asked. But … *money.*

"I get fifty thousand?" she asked, lifting her stump. "For this?"

"Per limb," Santana clarified, making a chopping motion above her elbow. "Has to be transhumeral." Santana must have sensed her resistance because she added, "I get it, Nike. I'm not entirely comfortable with parents using their children like ammunition either. But now … now you get to burn."

Nike flipped to the last page, where her name had been written in blue ink. Burner: Nike Highspire. There was a spot for the source too. Her dad would have signed for her all those years ago. She never had a choice then.

"I don't want to be a Burner," she said, holding the contract out.

Santana didn't take it. "What do you mean?"

"I'm not going to be a Burner. Find someone else."

"Everybody signs." Santana offered a red pen.

Nike ignored it. "Burning … it's …" She blew out her cheeks to mimic vomiting. "Ew."

"Don't you see?" Santana said, stepping forward to block Trayling. "No one will burn you ever again."

"I don't want to burn my father. No one should have to burn their family!"

Her dad stepped around the major, eyes desperate. "I want you to burn me."

"You can't mean that, Dad."

"Your mom and sister don't have lives because an alien infected them. If I can prevent that from happening to one other person, it's worth the cost."

"To you." Lose a limb and take home fifty thousand and save some people. He hadn't let her make that choice—and she was still out the fifty grand.

"To me," he said quietly, eyes downcast.

"I dunno, Dad, there's got to be a better way. We're in a fucking massage parlour—it's sick."

"It's covert," Santana corrected.

"Right. Why not just make it all public?"

Santana folded her arms and smiled, clearly feeling as though this was safe ground. "What do you think happens when the public has proof of an alien infestation that rewires the nervous system, causing catatonia for most people and creating new modes of energy amplification in a few?"

"You mean throwing fireballs?"

"I mean creating powerful weapons. What happens to our city when the world learns it's ground zero for the infestation?"

"Maybe I could afford real estate here one day?" Nike laughed; this conversation was insane, but that was the problem. "Maybe people should leave."

Her father touched her shoulder, and she sobered.

"We've done tabletop scenarios," Santana said. "At first, there would be chaos. Then, an influx of people seeking your powers."

Nike's gut told her Santana was right. "I'd be famous."

"For a minute," Santana agreed. "Then terminated by someone who thinks you're a demon—you can't stop bullets. Or you're kidnapped by foreign state actors. And when word gets out that living in Toronto means you could be infected by aliens?" She made a sound like an explosion. "You think the current civilian unrest is bad? Imagine the job losses. Sure, you might get your house, but it'd be in a war zone. And who knows what it would mean for the enemy? Would the raitgur stay? Or would they leave Toronto if their food source was driven away? Right now, we have them contained. Ten years ago, a meteor hit our stadium's center field. Ten years later, instead of a worldwide infestation, we've contained the only known alien species within a red zone with minimal casualties."

Her father cocked his head, intrigued. "You make it sound like a good thing."

Santana's face reddened. "We do good work. We keep the world safe."

"I bet the whole 'invulnerable to all but Burner fire' thing is pretty interesting to our military too, huh?" Nike asked.

"We're a team. What we have is working, Nike," Santana said, pressing on. "With the money you earn from spines, you can have a home here. Take care of your mother and sister. You can have time and materials for your art. That's what you want, isn't it?"

Was it?

"I think you've felt this coming, Nike. The witches you paint … you weren't a witch, but you've always thought of yourself as one, haven't you? What cures could come of this? What good? And you, Nike, the first source turned Burner, at the center of it all."

"The first?" Nike asked, surprised.

"We had no idea. This is all so new. You're the first source to ever come of age."

Nike was ready to challenge Santana further, but she caught her father's warning glance.

"We'll think about it," her dad said. "Keep those spines on ice."

Santana took the contract back, a lingering expression of disappointment on her face. "I don't want to lose you," she said. "But I need to assign the district, and I have capacity. You have twenty-four hours. And I'll remind you—you're now considered a weapon. Any illegal use of force will result in charges: arson, assault with a deadly weapon, aggravated assault, and more."

"No party tricks then?" Nike returned the major's stare before heading for the door.

"Wait. Can't believe I almost forgot." Santana's chest heaved as she hurried to a large stainless-steel fridge and pulled out a black leather case. "I want you to know, I think about Analia and Sabra every night before bed. This …" She hesitated, eyes shimmering. "I'm out of ways to trial this."

"What is it?" her father asked.

By the hope in his voice and the uncertainty in Santana's, Nike knew exactly what it was.

"It's untested, Trayling, and there's no way to know for sure."

"Give it to me." He took the case, tears in his eyes, cradling it like a newborn.

"Keep it refrigerated until you use it," Santana said. "Don't expect a sudden miracle. But it came from one of your samples."

He barked a laugh and shook her shoulder. "I knew it! You did it."

"Trayling, give it time. Chances are it won't work. Even if it does, there could be brain damage or other afflictions caused by the illness," Santana warned, but she finally smiled. "It's a start."

He hugged her. "Thank you. Thank you."

They left the parlour in silence, standing on the cracked concrete sidewalk. Her dad's face was gravestone gray, a spray of lines etched around bright, shining eyes.

"You can't break into the long-term care facility," Nike warned. "You'll have to wait until morning."

"I've waited eight years. I can wait four hours."

"Do you think she's bluffing?" Nike asked.

"About the cure?" he replied, cradling the case in his good hand.

"No, about reassigning the district. She's not going to hand the quota over to Fumo after what he's done."

"I'm not sure I care anymore," he said with a sudden grin.

"Not tested, Dad. You heard her. There's no way to know if it works." She worried about him getting his hopes up. Maybe about hers too. *To have a sister again. A mom!*

He put a finger to his lips and tilted his head toward home. After a block, her father said, "Santana will call in other Burners. Rosedale-Summerhill, Beaches-Danforth, High Park-Bloordale—someone will pick up the quota."

"It's not like we grow on trees."

"She won't want to lose us, but we're also pushing her. And we need her too." He held up the leather case as if it were proof against her doubts, and maybe it was. "I think you should sign."

"Dad, more than anyone on the planet, I understand what it's like to be burned as fuel." Nike skirted broken glass and a used needle. All around her were shards of things. Shards in her stomach. Shards in her throat. "I don't want a life of doing that to someone else. *Anyone* else."

Her father tucked the case back inside his coat before gripping Nike's shoulder. "Santana found me a couple of months after your mother's attack. Although, we didn't know it was an attack at the time. The psychiatrist had diagnosed Analia with sudden-onset catatonic depression. It wasn't even a thing, really—just the best they could figure out. But Santana had been watching for that diagnosis. And she found me. Gave me purpose. A path through the grief. Hope.

"I had two young kids, a sick wife with some nightmarish illness, and I was shattered. I couldn't even think about going back to work or pretending that everything was fine. I was about to lose you kids—both of you. My wife was in a four-bed ward in a public hospital full of overworked staff. Without Santana, I'd be a raving lunatic. Or dead. I think she can give you purpose too."

Her dad's words helped. The strength of his belief helped. But that was his life. Nike wanted to hear more about what happened to her sister— and to her. Dad seldom talked like this; he wasn't really a talker at all.

"A quota of ten raitgur spines a month for the rest of my life for a grand a spine."

"Matched to inflation."

"What, is there a union or something if there's a problem too?" She laughed. "Forget it. I'd know by now." She pressed a hand to her temple. The euphoria of burning had since worn off.

She imagined her future: bound to her father, living a secret, lonely life, walking the same neighbourhoods night after night, keeping her distance from friends, likely never having a family—because why would she ever inflict this life on a child?

"I didn't ask for this."

"No one does. It's a calling."

"What if it's not? The Italians aren't playing the same game. The government probably wants more out of it than eradication. What if we're just being used? We think we're figuring it out, but really, they've figured us out. We're being controlled. We're all fuel."

"Then, under those circumstances, it would be up to us to prove it."

Nike wasn't sold. She'd seen enough of the world to know it didn't change just because you proved something. When it came to change, proof had little to do with it.

"Okay," her dad said, stopping in a quiet spot between blocks, a stretch of glass retail windows where no one and nothing could sneak up on them. "Let's think short term. If not this, what do we do for money?"

"I sell my art. You can busk."

He rolled his eyes, and she sighed. It wouldn't be enough.

"We get real jobs. And I do art on the side."

"I'm not sure you're going to like that, and I gave up my securities licence a long time ago. I'm only qualified to be an Uber driver, and we don't have a car."

"Well, you can't Uber someone on a skateboard, but Joula has an old van she uses to transport finished pieces. Maybe—" She sagged, exasperated, remembering how she'd left Knocked Back and Sophie's recital of *It's a good job.*

"This may not work," he said, patting the case. "Likely won't. I know it. And the institution your mom and sister are in—that costs money too. Our house costs money."

"I don't want to be a Burner, Dad. And I'm not doing this for vengeance like you are. The price is too high. Even if I'm not the one being burned, it'll still mean my life."

"Vengeance?" he asked.

"You're not in this for vengeance?" It was her turn to roll her eyes.

He rubbed his face, fatigue etched into every line. "I don't do it for vengeance. Not by half. But being destitute won't make life easier either. Stay in the game. Give me a chance to figure out the bigger picture."

"Give you a chance." He was always saying that. *My district. My spine.* "I'm the Burner."

"Us. We'll figure it out. Together. Maybe we can clear this nest. Clear all of Toronto." His arm jerked as he gestured to the sweep of the city. They'd be up for military tribunal, but the idea appealed to her.

"Why didn't you clear it before now?"

"I thought we were," he said. "And maybe I was scared to think bigger." His eyes flicked to her stump and away.

"Because you didn't want to burn me?"

"Everything has changed. We can end this."

Nike considered. She couldn't imagine a lifetime of burning her father to a crisp, but what if there was a finish line? Eradicate the raitgur. Cure or not, they were a blight. No more burning.

Little Fuoco might have a chance at a normal life. But if Nike did nothing, Fuoco would lose her limbs as soon as Fumo ran out of her grandma. But that wasn't Nike's problem.

"I want to go to art school," she said.

"Fine." Her father agreed too quickly, and it made her suspicious. "That takes money too."

She knew it. "I have my time. My schedule."

"You're … you're the Burner."

"Didn't say I agreed to sign, though." Her father sighed. "How's the finger?"

"Hot."

"I left a bottle of painkillers in the cabinet."

"I don't want drugs."

"We'll see. Okay. If we do this, we do it my way now."

Her father hesitated. "If you don't sign, she won't pay."

"I'm not ready yet."

He nodded. He didn't have a choice, she realized. The part of her that might have felt sorry for him had long since turned to ashes.

"Dad?"

"Yes, honey?"

"I'm out tonight." She listened for his silence. Hoped for it. Sensed the tension as he worked to hold it.

Silence came, and so she filled it.

"Don't wait up."

Chapter Nineteen

At first, she'd thought she needed time to think. But what she truly craved was *not* thinking.

At this hour, the only option was an all-night rave Joula invited her to. Nike was mixing. The DJ mixed. The dancers mixed. Light mixed. The itching of her healing arm mixed with the taste of newly minted freedom and the savage energy she now recognized as part of being a Burner. She tried mixing drugs too, but they did little—as if her new physiology cooked through them before they'd barely grazed her mind.

Bodies pressed close as the lights strobed and the DJ blended the beat to a faster rhythm, drawing a cheer from the crowd. Nike raised her arms, snake-charmed by the thumping music. Blacklight ignited the looping glowpaint stenciled on her skin.

Joula had started the night across from Nike but had drifted off to grind against a muscular woman, her face buried in the woman's neck.

"I like this one," Nike said when Joula came up for air.

Joula smiled sadly. "Out of my league."

"Maybe you deserve this league."

They drifted apart again. Nike took more pills.

She grinned, feeling as though she dove headfirst into the night. Silver fire had shot from her hand. Fire had *shot* from her hand! Nike was all in for witchery. More pills.

"Rhymes with bitch!" she shouted at the pulsing light and laughed.

Something poked her arm. At first, it seemed far away, as if it was someone else's arm being poked, but the poking persisted. Then Joula was there, her smile wide and blindingly white.

The dancers pressed closer—too close now. Nike's chest constricted, her heart climbing into her throat.

"You okay?" Joula's eyes narrowed.

"Forgetting everything tonight. *Todos.*"

"How many did you take?"

Nike lifted her stump, realized it was out of fingers, and raised her good hand to show. "Dos." She'd popped two handfuls.

"Oh no, you're trying Spanish …"

"*Solo dos*. But they've done nothing. Seriously. I could take a bucket, and they'd do nothing."

Joula's tongue pushed out her upper lip, then her eyes widened as Nike suddenly heaved. The crowd leapt back, but Joula was caught, barf cascading down the front of her dress and legs.

"*Lo siento*." Evidently, Burner powers cleared her mind and blood but not her stomach.

"My fucking shoes," Joula shouted. "So hard to get them in my size!"

Joula grabbed Nike's hand and pulled her through the crowd, away from incoming security and into a parking lot crammed with cars, where they were hit by a rush of cool night air.

Nike made it three rows before leaning against a car still warm from its engine. She climbed onto the hood, curling into a ball. She wanted to be small. To be normal.

"No, no, we can't sleep here, girl," Joula said.

"I can't sleep," Nike replied. Her eyes darted beneath her lids. Her dad had only ever needed a couple of hours of sleep a night. She'd thought it a gift. Now she wondered.

Nike slammed her fist on the hood. The car alarm blared, headlights flashing. She started cry-laughing, rolling off the car and running with Joula until they hid behind a massive pickup truck, asshole-parked across two spaces. They slumped against the knobby tire.

Nike inspected her stump.

"You're getting past it. It's just a hand, right?" Joula's speech slurred. "God gave us two so we could lose one. Like tits." She stared at her cleavage and chuckled. "Well, I paid for mine. Maybe God fucked up a bit making me, but I fixed things."

"Is that why you make things? To remake them? Fix them?"

Joula cocked her head. "Maybe. I like to create."

"I do too." That might have been her issue with signing the contract. Artists created. Burners destroyed. "It sucks."

Joula nodded, then turned and punched Nike in the arm. "You know I'm making you a new one."

"A boob?"

"A hand! A hand for an artist. Even better—or at least a fix. You know in the future we're all gonna have bionic parts. Only poor people won't. Your new hand is gonna be *sweeeet!*"

Nike turned to her. "Really?"

Joula's gaze grew distant. "Yeah, I've been working on it all week. Carbon fibre and shit. Strong. For us night-roving-street-bitches."

"How strong?"

"Punch through this fucking truck."

"Switchblade?"

"Hand for an artist. What do you need a knife for?" Joula waved her off. "Whatever you want."

"Ultraviolet light embedded in the palm and a big-ass blade in the wrist." Nike leaned forward, thinking of raitgur and assholes. "Reinforce the knuckles."

"Dude."

"Can I change the colours? Match outfits?" Nike smiled at her stump. "This might not be so gross."

Something shifted beneath the car opposite them. Nike would have dismissed it as a rat—or her fired-up imagination—if not for the dark purple throb.

"Better than gross," Joula agreed. "Cool." She studied Nike. "You don't actually seem fucked up. No more than usual, anyway."

Nike crawled forward, planting her hand in a puddle of snottie when she leaned down. Her skin sizzled as she hissed, wiping it on the truck door before peering underneath.

"Spoke too soon." Joula sighed. "Whatcha doing, girl?"

A tiny raitgur huddled against a wheel like a stray cat.

"We gotta go," Nike said.

But the alien disappeared. When Nike turned back, it chittered on top of the truck bed, a foot above Joula. A jab of fear ripped through Nike's gut.

"No ... not her."

"What's wrong with you? One second, you're more lucid than I've seen you in a week. The next, you're like ... holing. Are you holing?"

"Yeah, whatever. Let's get out of here, okay?" Nike said, eyes locked on the raitgur, which was grooming its tentacles, rubbing one across the other. She'd say anything to get Joula out of range, but Joula was laughing. "Just come! Please. Please."

The raitgur's tentacles bent.

Nike grabbed Joula, wrenching her away, just as the alien smacked into

Nike's back. The sheer fabric of her clothes offered little protection, and acid screamed down her spine.

"Nike!" Joula shouted, shoving at her.

Nike caught the flash of purple and swung. Acid mauled her fist, but the raitgur was pushed off course. "You've ruined your last life, gelatinous snot nugget!"

"People are watching, Nike."

She kept herself between the alien and Joula. She couldn't let it hurt her friend. *So you're going to need to burn your dad.*

The raitgur's tentacles bent again.

Nike grabbed her friend's hand. "Run!"

Joula stumbled along beside her. "So messed up."

When they reached the edge of the parking lot, Nike stopped. Both of them were gasping for breath. There was no sign of the raitgur; the lot was full of better potential victims. Nike felt the weight of that, too.

"What's going on?" Joula asked, her gait faltering and her words slurring. Whatever she'd taken was catching up with her. "Tell me. I'm your best fucking friend. We can deal with anything." The word *anything* came out barely intelligible. Tonight wasn't the night for alien talk.

"I'm sorry," Nike said, breathing deeply. She was sorry for almost letting an alien infect the only person who truly cared for her. "I've been thinking about what comes next. I have to figure it out, like you did."

"Uh, you may see some independent woman, but I'm not here because I wanted to be. I'm here because it was this or … well, this was the only option. It was my family or me. They're no longer part of my life. I chose me. You can do it too."

Joula threw her arm around Nike's shoulders. "You paint. You're an amazing painter. Paint more."

Nike shook her head. "I have bigger shit, Joula. Shit I never asked for. All I want is to have a normal life."

"Normal doesn't mean anything. Normal doesn't exist. But all the drugs you're doing, all the alcohol—don't make that your normal. It's not getting you out of your current abnormal."

Joula studied her, and Nike realized she seemed older now, way older. Joula had had a tough go—parents who didn't accept her.

"I know. Okay. I'm not sure it matters anymore. Maybe normal is the new weird."

"And I once applied to college to be an accountant."

"Get the fuck out. Accountant?" Nike asked.

"I did. Almost did. Would've, if my abbi hadn't asked me what I wanted out of it."

"What did you say?"

"I said I wanted to earn lots of money. She laughed at me. Asked what I'd do with all that money, and I said I'd quit as soon as I could and spend time making my creations. She told me to go make." She squeezed Nike's shoulders hard.

"You smell really bad."

"Yup, someone barfed on me." Joula nodded. "Be careful about what comes next. What you think your goal is—it's usually just the way you hope to get what you really want. And even then, sometimes that goal's been so twisted by the world, it's hard to know if it's yours anymore."

"What if your goal is to protect your friend from aliens so you can go do art?"

Joula raised an eyebrow. "I'd say you're still fucked up. And to go make. Like, now."

"It's five in the morning." But Nike was already nodding; it wasn't like she could sleep, and Joula had kicked her out.

"That's what my abbi would say. If she wasn't dead."

"The dead stay with us," Nike replied.

"Deep." Joula laughed. "Paint tonight. Tomorrow, come find me here." She handed Nike a slip of paper with an address.

"What's this?"

"Your reward for making tough choices. Shut up and go before I change my mind."

Chapter Twenty

Dawn had yet to touch the slit of sky between the alley walls.

Giddy at the thought of soon being with her dad as he administered a cure for her family, Nike distracted herself by painting a favourite artist. The face was done, most of the swept-up hair, a flower sketched in, and the beginnings of a shawl. Empty paint cans lay scattered at her feet; fresh ones ranked near her bag. Her phone leaned against one can, its flashlight illuminating the wall.

Her finger ached from pressing the nozzle, the spray beginning to sputter. After a good shake, the stream was steady again—until the can crapped out entirely. She tossed it with the others and bent to study her remaining stock. None had the black cap she wanted. She grabbed a red for the shawl.

Something shifted in the shadows.

"Hello?"

No answer. She tensed, grabbed her phone, and scanned the alley. A boy, maybe thirteen, in a torn denim jacket and jeans, lifted a splayed hand against the light. She relaxed.

"Oh, hey. You a writer? I almost picked the spot over there." She shifted the light toward a relatively smooth cinderblock wall marred only by a scrawled squat-looking, black baseball bat.

He shrugged, and Nike went back to work, letting him watch. She wished she'd felt comfortable enough to stand and watch artists herself when she was starting out. Her first pieces had been terrible, with no sense of proportion or tone. But slowly, through trial, error, and YouTube, she'd learned. Now, she had her favourite brands of paint and nozzles, her own style, and a respected tag.

"This is a transparent red," she said. "Do you like transparents? You can make a line darker by layering it." She illustrated by adding a fold to the shawl without switching cans. "A can of transparent black will give you almost every shade of gray."

The boy seemed to be listening, so she continued. "You'll still need a matte black, but that's a pro tip right there." She chuckled.

"Who is she?" The boy pointed at the mural.

"Frida Kahlo. An artist."

"Why her?"

"Because she painted so beautifully, with so much detail. Her paintings were like her—feminist, activist, personal." Nike's laughter echoed. Was this what she wanted? To use art to be herself. To bring change. Was that her way of protesting instead of marches and signs? "No one told her what to do."

The boy's eyes hardened. "I do."

"What?" She stepped back.

In his hand was a small black club, like the one painted on the wall. "No one paints in this district without permission."

District.

Three more boys, no older than fifteen, had stepped from the shadows while she was distracted. Each held a black club, standing between her and her bag with its mace.

Slap, slap, slap. They beat their palms with their clubs.

Nike swallowed hard, making the connection between the tag and their presence. But instead, she channeled her dad's advice: *Don't feed the trolls.*

She shook the can of spray paint, the rattle covering the *slap, slap, slap* of the boys' clubs. One of them kicked over the other cans, then looked at Nike with menace. The others exchanged uncertain glances.

"You gonna pick that up for me, huh?" she asked, turning back to Frida. The hiss of paint almost drowned out the sound of furtive steps behind her.

A baton jabbed her ribs, and Nike tensed, unable to suppress a shudder. *Fuck trolls.*

"Not ticklish. And don't touch anyone without their permission."

"Listen—"

The boy didn't get another word out. Nike whirled, the can spraying a line of paint across his eyes, driving him back. His bat clattered to the ground.

"My eyes!" he screamed, clawing at his face with one hand while the other pulled a gun from his waistband.

He twisted the gun sideways, the barrel wavering.

"Someone beat the bitch, or I'm gonna put a new hole in her," he said, smearing red paint across cheeks flushed with anger and embarrassment. Tears tinged his voice.

The other boys froze, staring at the gun.

"Do it!" he shouted.

Tentatively, they advanced. Nike pressed her back to the wall as they came at her from the sides.

The first hit was a light knock on her shoulder. Then another, harder this time. Practice punches while the gun watched on with its single black eye. They hit harder. And harder.

Hard.

***

Trayling arrived before Chui's shift. Chui deserved to witness the moment Analia and Sabra woke, but he'd never allow Trayling to inject an untested substance into either of them. Even Trayling hesitated—but he trusted Santana and her team of scientists. They'd been working on the cure for ten years.

More than Chui, however, Trayling wanted Nike to be there.

The leather case trembled in his grip as he paced outside the center. A car rattled past. Crows cawed overhead. Every sound felt sharper, like he was burning again.

Trayling had texted Nike. Had called her. Had waited. The sun was rising, and Chui's shift started in fifteen minutes. Trayling couldn't wait any longer.

Too early for the florist, Trayling pulled a silver dollar from behind the duty nurse's ear instead of a flower. Even though it pained him to delay, he stuck to his routine, hoping to allay suspicion.

And then there he was before Analia, the curtain drawn tight around them.

Inside the leather case were two needles, two vials of clear fluid, and a message: *"Fill the syringes, deliver intramuscular, let me know. —S."*

Intramuscular meant a shot in the arm or leg. Easy, if not for his trembling hands.

Trayling filled the syringes. The alcohol swabs fought his pain-clumsy fingers, but within a minute, he had rolled up her sleeve and cleaned the injection site.

He glanced at the nursing station. The staff were focused on their screens.

Turning back to his wife, he exhaled sharply. "Analia," he whispered. "Come back to me, love."

Leaning over her, he stabbed the needle into her shoulder and pressed the plunger before pulling it out. He waited for a sign. Anything.

But it wasn't a shock he'd given her—it was medication. It would take time. All he could do was wait and hope that the clock had finally started.

Trayling moved on to Sabra, ignoring the arrhythmic bleats of the ward's monitors. "I love you, Sabra," he said, injecting her shoulder and quickly hiding the evidence.

A trickle of blood ran from Analia's injection site. He pressed gauze to it and tugged her sleeve back down, then repeated the process for Sabra.

Were they moving more? A nostril flare? Eyes rolling beneath their lids?

He dared to hope. Texted Santana: *"It's onboard. No change so far."*

Her reply was immediate: *"No change is good. Watch for allergic reactions. Ten minutes minimum."* As if Trayling was going anywhere. *"Patience, my old friend, and prayers."*

With the case, empty vials, and syringes hidden, Trayling pulled the curtain open and knelt beside Analia, taking solace in familiar territory as he waited.

His left hand throbbed too much to hold anything, so he cradled her hand in his right.

"Hey," he said, waiting for a response from his wife. Her silence hit harder today. "Being burned is better than burning Nike," he admitted, knees pressed to the cold linoleum. "But, boy, am I struggling. It's not just the burns. It's like I've aged ten years in ten days. No energy. I didn't realize what else burning gave me—or what being a source cost."

He paused, as if waiting for her to answer.

"You're right. I was holding back—Nike won't have to. That's why I never fully tried to eradicate the raitgur, I guess. Didn't want to hurt her. Not more than was necessary. Now nothing can stop us."

His hand tightened on hers. Was that a squeeze back?

He waited.

Nothing.

"You'd be so proud of Nike."

In the reflection of a stainless-steel water pitcher on her side table, Trayling saw Chui watching. The nurse went back to charting at another patient's bed.

Analia wheezed, her chest rising and falling. Trayling matched his breath to hers. Together. A prayer.

"The Burner burns. The Source gives of his body. Where evil goes, the flames shall shine, and the broken will rise again, cleansed by fire."

A throat cleared. Trayling looked up. Chui hovered at the soles of his boots.

"Early today. You good, buddy?" the nurse asked. "Never struck me as the religious type."

Trayling slipped Analia's hand beside her hip before turning back to the nurse. "We all have our own religions. Whether we call them that or not. We all need faith in something."

***

Nike came to lying prone, quaking with a cold that hooked into her bones. One eye was swollen shut, and her head ached from the blow that had knocked her out. She touched her scalp, and her fingers came away bloody.

Her clothes were on, but the contents of her backpack were strewn everywhere. She groaned, pushing herself to her knees, her head pounding. Her stump throbbed, the leather scuffed with sneaker treads.

"Bloody hell," she muttered, checking her pockets. No phone. No cards. No tips. Only bruised ribs that burned when she breathed too deeply—and the slip of paper with Joula's address.

She glanced up at her mural and stifled a sob. It took a few hiccupping chugs before the sob turned into aching laughter.

The boys had found her can of matte black and painted a mustache on Frida.

For a moment, she tried to decipher the time by the slant of light cutting between the buildings. Eventually, she gave up, gathering her spray paint into her backpack and hobbling out of the alley. Nike couldn't show up at the long-term care facility beaten, and she refused to let her father have the satisfaction of thinking she couldn't take care of herself. She headed for the Joula-cave, finally reaching the address as the sun peaked. Instinctively, she went to check the map on her phone, hand hitting her empty pocket before she remembered it was gone.

Across the road, two men in hoodies traded money, drugs, and fist bumps. A hooker—*sorry, Sahle*—a sex worker huddled at the corner of a windowless former brickworks. Her pimp leaned against his sedan, tapping on his phone, glancing up whenever a vehicle slowed.

The pink door Joula had described was embedded in the side of the brickworks, down a short flight of stairs. Nike shielded the worst of her bruises as she glanced up at the security camera. The door buzzed and opened onto another set of concrete stairs with a low ceiling. Only Joula wouldn't have to duck.

With one eye still blurry from swelling, Nike ran her fingers along the wall as she descended into the basement.

Brick walls covered with eclectic found art were lit by buzzing industrial lights. Eight pillars shouldered the open-concept ceiling, a maze of exposed pipes and venting. A laser cutter whirred, filling the space with tendrils of nutty wood smoke; several large 3D print beds laid down acrid black filament. Other equipment sat silent: the drill press, the arc welder, the circular saw.

"Welcome to my cave, bitch!" Joula exclaimed, pushing back from her work at a large drafting desk, her attention still on the screens bracketed to the wall.

"This is where you go," Nike said.

"My secret hideout."

"Why me, then? Why now?"

"Because a chick needs a place to paint. To create." Joula stood and leaned toward the stairwell, where Nike lingered in the shadows, knowing Joula would fuss over her face. "Honestly, I was pretty drunk," she said. Nike couldn't tell if she was joking. "I wasn't sure you'd make it in."

Nike understood. This was a gift—a gift of a kindred spirit. She wasn't sure she could live up to it. Maybe Joula wasn't either.

"How—how did you learn to use this stuff? How do you even have it?"

"My abbi left it to me. Just the basement. The neighbourhood wasn't so nice back then. As for the *how* part? Community, school, hard work. But, dude, why are you hiding? Are you still wearing glow paint?"

Nike wondered if last night counted as having slept rough. She stepped into the light and immediately regretted it. Joula's hands flew to Nike's face, clutching her cheeks.

"That hurts," Nike hissed, pulling away.

"What the hell happened?"

"It's embarrassing. Some assholes-in-training beat the crap out of me."

"Have you been to the cops?"

"They were, like, thirteen years old. Cops can't do anything."

"We should call them anyway."

"Seriously, Joula, I don't want cops."

Joula squinted at Nike, concern giving way to suspicion. She wandered back to her desk, picked up her phone, and dialed. Holding it up to Nike, she said, "Either you go to the police and tell them about your father, or I will."

"What? My dad? This wasn't my dad."

"This morning after painting, you didn't come here. You were at your dad's." Her voice tightened. "I've listened to every one of your lies and swallowed them. Not this time. I know the lies abused people tell, and I'm done."

Joula's suspicion was weighted by a heavy, lethargic sadness in her eyes.

"I was unconscious." Nike rushed over and grabbed her wrist. "There were four of them. Carried these stubby sticks, like what British cops use."

"Billy clubs."

"Yeah, and that's their tag too—a surrogate dick." Joula licked her lip, still unconvinced. "It's true! My cards, my phone—they took everything. All I had was your address."

Joula's finger hovered over the call button, as if tempting fate to decide for her.

"No more lies, okay?" Nike said quickly, then held out her stump. "*This* was about my dad. Or me and my dad, anyway." Joula stared at it. "I haven't told you everything. I'm sorry. But for good reason." Nike swallowed. "What I said last night was true. It's because of aliens. They landed here ten years ago."

"Don't fuck with me!" Joula screamed. "No, I'm not being fair to myself. I don't have to listen to this shit. I can't afford to be triggered by it. I've changed my mind—you can't be here."

Nike held her head. "I'm not lying. I'm not."

"I don't want to hear it!"

Nike shrank from Joula's furious torrent of Spanish, stepping back, tripping, and landing on her side. She cried out, curling into a ball as Joula continued to scream.

"I didn't believe in aliens either," Nike said softly. "Maybe out there, but not here. Not here. They glow and shit—it's so weird. Okay, I know this makes no sense, but I'm not lying."

The Spanish stopped. The laser cutter fell silent. Only Joula's heavy breathing remained.

Shuffling steps approached.

"Are you making this happen? All these injuries?" Joula asked.

Nike shook her head. "No. I'm not suicidal. I'm not psychotic. I'm not on anything. And I can prove it."

Joula snorted. "Fine. Where are these aliens? When did they arrive? Where's their spaceship? Why are you the only one who knows about them?"

Nike stayed curled. "Only a few people can see them. But I'm not the only one—there are seven of us, I think. The aliens are only in Toronto because they're territorial, and we keep their numbers low. They came here ten years ago on a meteor—the one that crashed into the stadium."

When Joula didn't respond, Nike opened her eyes.

Joula stood over her, hands on her hips, tongue pushing out the side of one cheek. "Invisible aliens." Nike nodded, swinging her legs around to sit on her knees. "Then what does it matter? If no one can see them, who cares?"

"They still hurt people. They suction onto people to eat. It makes them sick with depression. Like my sister and mom."

"Who were infected by aliens." Nike nodded, wondering if they were waking at that very moment. "How do you stop these aliens?"

"I can shoot fire out of my hands. Or energy of some sort, at least."

"Go ahead. I'll give you a million dollars if you can shoot anything out of your hands. I don't care if it's gumballs."

"I can only do it when my dad's here."

"Convenient." Joula laughed, sharp and mean. "You can only prove your story by having me bring you into contact with your abuser—I'd never do that to you."

"He's my source. I set him on fire, and then I can do it. I know it sounds crazy."

"Sounds like a shit superpower."

"Yup. I used to be his source." Nike held up her stump. "I know just how shitty."

"All those burns were—"

"My dad frying aliens. The government paid—"

"Your father burned you to earn money? He got to be powerful, and you got hurt?" Nike forced a nod. "You were his battery pack. Aliens or not, it's still abuse."

"It's not."

"You conveniently limit the number of people who can see them to a few other lunatics and make the whole thing a big secret."

"But it's true."

"They're just invisible. Got it." Joula was working herself up again. "You know what's not invisible? You. Your burnt hand. Your beat-up face. I see that. And I see you walk back out into that again and again. When will you decide you're worth more than this?"

Nike didn't have an answer.

"What do they look like?" Joula picked up a stylus.

"They're real."

"I'm going to need to see those gumballs before I can agree."

"Sahle knows. He came to me at work. He wanted help with someone who got sick with it."

"You told Sahle?" Joula waved off the question, but Nike caught the hurt. "Never mind. How is his friend?"

"I didn't go with him … I was working."

Joula whistled. "You messed that one up. He's one of the good ones, you know?"

"I'll text him. I promise. Once I have a phone. Please."

Joula pulled the tablet from its mount. On the screen was an image of a prosthetic.

"Is that my arm?" Nike asked.

"I need more time," Joula muttered.

For the first time, Nike noticed the scattered fragments of plastic. "The stuff your gear is printing—are they components for my arm?"

"I'm prototyping. Not even close to done."

"It's okay. I can't use anything until my arm is fully healed. But thank you."

"I wanted to make you whole." Joula's voice cracked.

Nike leapt up and clutched her in a hug, ignoring her bruises.

"Shit, Nike." Joula squeezed back. "It's going to take serious cash. The materials alone will run into the thousands."

"I earn money killing the—"

"Aliens, got it. Whatever. Listen, where are you going to stay?"

"I thought you were starting to believe me."

Joula looked away. "You thought wrong."

"I'll stay at my dad's." At Joula's wince, Nike pressed on. "What? I don't have cash yet. Knocked Back didn't work out. Where else can I stay?"

Joula sagged. "I can't let you stay with him."

"He's not my abuser. If anything, I'm his abuser now."

Joula glared, and Nike shut up.

"Remember, I don't believe you. I think you either have psychosis or you're covering for long-term abuse. Neither is good news."

Nike bit her lip. "The fireballs—they're not that big. More like a fire marble. My dad launches the big ones. Or used to."

"Light a match with your mind, and I'll believe you."

"It doesn't work that—"

"Just saying. Gumballs."

"Right. Don't believe."

Joula slammed her fists on the table, making Nike flinch.

"Do you know how this makes me feel?" Joula's eyes burned with betrayal. "Sick. Powerless. It brings back every terrible thing that's ever happened to me. It's not about what I believe. It's about what I *know*. I know that what happens to you doesn't happen when we're together or when you're at my place."

She waggled a sharp-nailed finger at Nike.

"Here's what you're going to do. You're going to keep yourself safe. No burning, no black eyes, no blasted-off fingers. You're going to find a place to live and work. Once that's all happening, then you can start saving people and killing invisible aliens." Joula shut her eyes and swiped away tears. "Stay here. Not with me, but here."

"Really?" Nike threw her arms around Joula. "I love you."

"I love you too. You fucking crazy bitch."

CHAPTER TWENTY-ONE

Nike slept for a couple of hours, waking with her face and arm throbbing but feeling fresher than she deserved. Beside her, Joula snored in the Murphy bed. She'd stayed. Printers hummed, building parts for Nike's prosthetic. On the floor by the bed, next to a lukewarm ice pack, was a phone and a yellow sticky note.

I was keeping this for parts. SIM card is good.

There was a number below it, followed by: *Text him.*

Nike's smile cracked a scab on her cheek. She texted her dad first: *New number. Did it work?*

The reply came soon after: *Waiting. You safe?*

Yes.

She ignored her dad's follow-up and texted the number Joula had provided: *I'm sorry.* And then: *This is Nike.*

Sahle: *Meet me under the Gardiner at Jarvis ASAP.*

She beamed, waiting for more, but nothing came. She replied: *On my way!*

The Gardiner was the elevated expressway running near the shore of Lake Ontario. It wasn't an ideal spot for a second date, but Nike would have gone back into the sewer if she had to.

She rolled out of bed slowly, trying not to wake Joula, who stirred anyway, bleary and groaning.

"Do you have another board I can borrow for a couple of hours?" Nike asked.

"Where are you going?"

"I have an apology to make."

Joula grinned. "You look like hell."

"Thanks, Mom."

"Would your mom be helping you get laid?"

"Sis, then."

Joula propped herself up on an elbow. "I like that. I've always wanted to be a sister."

Emotion clumped in Nike's throat at the thought of sisters—would Sabra wake? She leaned in for a hug, but Joula shrugged it off.

"Careful on that board. I may have installed a turbo."

The turbo pushed the speed over sixty. Cars, potholes, and gutters blurred past—welcome distractions to Nike's racing heart as she thought about Sahle. She'd imagined this meeting a dozen times since Knocked Back and knew that no one was hooking up today under a freeway. But that wasn't what sent her pulse surging.

In one scenario, Sahle's wide eyes flicked to her stump, and he looked at her like one of his homeless to be helped. In another, he laughed at her missing hand and said, "As if I'd want a one-handed chick!"

She didn't have a good scenario.

Few pedestrians wandered under the Gardiner, a common refuge for the unhoused. Blue and orange tarps covered heaps of belongings. Nike slowed and grabbed her board as she hit the gravel marking the start of the encampment.

Here, she texted Sahle.

Picket signs from protests lay scattered between tents, reading *Hope for the Homeless, We Exist,* and *No Penalty for Poverty.* A woman looked up from where she heated water over a camping stove. Her eyes scanned Nike briefly before returning to the flames.

Sahle: *Over at the pillar. Yellow tent.*

Massive concrete pillars propped up the aging highway. She snaked through refuse and used Narcan dispensers. Some shelters had metal poles, camping mats, and sleeping bags. Others were just piles of old blankets on cardboard with barely discernible human shapes inside.

Sahle stood near a newer-looking yellow tent. He waved her over.

Drawing a deep breath, she waved back with her stump. His eyes landed on it, widened, and then his face twisted.

"Nike, are you okay? What happened?"

He didn't vomit, but she wanted to hide from his pity in one of her graffiti-covered alleys. She would never be anything but another case for him.

"A burning. A bad one. But it's over. My dad can't do it to me anymore."

His expression darkened. "Then maybe it's too late."

"What do you mean? Why are you here?"

"Remember Dan?"

She nodded, and he unzipped the tent flap to reveal a man sprawled on the ground, arms stretched wide. Bright pink sneakers stood out against his slack, pale form. His eyes were open, and his chest rose and fell.

"Is it that illness? The awake-coma?" Sahle asked.

The man's expression mirrored her mom and sister's. "Could be."

Nike broke away from Sahle's gaze, scanning the freeway's underbelly for raitgur. Moisture seeped through cracks in the concrete, but she couldn't tell if it was from snotties or if it was just wet.

"The people here call it the jitterbug." Sahle pulled his phone from his pocket and played a video tagged #jitterbug.

On it, a woman's voice narrated, "Oh my God, check this guy out. This guy is soooo jitterbugging." The video showed a man lying under an overpass, seizing until he slumped.

"There's more like this," Sahle said.

"That's it," Nike said. "I've seen it. That's what it's like when someone gets infected."

"Was there anything? In the video, I mean—one of the …"

Nike shook her head. "Aliens don't show up on video."

Sahle looked back at Dan. "Can your dad do anything?"

"Not now. Not for him. This is the disease. He needs a hospital."

"Can a hospital cure him?"

"No, but it can keep him alive until there is a cure." She hesitated, wondering if she should mention the one Santana had given them, but decided against it.

Sahle's disappointment hung heavy under the freeway's shadow. "This is the third case like this. Dan didn't show up at the shelter, so I went looking for him and found him here. This isn't anywhere near where he usually camps." His hands clenched into fists. "It's like someone dragged and dropped him here."

Nike thought of the man her father had pulled from the Promise Complex rowhouse—how he'd seemed out of place. Who was moving the victims, and why?

"You shouldn't be here, Sahle. It's dangerous. If you see someone doing that jitterbug, it means there's an alien right there."

Sahle frowned. "You think I should just leave people to be attacked? Run away?"

"You can't see aliens," she whispered. "You can't stop them."

"But you can. You can stand guard for these people, right?" He shook his head, frustrated. "What am I saying? You can't fight them. I can't ask you to be an early warning system. I'll call an ambulance."

Nike hesitated. He turned away. "Actually, I can fight them now."

Hope returned to Sahle's eyes. "You can?"

"Yeah. We flipped. My dad and me."

He clutched her shoulders. "Kill them, then. Do it!" The look on his face was the same one Joula had when she'd told Nike to go paint. "You have such a gift."

She trembled as his fingers drifted closer to her stump. She shut her eyes, feeling his warm breath on her cheek, his hands slowly moving down, over her triceps, the elbow, pulling her arm from where it had found its way around her back.

"Can I?" he asked.

She nodded.

His fingers found the tip, tender, a whisper of a touch. He shuddered, and she pulled away.

"I'm sorry," he said.

Pity.

"Me too. About your friend," she said.

His gaze swung back to the tent. "I want to help, but I can't. I've never not been able to do something. Anything. Nike, I've never felt so helpless."

As he began to quake, she drew him back into her, pulling his head to her neck like no other man she'd ever known.

Chapter Twenty-Two

Ambrose had couriered a stack of papers to Trayling's townhome. A new map covered the kitchen table, identical to the one pinned to the wall. Ambrose's yellowed foolscap pages, covered in fading ink and loopy handwriting, were spread across it. The data provided a welcome distraction as Trayling waited for news about Analia and Sabra. From a package of adhesive dots, he carefully marked the locations of rait-gur takedowns from years ago. On each dot, he wrote the spine length, which varied widely. At the top of the map, he had written: *Raitgur Distribution – Pre-Districts.*

Ambrose had described locations using landmarks, but stores had changed, rooming houses had been torn down, and condos had sprung up everywhere. Interpreting the data was slow and methodical. Trayling found an odd satisfaction in peeling off each tiny dot and pressing it onto the map. By the time he broke for dinner after his third coffee, the dots had begun to form a cluster.

The front door slammed. Trayling's hand instinctively went to the knife.

"I need cash."

Nike, face bruised but grinning, blew into the kitchen wearing jeans and a sweatshirt. "Can we burn?"

"The cure hasn't worked yet."

She paused. "I'm sorry."

He nodded, finally admitting—if only to himself—that the injections might fail. "It hasn't killed them either. What happened?"

"I need money. Can't it just be about that?" She hesitated. "Joula's making me a prosthetic, and I want to find my own place."

"I meant the bruises."

Aside from the deep purple swelling around one eye, her skin and hair glowed with the unmistakable sheen of a Burner.

"Oh. I got jumped after the rave. I would've texted, but they stole my phone."

Trayling unlocked his own phone and opened the tracker app. "It's in the Financial District."

"That's creepy, Dad."

"It's helpful when your daughter sends texts like 'help' or goes to raves."

"Are we going to burn?"

"Is Joula okay?"

"What? Oh, yeah, she wasn't with me. I was painting."

"At night?"

"Yeah, Dad. Think about it. Do graffiti artists usually work in daylight? It's illegal."

"Alone?"

"I'm fine, thanks for asking, and yes, I was alone."

"Where was Sahle?"

"Now you want Sahle? Shit, Dad."

"Don't swear. I don't think it's smart to be heading out alone at night."

"So this is my fault?" She pointed at her face. "Would you be saying this if I were a boy? Would Sahle be a problem if I were a boy? Or would he just be a conquest? Maybe you'd let your son join some stupid gang and beat people up?"

"No. Sahle—"

"There is no Sahle!" She raised her stump, recalling Sahle's pity, his shudder. "You took care of the Sahles. Now I need a guy willing to take a discount."

"Don't say—"

"Let me … let me be sad about what I've lost. Just because you're prepared to mangle yourself doesn't mean I ever was."

Trayling shut his eyes.

"I need money. Let's hunt."

It seemed safe to open his eyes again. He tried to mask his rising excitement at hunting with his daughter by slowly adding another red dot to the map. "There's a meeting first."

"A meeting of?"

"Burners."

"There *is* a union?"

"Call it whatever you like."

***

135

Located in the Financial District, the restaurant was called Old Money. Nike hated everything about it, from the name to its brown pillars, gold frosted windows and massive old bank doors. The wound on her arm had moved past the constant-throb and then the nearly-constant-throb stages to the *so itchy* phase. At least the icepack from Joula's had helped with her swollen eye. Despite her injuries, she'd never felt more alert.

She felt guilty about the fight with her father, but she hadn't wanted to give him the satisfaction of thinking she might consider taking the role for anything other than cash. She definitely wasn't about to suggest that Sahle had half-convinced her with his protecting-the-homeless code. She wasn't doing this for a boy. For Joula? Maybe. In any case, Nike needed money, and it was worth a shot at finally being free of her dependence on her father—so long as he kept that smug, prideful expression off his face.

A sign on the restaurant door read "Private Party," but no one had gone in yet. Other Burners and sources smoked, leaned, or loitered outside Old Money.

"We're waiting for Chuck," her dad explained.

The pairs were obvious couples: Burners with healthy, taut skin, minus the odd acid lash; sources, gray and diminished, with hair like straw. One pair stood off to the side: a Southeast Indian-looking guy in plaid and a trucker hat, gripping the shoulder of a boy with a striking but sallow resemblance to him and a bandaged hand.

"That's Ari and Farhan," Nike's father said, quietly providing details.

An older woman in a wheelchair wore a silver foxtail cape. Nike had seen her through the massage parlour windows before, but her dad didn't remember her name—only that she was the source for Sylvain, who Nike knew was a real estate agent or interior designer or something rich like that.

She wasn't the only well-dressed woman, though. Lena stood almost as tall as Nike, with cheekbones sharp enough to stab. Her white hair, sequined black-and-white dress, and translucent purse suggested a black-tie event. On either side of her, two burly, gray-bearded men smoked angrily, as if daring anyone to touch her. Both wore custom gloves with only thumbs and pinkies.

"Bodyguard sources?" Nike asked out of the corner of her mouth.

"Her father and uncle. They're identical twins."

"And him?" Nike's eyes flicked to a young, good-looking guy standing across the street on the steps of an office building. Behind him, a digital display flashed stock index levels. They'd passed him on the way, but she'd been too distracted by the crowd in front of the restaurant. In jeans and a collared shirt, he stood just far enough away to be an outsider—but close enough to be suspicious if he wasn't. Nike hoped he was part of it. He seemed normal. Alone. And good-looking.

"Don't know him."

"What are we here for?"

"An old friend called a meeting to help gather data on raitgur movements. You remember Ambrose?"

She nodded. Of course, she did—she remembered Ambrose feeding her sugary Shirley Temples while she waited for her dad at a meeting like this years ago.

"With any luck, we can figure out the raitgur ranges, how many we're dealing with, and their main runs. We'll find their nests."

"Nests, plural?"

"We don't know yet. But I think so. Otherwise, Burners couldn't hit their quotas so far from Fumo's district. Once we know, we can destroy them all."

Santana wouldn't like him going over her head, but Nike wanted an end to this as much as her father did.

"Why are we whispering and not talking to them?"

"Rules. No talking until sources and Burners are separated by the vault. So we don't kill each other. Some Burners can reach their sources better than others, but none through a metal wall."

"Oh." That explained the narrowed eyes. "But why aren't you all friends?"

"There's a reason I stopped bringing you to these. They come with risks. Every single person here has tossed a fireball at another Burner— or their source. Me included."

Nike had been ten the year of the districts. She remembered fights over spines, her dad shielding her from what she'd thought were stray blasts. The recent memory of the Italians wasn't so hazy. Maybe the blasts hadn't been so stray back then either.

The bank doors creaked open, revealing a man in his mid-thirties with a pinched face, oiled hair, and a white tuxedo. Chuck. Her father caught her glance between the man and Lena and said, "No relation."

The group began filing inside slowly, each pausing for a moment before stepping into the dark restaurant.

Her father went in first and stopped to be patted down. Then it was Nike's turn. Chuck, grinning, took his time.

"Welcome, Burners. Sources, take a table and help yourselves to refreshments," Chuck said with a hint of a Southern accent.

Inside, the restaurant was elegant. Tables were cleared and laid out, ready for the next day. Soft music played, and a polished mahogany bar gleamed along the right side of the room. Crystal stemware refracted rainbows.

"Keep Dottie away from the good stuff," Chuck said.

Nike's dad snapped his fingers as if suddenly remembering her name and mouthed, *Dottie.*

"Fuck you, Chuck," Dottie said from her wheelchair.

"Sylvain, Farhan, Nike—nice shiner—and ... who's the Chinese guy?" Chuck asked, motioning toward the man standing apart.

"I'm not Chinese. My heritage isn't even Chinese," the man replied.

"Heritage, huh?"

"My name's Huey."

"Doesn't sound Chinese."

"Because. I. Am. Not. Chinese," Huey said, lifting an eyebrow.

Burners and sources separated, and Nike was struck again by their differences. The sources were washed out, colourless, and sickly. It wasn't just the pain or amputations—they seemed older. Her father too; his glow was gone. It was hers now. In the bar mirror, she noticed her bruising had already faded from purple to green and yellow.

Huey was somewhere in between. He didn't look sick, but he also lacked the feverish, manic sheen that filled all the Burners' eyes.

Sylvain approached her father. "What happened, Trayling? Did Chuck say Nike?" She nodded toward her dad's hand.

Trayling shrugged. "We just ... flipped."

"Too bad. You were interesting."

"Is everyone an asshole?" Nike asked her dad, loud enough for them all to hear.

Huey laughed, and she decided he might be worth meeting.

"Sylvain, Farhan, Lena, Nike, and Hue," Chuck called out, waving.

"Huey," Nike and Huey corrected together.

"Thank you," Huey said, smiling at her.

"It's ridiculous," she replied.

Chuck was already leading Lena and Farhan into the back. Her dad nudged for her to follow.

"Nuh-uh, this is your meeting. Not mine," Nike said. "I'm not going in with them."

Trayling grabbed her arm. "This is the way. The meeting is for Burners. Follow Ambrose's lead, pay attention, stay quiet, and try to remember everything."

"I just want to get out of here, make some cash, and get a new hand."

"Then I suggest you get what we need, and then we can leave."

She winced. "What are we here for? What am I supposed to remember?"

He rolled his eyes. "We need data. If we know where the raitgur are, we can find them more easily. Everyone wins."

"Location data. Got it."

Chuck guided her by the elbow through the doorway of a bank vault. Inside, a long black granite table held empty water glasses. At the far end sat a one-armed Black man—Ambrose. He'd helped her and her father when they'd first started hunting. Kindly, very large, and a bit irascible. He winked at her, and she smiled.

Chuck took the head of the table and waved her into the seat beside him, despite the table being large enough for twenty. She looked at the far side, toward Huey, who scanned the others.

The door behind Chuck banged shut, the mechanism taking several complicated clanks to seal.

"Nothing gets in here, nothing gets out," Chuck said.

"How melodramatic," Sylvain remarked.

"Fumo snubbed us," Lena said.

Sylvain waited for everyone to sit before elegantly lowering herself into a chair. Farhan stared at his rough hands, moving them awkwardly as if unsure where to place them.

There wasn't even wine—just a pitcher of water behind Nike. But of course, they were all Burners.

"Get me a glass too, hun," Chuck said. It took Nike a moment to realize he was speaking to her.

"Why you here, Huey?" Farhan asked.

"I invited him. He's a new Burner. I found him," Sylvain said, as if it were a point of pride.

"Didn't notice a source?" Farhan asked.

Huey swallowed. Sylvain smiled at him. "I know he's a Burner because I watched a squid practically climb down his throat while he sang karaoke. He didn't even blink."

"Could be a source," Farhan muttered, his hands twitching again.

Huey slowly stood and pulled up his shirt, revealing chiseled abs half-covered by a bandage. With a jerk, he tore the bandage away, and Nike sucked her teeth. Acid burn—a bad one. Definitely a Burner. A Burner with no source.

"Who cares why he's here? Why are *we* here?" Lena demanded. "Let's move this along. I have a reception with the Russian Ambassador after this."

"Water?" Chuck waved at Nike again without looking her way. She cracked her knuckles, wondering if she could take him by surprise. Maybe with the water pitcher across his skull.

"I called the meeting," Ambrose said.

It was as though no one else had noticed him. Farhan jerked back, and Lena's scowl deepened.

"Why is a source allowed here?" Lena asked.

"Because his daughter is dead," Sylvain said. "He's a source with no Burner."

"Which is nothing," Lena snapped.

"Except that I'm immune to both the acid and the infection," Ambrose replied. "Most of you remember my daughter, Emily. Since she died, I haven't had much skin in the game. Nothing to gain. And that's the agenda—I want to help. If you share your district's data on raitgur movements, I can help you. I miss the hunt."

"You miss the hunt," Chuck said skeptically.

"I do."

"I have tears in my eyes," Lena said, deadpan.

"What kind of help?" Sylvain asked.

"We want to—" Nike started, but Ambrose interrupted.

"Nike, for your first meeting, why don't you try listening," Ambrose interrupted.

Nike shut her mouth and glowered at the tabletop.

"Good, you have time to get me water," Chuck added.

Lena tracked Nike. "You're involved with Ambrose? Trayling's girl?"

Nike realized her mistake. Ambrose had called this meeting for a reason, and her job was to stay quiet. "We means me and my dad. We want to keep our district to ourselves." She tried to hide her embarrassment by fetching the water and pouring glasses for herself and Chuck.

"Thatta girl," Chuck said.

"As I was saying," Ambrose continued. "Efficiencies. I can link up raitgur runs from one district to another. I can run simulations and forecast where they'll be and when. You all want to meet quotas, and you all want to keep your late-night roving to a minimum."

"This doesn't sound like a good idea—everyone knowing everyone's business," Chuck said.

"Oh, I don't know. Dottie's getting hard to push around. I'd be interested," Sylvain said. "Is Trayling going to hand over his district to Hue?"

"Huey," Huey and Nike said together.

"It's my district," Nike said firmly. "Trayling is a source. The territory is the Burner's."

"Yeah, what is that all about? How did Trayling make that happen?" Chuck asked, his gaze hot with suspicion and a note of worry.

"He didn't do anything. It just happened," Nike said.

"Just happened," Chuck repeated with a sniff. "Could it happen to the rest of us?"

"Are you working together too?" Lena accused, her gaze darting between Huey and Nike.

"You've signed the contract, Nike? Hadn't heard," Sylvain said.

When Nike shook her head, Farhan rose to his feet. "If she hasn't signed, why is she here?" He pointed to Ambrose. "No Burner." Then to Huey. "No source." And finally to Nike. "No contract."

Chuck turned to her. "Why are you here, hun? You were saying earlier?"

Ambrose started to cut in, but Chuck raised a hand to stop him. "Why haven't you signed? Hue, you signed, right?"

Huey didn't say anything, only nodded.

All eyes burned into Nike. Ambrose gave a small shake of his head, hard to interpret. "I wasn't sure I wanted to sign my life over to a government more concerned with controlling the aliens than getting rid of them—or whether I burn dear old Dad," Nike said.

Silence greeted her statement, followed by a snort from Ambrose.

"Liberal shit," Lena muttered, shooting to her feet to lean against the table. Nike slid her chair back.

"We're not getting rid of them?" Huey asked.

Sylvain looked to Chuck, who looked to Lena, who looked to Ambrose. Ambrose made a flicking motion with his wrist, as if tossing his cards onto the table.

"And what, pray tell, do we do when there are no more spines to harvest?" Chuck asked. "Or do you think this restaurant actually makes any money?"

Nike swallowed but straightened. "Then we throw a fucking party."

"Get out," Chuck snapped, hitting a button inside his jacket and triggering the locking mechanism on the door.

"What do you mean?" Nike asked.

"Until you've signed and have skin in this game, get out."

"I've got more skin in this than you do!" Nike shot back, shoving her stump toward his face. He swatted it away, and her world spun.

The vault door swung open.

"Pilot!" Lena called.

Beyond the vault, both of Lena's sources lit their limbs, and her hands swelled with magma.

"That won't be necessary," Ambrose said.

"Dot!" Sylvain cried, and her hands flared white.

"I'm not going to do anything!" Nike said, but her hand was already a mitt of flames, her dad a step ahead of her.

"Easy," Ambrose cautioned.

All the Burners' hands suddenly ignited. Huey pressed himself against the wall, eyes wide.

"I can't control it yet!" Nike yelled and bolted for the vault door.

In the dining room, a young girl played on an iPad. She looked up at Nike, saw her flaming hand, and reached across the table to ignite her fingertips with a candle. "Daddy?"

"Yes, Charlotte," Chuck said. "Let's take this to the street, kids. No one needs to get hurt. Here."

Trayling opened the front door wide, giving Nike a questioning look as she passed. Fresh night air blew in, but everywhere around her glowed with heat.

Gathered on the street, the Burners surrounded Nike and her dad.

"If she hasn't signed, then there's nothing protecting her," Lena said.

"And Trayling's district is available," Farhan added.

A security guard for the office tower across from the restaurant unlocked the deadbolt and opened the door, a heavy flashlight in hand.

Immediately, the sources snuffed their flames, leaving everything in relative darkness. The Burners jogged off in separate directions.

"What the hell happened?" Trayling asked, standing in the suddenly empty street, his finger still smoking.

"I told them we wanted to destroy the raitgur, and they made it seem like I'd threatened their lives," Nike said.

"Why would you do that?"

"I didn't realize everyone liked the aliens so much."

"Because you've never had to pay for groceries. I said to let Ambrose take the lead."

"Yeah, well, Chuck is a prick, and Ambrose kept talking over me."

"To stop you from saying what you did!"

"I'm sorry. Okay. But you were never going to get your data, not from them. Can we just burn a few aliens and then figure it out?"

Her dad sighed. "Yeah, we can do that."

They walked off in silence.

"And you're right," he continued. "Chuck's a prick. Tonight will give us a chance to research, start a grid."

Nike stopped. "No. I don't want to wander all night. Spadina and Dundas. We wait for them to cross from Fumo's district, we burn, and we're done."

Her dad looked ready to argue, but Nike didn't have the patience for it tonight. "And then I'll sign."

"You sure?"

"I have to buy groceries, and everyone seems to think our district is up for grabs. We'll split the cash."

Nike stopped at an entry to an alley. On either side, like columns to an Ancient Egyptian temple, were painted Billy clubs. Her fingers spasmed into a fist as she stared at them, jaw muscles tightening. The pain an echo of their blows.

"See something?" Her dad peered into the darkness.

If she told him, he'd charge in and get shot.

"Maybe." Settling that score would have to wait. She threw down her skateboard, and her dad followed. Even though the turbo on Joula's board meant she outpaced him, she could tell by the smile on his face that he was enjoying this.

At Bathurst, they slowed. "Walk from here," her dad said.

Nike struggled with competing emotions. Her hand tingled in anticipation. She was excited to feel the surge of energy again. But tonight would be the first time she burned aliens for money. She would be burning her father for profit and, she admitted, maybe a little for Sahle.

Although her relationship with her father might be improving, it wasn't like the old days when she'd clamber up for a piggyback ride and steer him by the ears. He was going to lose weight tonight. If she was burning him for money, she owed it to him to reduce the burn however she could.

"I found something on Chatelaine," she said.

"The magazine?" he asked, not looking up from the sidewalk's cracks.

"Website. It's a relationship test." She flushed. "It's supposed to be for romantic relationships, but I thought … we could try it while we hunt?"

For a moment it seemed like he was about to dismiss it, but then he laughed, his eyes brightening, and it lifted her spirits. "Sure, hit me up."

She drew out her phone and found the tab. "Here's the first of the *Test Your Relationship Skills* quiz … Do we ask each other open-ended questions?"

"Open-ended like … how's your night going?"

"Super normal. Yours?"

"Good." He shrugged. "This is easy. Next?"

They laughed together.

"All right, here's another," she said. "Do we read each other's body language?"

"You look …" Her dad's head bobbed left and right as he inspected her. She reflexively hid her stump, then stopped herself. "You've always had really good posture."

"Posture. Wow, very observant. You're slouching. Makes you look older and tired," she told him with a smile.

"Thanks. I bet honesty is in there somewhere. Moving right along."

"Do we set aside time to talk?"

He waved his arms. "Does hunting aliens count?" They'd reached the outskirts of Chinatown, Dundas's busy retail strip to the east, alien trails to the west.

"You used to shush me on a hunt. And, when I couldn't talk, all I would think about was when the burning would start."

He slouched a little further. "I didn't know that."

She continued with the quiz as he scanned for traces of their quarry. "Do we tell each other what we want?"

"You wanted me to stop burning you," her dad said. "Is that what it's asking?"

"Not sure these were written for us," she replied. Time might have been passing, but she didn't feel any closer to her father.

"Nope."

"There's another article on how to fix a bad relationship."

He swallowed. "Bad, huh?" His gaze drifted to his own hand—the one she would burn tonight.

"Yeah, top five ways." When he didn't respond, she read the first. "We're supposed to spend more time together." More of the same.

"I'm totally okay with that," he said. "That is what I've been asking for all along."

But he hadn't been asking for time to help with her schoolwork, or to go to a recital, or even to have a board game night; he'd only ever wanted time together hunting. Burning. She didn't say that. Instead, she read the next. "You're supposed to imagine me being amazing. And then talk to me as if I am."

"I don't?"

"You mostly criticize."

"Then I'm sorry." He reached up and grabbed her shoulders, his gray eyes locking onto hers. "You are amazing. Even if I haven't told you enough, I am so proud of you."

"Thanks," she whispered.

He broke away. "That was a good one. Are you supposed to do the same back?"

She swallowed, watching cars roll over a patch of desiccated fur. "Moving on."

"Ouch."

"Problems are solutions," she read.

"What does that even mean—problems are solutions?" He snorted, but his eyes tracked something. "I can still catch wisps of them, I think."

"You take the phone." Nike handed him the screen of questions, hoping they'd have some sort of breakthrough before the burning began. "I think it means that the problem is a solution to another problem that didn't work out well."

"Oh, so the reason I burned you so much is because we were angry with each other, and we were angry with each other because ...?" He pointed toward a telephone pole, but she'd already spotted the alien. A raitgur shimmied across the telephone line.

"Because you're not treating me like an adult," Nike said.

"And you're not respecting that you have responsibilities as an adult. You aren't reliable."

It was heading directly toward them.

"Because I want to be out of the house and not feel tied down," she said.

"And I ... I'm afraid to let you go."

"But you can't always be there for me. You won't be."

"And I want you to be happy."

"Me too," she said.

He hugged her then, letting the foot traffic flow around them. She stood rigid.

The raitgur passed overhead and clung to the insulators at the end of the wire. Trayling must have read her body language because he asked, "Ready to burn?"

"Yeah, I think I am. You ready to be burned?"

"You want me to—"

"Shhh. My turn to say it," she said. "Light up, Dad."

They took down the first alien in the close quarters of a deep, vacant shopfront doorway. Nike was almost able to reach out and touch it. The second they chased into a long alley as it scrambled, clinging to the mortar between the bricks. Her first throw missed, and even in the panic of nailing the little shit, she caught her father's smirk. Why the hell was he smiling as he burned? Nike flared his finger, formed another marble of energy in her palm, and heaved it with all her might. Flubbed it again, and her father chuckled harder. Still, the blast shattered the alien against the wall, the creature's tentacles shriveling until only the spine leaned against the bricks.

"What the hell's wrong with you?" Nike said.

"I never taught you how to throw." He held up both hands, as if expecting her to punch him. "I'm sorry, I'm sorry. I'll be back in a sec."

He smothered his hand and disappeared while Nike went to retrieve her second spine of the night. He returned with two oranges, tossing one to her. She fumbled it, catching it between her forearm and stomach. "I'm not hungry," she said.

"Throw it to me."

She did—a sad lob. "What? We never played catch," she said.

"I know, and I'm sorry. The way your powers work, you'll need to learn how to throw." He nodded. "Throwing uses the whole body, not just the wrist."

"Pretty much the opposite of what I'm doing then."

He demonstrated, looking like a pitcher on a mound. His orange shot down the alley and ricocheted off a dumpster. "The key is balance," he said.

She tried. The orange arced halfway to the dumpster and then rolled.

"Good, better. Use your hips more—don't open your arms before the hips."

She retrieved the orange, and the next time she threw, it rolled to touch the dumpster. He clapped. After a few more throws, she was already pitching the orange twice as far. Still, she struggled under her father's pleased gaze.

From around her neck, she pulled the chain with her bite guard. She handed it to him.

"Thank you," he said, shaking it. "But I'm going to wash this first."

For the first time that night, she allowed him a genuine smile.

Chapter Twenty-Three

After the hunt, Trayling left his daughter at the massage parlour, waiting until she entered safely before heading to one last stop, despite his heavy fatigue. The ten gallons of gray paint he'd hidden in a garbage bin covered less of the cinderblock wall than he'd hoped. The rough texture soaked up the paint like a sponge as he rolled it on.

When he finished, oilskin splattered, his good hand spasming, and his nostrils full of latex fumes, he had managed to cover a hundred feet of wall as high as he could reach in only fifteen minutes. He wasn't much of an artist, but this kind of painting was his forte. It being after midnight, only a few people had muttered snide remarks to one another as he did it, but no one had stopped him, even though he covered the work of dozens of authors. An asshole move.

It was a gift to Nike. A hundred feet of fresh canvas. An opening. An acceptance. He knew there was still work to be done between them, no matter what Chatelaine said. The burn tonight had been better than the first time, but his finger had cooked lower over the course of three spines.

After a short ride, Trayling staggered into the house. It wasn't just the pain keeping him off-balance—it was the exhaustion. Night and day blurred together as his eyes watered with fatigue. His thoughts fixated on ice, food, and bed.

When the door clicked shut behind him, a drawer snapped closed upstairs. Trayling froze, the pain forgotten.

Someone was in the house.

The living room was tossed. Ambrose's papers scattered, the map on the table shredded. Upstairs, a flashlight beam skittered across the railing.

"No one. Nothin' more here. You?" called a voice from upstairs. There were two of them. "Enzo?"

"I got something," replied a rough voice, close and threatening.

The lights went out. Trayling spun to reopen the door, but someone grabbed the collar of his coat and hauled him backward.

The thug from upstairs rattled down the steps. Trayling was already toppling backward in his attacker's grip, wrenching left and right to try to slip free of the oilskin as he was dragged through the living room.

The dark shadow of the second man loomed over him, and Trayling kicked out at his kneecap, connecting. The grip on his collar slackened, and something hard struck his head.

His vision swam. They had to be Fumo's men. Who else would target his maps and notes? *No one.* Who else would be after him? It gave him a chance.

Beneath his coat, Trayling fumbled for his palm light and switched it on. "You've seen what Fumo can do?" Even he was surprised by the steel in his voice.

Keeping his hands inside his coat, the light filtered around his fingers, creating the illusion that he could still produce fire—that he was still a Burner.

"Oh, shit—" The grip on his collar released.

Trayling rolled, keeping his hands in motion to maintain the ruse.

"—go, go!"

The intruders sprinted for the door.

"Hadouken!" Trayling shouted after them.

He collapsed to his knees as the adrenaline drained away, listening for evidence of their return. They'd almost had him. Almost.

The front window shattered, glass spraying inward, showering him with fragments. Something hard clattered onto the floor, and the pungent smell of gasoline mingled with the blood clogging his nostrils.

A second Molotov cocktail smashed against the windowsill, igniting a curtain of flames that roared into the living room. Trayling tried to rise, but his strength failed, dropping him back to the floor.

He reached inward for panic, for anything that might push him up, but found only ashes.

***

Nike had helped her father to the door of headquarters. It was hard not to notice how much older he looked, his face drawn and creased.

"Use the afterburn ointments in my burn kit," she had reminded him.

"Yes, yes," he'd replied, rolling his eyes.

"You've watched me do it a hundred times. After the ointment, use cling wrap to keep it sterile—and don't be stingy with it."

"Yes, yes."

"There's nothing worse than an infected burn," she added. "It smells like rot. How was it, anyway? The burn?"

"Real good," he said. "I'll wait for you. We can talk after."

She hesitated. "Not tonight, Dad. I'm staying at Joula's. Let me know if you hear anything about Mom and Sabra."

He might have covered the hurt in his eyes, but it showed in his gait as he slunk away.

Before she could open the door, he turned back. "Nike?"

"Dad?"

"Stop by the alley with all the graffiti later."

"What for?"

"Just do it."

She nodded, and he continued off. She stepped inside.

A part of Nike wanted to go home, sink into her own bed, and sleep for as long as her Burner mind would allow.

The massage parlour smelled of coconut oil—a nice touch. Tyler greeted her warmly.

"Girl-to-girl, I like your dad, but it's nice to have you here."

And it was nice. No more receiving tips for showing skin; now, she'd make money by burning it.

When she passed through the waiting area into the hallway beyond, the air shifted—cold, dry, and odourless. The door at the end was solid steel, and as Nike made her way towards it, the sound of her steps echoed between the unadorned walls. Something told Nike that if she knocked on them, they'd sound like metal too, a reminder of Chuck's insistence on security. That was why she'd never been allowed in here with her father.

The retinal scanner didn't respond to Nike's eye. She knocked.

Santana threw the door open and laughed. "Nike! Welcome. Any word about your family?"

At the lowering of Nike's gaze, Santana's shoulders slumped. "Well, it's early still. Not my only option. How was the hunt?"

Nike showed her the spines wrapped in leather. It had been a good hunt. Three spines in three hours, simply by staking out the raitgur's travel artery. The hardest part had been tracking them to a location free of spectators and not losing them in the process.

"Three," Nike said. A thousand dollars an hour. The thought eased the tension in her neck. Money solved a lot of problems.

"Oh my God, are these your first? Let's see them." Santana took the leather roll and eased it onto a steel table as if it were precious. "I like the leather, certainly more stylish than plastic bags, but I worry about contaminants. Use the bags, please." She unrolled the spines. "These are nice. Really nice."

To Nike, they looked the same as the ones her father had captured, but she didn't have much experience.

"Listen," Nike said, trying to sound casual, not wanting to upset Santana, who she instinctively liked. "I want to do a good job and could use some info on movements."

"Sure, what kind?" Santana asked, studying a spine as if trying to see how straight it was.

"Raitgur movements," Nike clarified. Santana paused, and Nike pressed on. "Like where they were taken out. I don't care so much about size—just want to blow past quota."

"Saving for something?" Santana asked, pulling out a measuring tape to gauge the length.

"College, actually."

"Any particular features of this specimen you can recall, prior to termination?"

"Termination?"

"Yes. What did it look like before you fried the sucker? Burners tend to see the aliens differently."

When Nike didn't respond, Santana elaborated. "Look, the spine—or what we call the spine—has two flat sides, a serrated edge, and a smooth edge. Why?"

"Means they have a front and a back."

"I knew you were smart." Santana grinned.

"I didn't notice anything, but I'll do a better job next time."

"Trayling tracked everything. You want data, ask him."

"What? Oh, right. But he doesn't have data outside my district. I want to get a sense of flow between districts."

"I like to keep the districts competitive. Good for quotas and morale. Don't want Burners getting jealous, right? You've heard the stories about when they were in competition."

"Wouldn't it be better for quotas if we helped each other?"

Santana lowered the spine and turned to Nike, her dark brown eyes sharp and assessing. "Between you and me, all districts aren't equal. Some have more raitgur than others. The less data out there, the less complaining. The less complaining, the better for me." She pressed a conspiratorial finger to her lips.

"Where does our district rank?"

"Yours is about average."

"Fair enough," Nike replied, realizing Santana couldn't—or wouldn't—say otherwise.

"How was the burn?" Santana asked.

It took Nike a moment to process the change in subject. "Good. My dad and I are doing better. I think he's finding it hard, though."

Santana raised her eyebrows and shook her head. "Not all Burners make great mentors. And your father isn't even one anymore. I could make some introductions."

Nike laughed. "What, like Chuck?"

Santana's sharp eyes flashed. "You know him? Right. Maybe not Chuck. Who would you want? Lena, perhaps. Another strong woman. She burns her father too."

Nike swallowed, unsure how much to reveal but knowing the Burner meeting couldn't possibly stay secret.

"I don't really know them very well."

"But you've met them?"

"Yes. Wanted to, before I signed the contract."

The ferocity in Santana's stare dimmed. "Of course. Due diligence."

Something weird itched at Nike's hand.

"Who called the meeting?" Santana asked.

"Our ex-mentor, Ambrose."

Santana smiled, and the tension left her face. "I can't give you the data you want, Nike."

Nike bit her lip, trying to bank the hot anger rising in her. "How can we defeat the raitgur if we don't have data?"

"Your job is to control the population, to keep the aliens below reproductive size. My job is eradication."

Nike drew herself to her full height, forcing her thoughts away from her itching hand. It felt as though a fingernail scratched and scratched into her palm. Energy rippled through her. "Like the nest in the Trinity Bellwoods District?"

"Yes, like the nest. You were right. A nest does exist there, and Fumo will eliminate it."

"He will?" Nike's breath caught. If it was the only nest and they could clear it, maybe this wouldn't take as long as she feared. She could work her way out of a job. If only her hand would stop itching, she could concentrate. She rubbed it against her hip but, with the glove on, it didn't help.

Santana continued, "There's nothing complicated about the raitgur. They want to feed and breed, like every other predator. No conspiracy. No raitgur factory."

"And if Fumo doesn't?"

"Then it's yours."

Nike forced a smile. "Great, I guess."

She needed to stop the itching. Tugging her glove off with her teeth, she inspected her palm, expecting it to be red and raw. Instead, it glimmered. She closed her fingers and wiped the surprise from her face.

"It's weird, isn't it?" Santana said. "How clearing the nest won't do Burners any favours. Spines will be harder to come by."

Nike shrugged. "A normal life. Not having to burn my dad. It'll be nice."

The itching intensified, a euphoric energy flooding her skull.

Santana broke away to her desk, gathering a sheaf of papers and a pen. Nike checked her glittering palm again, holding it close to her stomach to shield the glow.

"Sign here," Santana said. "You'll find payment in the following account." A card and a numbered digital currency account were clipped to the contract. "Maybe you can think of me as your mentor, Nike? I'll see you here tomorrow morning with Trayling."

Nike turned away to sign, hiding her hand, fear fed by the glow. "Why do you want to see my dad?"

"Because tomorrow is testing day. Every Burner is different, and if the government is going to wipe out the raitgur, we need as much data on them—and you—as possible."

With the papers signed, Nike rushed for the door.

"We'll have some fun, Nike!" Santana called after her.

Nike caught the wistfulness in Santana's voice, but panic clawed at the edges of her Burner-fed glee. Fear for what her glowing palm meant.

Every door she passed through amplified the electricity swelling in her hand. She hopped on her board, kicked the turbo, and shot away.

The glowing palm. The rising power. It could only mean one thing.

Her father was on fire.

Chapter Twenty-Four

Two blocks from her home, an ambulance sped past, lights flashing.

"No, no, no," Nike whispered, surging full-out on her board.

Three fire trucks were parked on her street, their whirling lights casting chaotic patterns across the townhouses and trees. Hoses uncoiled as firefighters swarmed her house. Nike abandoned her board in the gravel yard and ran past the emergency crews.

"Whoa!" A firefighter caught her bad arm at the bicep. "You can't go in there."

"My dad!" she gasped. "He's burning!"

"We'll get him," he assured her.

Nike glanced back at the other firefighters, who stood in a loose cluster, discussing strategy. She struggled in the man's grip, but he held tight.

"The team will go in," he said.

With a scream of pain, she corkscrewed her arm and managed to pull free, leaving her leather sleeve and bandages in his hand. Then she was past him, her hand ablaze. Without breaking stride, she hurled a ball of energy at the front door. It blew inward, smoke and chaos obscuring her actions.

Inside, the foyer was thick with poisonous, yellow-tinged haze. She dropped low, coughing as she crouched beneath the smoke. Behind her, firefighters yelled, but their words drowned in the roar and crackle of flames. Waves of heat forced her to shy away, her skin stinging with the all-too-familiar pain.

"Daddy!"

No response. Only smoke and fire.

She ducked lower, hacking, eyes streaming. Smoke billowed down the stairwell, making it clear nothing on the second floor could survive. *The maps,* she remembered—he was always in the living room and kitchen with his maps.

"Daddy."

She crawled toward the living room, where fire had poured through the shattered window and raced up the walls into the ceiling. Still no sign of him. The air was heavy with smoke, making the search nearly impossible.

She had one tool that might help her find him, but it always came at a cost.

Willing power into her hand, a column of flame blazed magnesium white, cutting through the smoke to reveal her father's location on the far side of the room. She clamped off the energy, and the flame vanished.

"Dad!"

She jumped between melting patches of carpet, keeping low. Her father lay sprawled on the floor, flames licking at his arm like a log in a fire. Nike tore off her coat and smothered the flames, tucking the fabric tightly around him. With the fire dampened, she grabbed his unburned arm and began dragging him inch by inch toward the door.

He was heavy and barely conscious, his legs twitching feebly as she hauled him. She kept her eyes away from his charred arm, focusing instead on the task. The heat pulled tears from her eyes as her skin tightened, baking.

Shadows appeared at her shoulders, emerging from the haze, hulking—firefighters in their gear. She croaked for help, and they scooped her and her father up, carrying them out into the night.

"Is he okay? Is he okay?" she rasped as they descended the steps. Normally, she could smell the neighbour's roses here, but tonight there was only the acrid stench of burnt plastic.

"We've got him," a firefighter repeated over and over, her words echoing through her mask.

Nike was handed off to a paramedic, who wrapped her in foil. She craned her neck toward the ambulance where her father had been taken.

"We'll get your dad cool," the paramedic said. "He's safe now."

"Are you the homeowner?" another voice asked.

Nike didn't bother to look up. Perhaps the paramedic waved the person off, as they didn't ask again.

The paramedic stared at her stump, bleeding where the firefighter had stripped away her sleeve and reopened old wounds.

"That's not from tonight," she said.

"You poor girl."

Four fire trucks strung hoses from every available hydrant, pouring water on their house and the neighbouring roofs to prevent the fire from spreading in the dry summer heat. Nike knew her home would be reduced to cinders—her room, her father's maps, everything.

A groan came from the ambulance, and Nike stood and craned her neck to see inside. "Dad!"

"Here. I'm here." The groan broke into a fit of coughing.

The paramedic handed Nike a water bottle, and she downed it, the fluid sluicing through her parched throat.

A door slammed. Ambulance lights flashed.

"What's happening?" she demanded.

"They need to take your dad to the ER."

"Let me go with him." Nike shoved past the paramedic to the rear of her father's ambulance, where he sat upright, a blood pressure cuff on his good arm. Another paramedic was cutting away the charred remnants of his sleeve with what looked like kitchen scissors.

"Dad!"

She grabbed the door as a firefighter fought to shut it.

"Get her out of here," the paramedic shouted.

When she hauled on the door handle, the paramedic punched her in the face. Nose exploding, she stumbled back, caught by the firefighter who stared with her after the departing ambulance. Its door slammed as it lurched into the crowd.

"What the hell," the firefighter muttered, stunned.

Nike's mind raced. The scissors. The punch. Sahle's story about bodies being moved. Her father's confusion about the victim relocated from the alley to the Promise Complex rowhouse. Who better to move bodies than a paramedic?

Whoever was behind it, they had her father now.

Nike rolled from the firefighter's grip, grabbed her skateboard, and slapped it down. The ambulance had been slow to weave through the artery clogged with people and emergency vehicles, but now it turned onto a side street. Nike kicked off the ground, cranking her board's electric engine.

She followed, keeping low and out of sight of the mirrors. When the ambulance turned again—away from the nearest hospitals—Nike stomped on the board, triggering the turbo, crouching as she accelerated.

A shot of sirens gave the ambulance a pass through a red traffic light. Nike followed, ignoring the screech of tires and honking horns, closing the gap until she reached the ambulance bumper, where she slowed until she matched its pace. She snatched at the door handle, missed and nearly overbalanced, and tried again. The ambulance turned once more, and she swung with it, bracing as she whipped, hitting the rear with her shoulder when it straightened and braked suddenly. Her fingers closed around the handle. She clung to the back and pulled, even as the ambulance accelerated once more, wrenching her arm.

The door opened.

Her father blinked at her in shock.

"Get out," she hissed.

He glanced toward the two men in the front, whose focus remained on the road.

"They're not paramedics," she said.

He hesitated.

"Trust me."

The ambulance slowed. They were running out of time.

Her father finally moved, sliding to the rear of the gurney. The ambulance switched lanes, swinging her out with the door. Her father caught her wrist and held, with his legs hanging over the transom. She swung back, until his feet dangled above the board's deck. He climbed onto the skateboard. Nike steadied herself, bracing between his legs.

"Ready?" she asked.

The board took his weight, and she released the door. As the ambulance turned again, they rolled straight, leaning back, decelerating. She helped her father to the sidewalk.

Down the side street, the ambulance disappeared into an old automotive garage with two full-service pumps. The garage door slid down as the side doors of the ambulance kicked open.

"I don't think the quality of care would have been high," she said. "But the wait times are short."

Her dad leaned on her as they hobbled through shadows toward the gas station. This late at night, no one manned the pumps, but the lights were still on inside. She watched from the other side of the road as the fake paramedics hustled to the rear of the ambulance.

"You okay for this?" she asked, indicating her palm. Her father had never asked, he'd always just told her. *Light up.* But this would be her way.

Trayling fumbled at his neck, pulled the leather bite guard and fit the scrap between his teeth. Nike swore at his charred arm. "It's more superficial than it looks. I'm ready." He lit, flesh catching easily like hers used to.

"The people in there, they're not aliens," Nike warned.

"They burned me. Burned our house. Destroyed my data and your art. If you'd been a minute slower, I'd be dead. If you'd been with me, we both would be. It was a hit job."

"Assholes."

His breathing quickened, and she smelled him cooking. She hunched, molten energy pooling in her palm. Her father opened his coat to shield their flames.

Nike spun and unleashed her power. The energy struck the garage door, crumpling it. A beat later, the windows exploded. They pulled up their coats against the shower of glass, both having snuffed their hands.

The pumps blew, flames jetting a hundred feet into the air. Plumes of smoke, purplish against the city's night, poured higher still. The ground jumped and the thunderous wave of heat bowled Nike back, the shock shoving her toward the alcove of a storefront doorway.

"Dive," her dad gasped, then shielded her as the pumps crashed nearby. A pause, and then the night was filled with shouts and sirens.

"Quick," she said, pulling him to his feet. "Let's go."

They leaned on each other now, keeping out of the glare of the already gathering phone cameras, slipping away into the night.

This felt like war.

***

Without anywhere else to go, Nike took her father back to Joula's makespace. She wasn't sure it was a good choice. While she treated her dad's arm, Joula stood watching, arms folded across her chest like a prison guard.

Joula had arrived shortly after ten in the morning, saying nothing about the Murphy bed pulled down, the remnants of takeout scattered around, or Nike tweezing coat fibres and dead skin from her dad's arm. She didn't respond to Nike's greeting, only glaring at her father.

Nike hadn't realized how much damage he'd taken at the garage. His fingers were mostly gone, the remainder red and raw.

"Shit, Dad. I didn't know it was this bad."

"It makes it easier to light up," he said with grim humour.

"What the fuck am I looking at?" Joula demanded.

"Joula, nice to see you," Trayling said, to which Joula only hummed in response, her expression stony.

Trayling glanced at Nike as if for help.

"She thinks you abuse me," Nike said, peeling away a charred strip of cloth. Her dad hissed in pain.

"I did," he said finally. "I used you, hurt you, and I did it again and again for years. I'm sorry."

It was the first time he'd admitted it, and Nike struggled with how his words seemed to soothe old wounds, despite her not being ready to accept them.

"Am I abusing you now?" she asked.

"I'm a willing participant who's forty-five years old. It's different."

"But you had to do it."

"Because aliens," Joula interjected.

Her dad shot Nike a glance.

"She was going to call the cops," Nike explained.

"And you believe her?" Trayling asked Joula.

"I believe it wasn't you that assaulted her. I found the hideout for those Billy Club Boys, so she wasn't lying about that."

"The who?" Trayling asked.

"The assholes in training who beat me," Nike replied, plucking another fibre from his gooey forearm.

"And I talked to Sahle," Joula added.

Nike looked up, startled. "You do believe me."

"So you have been seeing him?" her dad demanded.

Joula ignored Trayling entirely. "I don't think you're lying."

Nike had no patience for word games. "But?"

"But she doesn't trust me," Trayling said, shrugging off Nike's attempt to wrap his hand. "Not yet. Show her."

"There's going to be nothing left of you," Nike protested.

"Only for a moment." His fingers deftly retrieved a lighter from his pocket, and in a single motion, he struck it and lit his hand.

Joula stared, eyes wide. "What the hell is happening?"

"You sure?" Nike asked her father.

"Do it."

Nike drew on him, and her hand glowed, energy kindling in her palm.

"Get. The. Fuck. Out!" Joula ran closer, hovering over Nike's hand. Her eyes shone as her fingers reached hesitantly. "Impossible. Can I touch it?"

Nike snuffed the flame, and Trayling smothered his hand.

"Not recommended," Nike said.

"That's …" Joula trailed off. "I know what I just saw, but I can hardly believe it. Whoa! What else can you do?"

"What do you mean, what else?"

"Just that's amazing! Fire. Hands. Boom. Wow! I get your burning witches now." She clutched her head like she was trying to contain her thoughts.

"I'm not a witch. Really."

"I have so many questions … It hurts him, but not you? And it's not equal, right? He burns a little, and you … augment it or something?"

"Something like that. And if we're not getting along, it *really* hurts him."

Joula's eyes swept over Trayling's injuries. "You two aren't doing so hot …"

"Actually, this is better than before," Trayling said. "I think saving me was good for us. That, and Chatelaine."

Nike turned to Joula. "The worse our relationship, the worse the burn. But he's mostly burned because someone tried to kill him last night."

"So. Weird." Joula hustled to her computers, turning them on. "I want in."

"What?" Nike asked. "I just told you someone tried to kill my dad. It's only a matter of time before they come after me. We have to leave so you're not targeted."

"Don't care."

"No," Trayling added. "You're not in."

"But I can help," Joula argued. "I know I can't be a sidekick, but I can be the side-sidekick!" She pointed at the computers. "The techie! Every team needs a techie."

Nike considered. The thought of not having to work alone with her dad was appealing. "She is pretty good," she said.

"No! Let's sleep. Talk later, sleep or I'm going to—"

"You sleep, Dad. I barely need it anymore."

"Here's the design for the prosthesis. I've already printed the proto-type," Joula said, waving toward the 3D printers, where plastic pieces were scattered. "I was already doing the job; I just didn't know it."

Nike stared at the prosthesis on the screen. "You gave it a retractable sword?"

"Yeah. Figured you'd have more power if your whole arm was the sword. Besides, swords are cool." She clicked, and an image of a raitgur appeared on the screen.

"You have a picture of one!" Trayling leaned closer.

"Sorry, artist's rendering," Joula said.

"That's what it looks like. Three more tentacles than that, but the light inside—that's right. The light defines it."

"Can't fucking believe these are real," Joula whispered.

"One was almost on your shoulder at the rave," Nike said.

On the third screen, a map appeared, dotted with black markers. "I mapped social mentions of Billy Clubs in Toronto and triangulated their activity to find …" She switched to a street view, revealing an alley entry Nike recognized from the Burner meeting.

"Chuck's district, Dad."

"Guess we won't be getting data from him either."

"Dad, Joula can do this for your data. With her on our team, we won't have to beg for help."

"I love data. Feed me," Joula said rubbing her palms.

Trayling lay back on the bed and looked in serious danger of passing out. "Not on the team. And there is no data. The fire destroyed it."

Nike pulled out her phone, swiping through her feed until she found the photo she wanted. She held it up. On it, Nike was making a kissing-face selfie. Her dad looked back. "Look closer," she said, zooming in to reveal maps and charts on the wall behind her. "It's your data."

Trayling blinked. "A start."

"Glad someone is on these things?" Nike teased.

Her father rolled onto his side.

"You don't know where the aliens are, but do you know where their victims lived or were found?" Joula asked. "If they're territorial, the attacks will cluster, right? It might even give better insight into their movements."

Trayling didn't turn but he said, "Won't work. Their victim diagnoses will be mixed with diagnoses of other real depressions, overdoses, and other deaths or illnesses."

"Give me enough data, and I'll find the anomalies," Joula said.

"Sahle said the homeless call it the jitterbug. If we track that hashtag by location, it could fill in some blanks too."

"Good idea!" Joula said. "I'll write some code."

"But we really need the other Burners' data," Nike added.

"Names and addresses," Joula said.

"Of what?" Nike asked.

"These Burners."

"And then what?"

"I'll hack them."

"No way. Hacking will be tracked," Trayling said sleepily. "We stay in the shadows."

"Hacking is by definition behind the scenes," Joula said.

"Chuck owns Old Money," Nike said. "He might keep information there."

"Stay in the shadows," Trayling repeated firmly. "I'll see Ambrose before stopping by Analia and Sabra's to check on them. He may have had luck, and he's not responding to messages."

Maybe it was the fire. Maybe it was the drain of being a source. But it was hard to see the hope absent from his eyes.

"You're hurt, Dad. Rest. Let me visit Ambrose."

Her dad hesitated.

"It's daylight. No raitgurs out, and the Burners are all tucked in their beds."

Finally, he nodded. "Meet me at the clinic. Maybe Nurse Chui has access to patient data."

"Then we can go to headquarters for testing," Nike said.

"Headquarters," Joula whispered. "This is amazing."

As Trayling started to snore, Nike scribbled the address for Old Money on a notepad beside Joula, who patted her on the ass.

"I can't believe I'm a side-sidekick," Joula said. "I'm on the team, right? Right? Alien hunter—yes!"

Chapter Twenty-Five

The rideshare dropped Nike at the gate. A chain-link fence bordered the parking lot of the small yacht club, police tape hanging in tatters from its galvanized links. The driver raised an eyebrow at the scene.

"Can you wait for me?" she asked.

He hesitated.

"I'll only be a few minutes, and you need to drive back into the city anyway. Might as well get paid for it."

He nodded and picked up his phone as Nike opened the passenger door.

Beyond the fence, a woman in a raincoat was hosing down the hull of a sailboat pulled up on a trailer. Security cameras studded fence posts, aimed at the lot and harbour. Wire rigging clanked against masts swaying in the wakes of passing boats. Closer to the lake, the air turned cooler and tasted of seaweed, rotting fish, and ash.

Nike paused at the gate. A chain and an open padlock dangled from the fence. The original lock had been melted to slag, the brass pooled and hardened on the concrete below.

The woman looked up as Nike opened the gate.

"When did this happen?" Nike asked, pointing at the melted lock.

"Two nights ago," the woman said, shutting off the hose. "Arson. Police are investigating. Looking for an amputee."

Nike instinctively glanced at her wrist.

The woman shook her head. "You don't look the type."

Nike was relieved she'd left her flame-fringed coat at Joula's.

The woman continued, "I'm thinking ex-military. An amputee killing an amputee. The victim was a war hero." She turned the hose back on and moved around the hull.

A couple hundred boats filled the marina, protected by a breakwall tipped with a small lighthouse. The docks branched off from the spine of a central boardwalk, and Ambrose's houseboat was moored at the far end. Even without her father's directions, Nike would have recognized it. A switchback wheelchair ramp connected the boardwalk to his narrow dock.

Twenty berths along, police tape surrounded the houseboat. Its windows were broken, and the fibreglass hull was bubbled and charred. Through the cracked glass, Nike spotted the remains of a wheelchair.

She checked to make sure the woman was still busy cleaning, then took a photo and sent it to her father: *"Something bad happened to Ambrose. I'm sorry, Dad."*

The reply came quickly: *"Check aboard. Had to die for something. Maybe they didn't find what they were looking for."*

The woman in the raincoat was using a broom to brush down the hull of her boat. Nike ducked under the police tape. Glass crunched beneath her feet, the boat rocked gently, and the lines creaked.

An amputee and a melted lock. The list of likely murderers wasn't long. They were clearly pushing Fumo's buttons.

Onboard, the houseboat felt claustrophobic. Much of the interior had melted, with shards of glass fused to the floor. Nike imagined a Burner blast flooding through the windows, the old source going up like a torch.

The houseboat was a single level, accommodating Ambrose's disabilities, so anything hidden would be within reach. Nike had never seen Burner fire do this much damage. Her father's fireballs were like basketball-sized spheres of burning pitch, while her own grenades were marble-sized. Fumo or Lena must have done this—Fumo with his dual sources, or Lena with her magma-like fire.

Beer bottles and tinfoil meal remnants cluttered the space. The fire had cleaned up the rest. Charred maps in the helm's compartment were nautical charts, not the data her father was hoping for. The drawers beneath a burnt bunk were filled with clothes.

Would Ambrose have hidden anything in the engine?

Nike yanked open the door to the bilge. The fire hadn't reached this part of the boat. The engine and bilge, half full of water, were intact. She scanned the space, but nothing was floating or lying on the bottom.

Where would Nike keep something safe? *My burn kit.*

Ambrose had taught her to always carry a small, waterproof, metal container with essentials: matches, a lighter, painkillers, a quick-freeze gel pack, and a bite guard. He'd helped her make her first guard. Back then, it and burning had held an almost religious significance to her. She'd burned designs into each of her guards, keeping them even after she'd bitten through. Ambrose wouldn't have gotten rid of his, not if his daughter had died while he was still her source. Nike's burn kit was the size of a small can of spray paint. Fire, medicine, and cold. *Ice.*

The food cans in the fragment of a kitchen were scorched of their labels. The fridge was warm and filled with beer and eggs, limp vegetables and a small carton of spoiled milk. In the freezer, she found a small jewelry box. His daughter's. In it, he kept mementos of her with his past life, all arranged neatly together. A couple diamond studs, along with two cigars, waterproof matches, a fitted rubber mouth guard, and a memory stick. *Bingo.*

Nike pocketed the memory stick and wiped the box clean of prints before putting it back.

When she turned around, the woman's head was framed in the window, startling her. Nike let out a small scream.

"Scared me," Nike said, laughing nervously.

The woman chuckled. "Thought I'd check on you."

"He was an old friend of my dad's," Nike blurted. "I was supposed to be looking in on him."

The woman squinted. "I've been here four seasons and never seen you."

Nike shrugged. "I didn't do a good job."

The woman held her phone, and Nike couldn't tell if she'd been using it. Were the cops already on their way?

Her rideshare honked.

"Gotta go," Nike said, climbing out the door, amazed that Ambrose had been able to navigate it with his wheelchair. Outside of the reek of burnt fibreglass and away from that woman, Nike took a deep breath, happy to escape what had doubled as a crematorium.

"I hope you get him," the woman called after her.

"Who?" Nike asked over her shoulder.

"The killer. Ambrose only ever wanted to be useful. He was a good man, and they burned him so bad he was nothing but ash."

Nike nodded. "I gotta go."

She hurried down the dock and into the waiting car, ducking low in the seat as the driver pulled away from the harbour.

She arrived outside the care center to find her dad sleeping on a bench. His trench coat, worn Docs, haggard beard, and bandaged arm gave him the look of a homeless man—only the electric skateboard set him apart. His swollen, scraped knuckles brushed the gravel.

"You need to keep that elevated," Nike said. "And on ice."

He turned, eyes a little cloudy. "Thanks for the advice."

"Would've been nice to hear it from you instead of figuring it out myself."

"I've got a lot to apologize for," he said, rubbing his eyes. "Let me know when I'm getting close."

She sighed and held up the memory stick. "I found this in Ambrose's burn kit. I'll get it to Joula—she can break any encryption."

He shook his head. "Who the hell feels threatened by a one-armed, legless man, Nike?" When she didn't reply, he swallowed. "It's scary."

It was. Every passing car. Every pedestrian. They all seemed as likely to nod and wave as to pull out a gun and fire.

"So, I'm here," she said. "Don't know why, but I'm here. Any change in them?"

"No change."

With his legs off the bench, he paused to recover, then stood, pausing again. His face was gray with pain, and his hand was clearly swollen.

"Got any of those pills?" he asked, his lips tight as he bared his teeth.

"Sorry, Dad, not on me."

He nodded. "Let's go."

The nurse greeted her father at the nursing station, waving him through and eyeing Nike with interest before returning to her computer screen. Her father hurried ahead, going down on his knees to pray at the bedside. Resentment surged again. Their only church had been an alleyway and the only thing he ever worshipped was Burner fire.

His lips moved; her mother's didn't. She just stared on, her eyes dry. A husk. Not cured. Nike knew it in her gut.

"Nice to have you back," Nurse Chui said to Nike, and Trayling snapped out of his reverie.

"Nike's here because she's doing a summer school project on depression in the city and different rates in different neighbourhoods. Can you help her with some data?"

Nike nodded, catching on. "Yeah, like where all these people lived before they were diagnosed, that sort of thing." It didn't seem like much of a reason for a visit, but Nike was relieved.

The nurse frowned, thinking. "Patient data is off-limits, but there's a researcher—Dr. Polanski, I think. You could try her. She studies aggregated patient diagnoses across a number of metrics, including neighbourhood, race, gender…"

"Polanski, got it," Nike said. "I'll text my research partner and catch up with you later, Dad."

"Hold on."

He gripped her wrist until she sat at the edge of Sabra's bed, feeling her sister's presence behind her.

Trayling looked at Chui and then back at Nike.

"I'll give you a moment," the nurse said, stepping away.

"I want you to understand why I'm doing this. Why we're doing this," her father said after Chui was gone. His gaze returned to her mom and sister.

"I get it. I know why you are, Dad. Maybe one day a cure will be found, but ... until then, they're gone."

"They're not," he whispered. "Sometimes ... sometimes I hear them speak to me."

At his admission, a prickle of fear crept up her spine.

"And even if they *are* gone, I want you to know that I'm willing to cover the cost of stopping the spread of the disease to anyone else. This could be anyone's wife, anyone's daughter. I'd do anything to have your mom and sister back—and anything to destroy those who did it."

She held up her arm. "I know."

"I'm asking you to do even more than that. If it comes to it, destroy me. To stop the raitgur, do it."

"That's not going to happen. You said it yourself—I'm not burning you as much."

"Ambrose is dead. They firebombed our house."

"Sylvain?"

"She isn't replying to my texts. I think someone got to her, too. We can't trust any of the other Burners. Do we really know what we're facing?" He shook his head. "But it means we're getting close. Promise me you won't hold back."

"One step at a time."

"Burn me."

His fingers clamped painfully around her wrist.

"Fine! Fine."

He let go.

Nike didn't like how her sister was positioned like some doll, smelling of talc and urine. She lowered Sabra's arms, pushing past surprising resistance.

"She looks like Mom."

Her father didn't say anything.

"How'd it happen? The infections?" she asked, letting the question hang between them.

Sabra's mouth gaped, her lips dry and crusted.

"We were together," her father said. "Your mom and me. This was early on in the raitgur invasion. Only a year or so after the meteor, and they were just figuring out Burners. It was night. We were heading under the Gardiner Expressway, wanted to walk along the lake. We'd go for long, long walks."

He bit his lip, his eyes far away. The sounds of the ward faded as he spoke.

"One was waiting, I guess—I couldn't see them yet. Maybe more than one. Caught us as we passed. Analia went down seizing, and that was it. I called the ambulance. I was investigated, too. A few days later, I started seeing things … I thought I was going crazy. Until Santana found me."

"And that's why you hate Fumo so much."

"He was there. He was tracking it. He could have stopped it."

Nike frowned. "Why you and not Mom?"

"Why am I immune? Genetics, I suppose."

"It's not really an immunity, though. I mean, it still changed you. Changed me."

Her father turned to her, his eyes sharp with interest. "You mean like maybe the infection jumpstarts something in some people but burns it out in others?"

"I guess."

"And, if we switched, maybe their condition could change, too?"

Nike shook her head and shrugged. They'd had conversations like this before, and he always got too excited. Too hopeful.

"Maybe. But I was actually wondering about Sabra and me. How'd we get infected?"

Her father turned back to her mother. "That's a story for another time. We need to hurry to Santana. The military likes keeping things punctual."

While her father finished feeding her mom, Nike turned to her sister and her dead, dead eyes. How much of her hand had Nike lost for these all-but-dead people? Would she have been burned at all if their lungs had stopped, their hearts? Or was it hope that had burned her?

Nike forced down the wish that they hadn't survived—hammered it right down.

"I'm going to get a new hand," she told her sister instead. "Better than new."

Sabra's arm had lifted a few inches. Nike pressed it back lower. As she did, her sister leaned forward, her head tilting, and Nike froze under her gaze.

She remembered why she'd stopped coming here. It had been after a burn and a sundae, and she'd talked to Sabra about running away from home. Nike had sensed betrayal behind Sabra's eyes.

Nike feared the idea that her sister was still there, somewhere, listening—because that was worse than being gone. It meant they were both stuck in a living hell.

They talk to me, too, Nike thought, but she would never dare admit it.

Chapter Twenty-Six

Corporal Tyler followed them, her hand firmly planted on her sidearm. "Standard procedure," Tyler said. "Testing is the only time a source and Burner are allowed in the building together."

Room number two opened to Tyler's retinal scan, and she waved Trayling in before shutting the door behind him, muffling a tinny-sounding Santana.

"You're in the next," Tyler explained.

The mechanical lock on room number three clicked, and the door opened to a narrow chamber that seemed to run the width of the facility—about twenty yards. At the far end of the corridor was a target. From her setup in the corner, Santana gave Nike an encouraging wink.

"It's a shooting gallery for Burners," Nike whispered.

"Smart girl." At a small bar table, Santana operated several computer screens. "You ready, Trayling?" she asked, using an intercom.

One mirrored window faced the laboratory, and another looked into an adjacent room where her father sat facing them. His burned hand was held between two vertical metal plates, the bandages already removed. A glass of water rested by his elbow.

Her father nodded.

"The diodes will take a variety of measurements. I have Nike here with me." Santana released the intercom button and pointed to the end of the arcade. "That is a very special target. It will measure heat, force, chemical makeup, amperage. We'll get a real sense of what you're capable of. You ready?"

"My dad's pretty burned—we were attacked last night. Can this wait? He's been through a lot."

"I'm sorry the medication didn't work." Santana shook her head, and Nike's stomach sank. If it was going to work, it should have by now. "Testing can give us a sense of what we can do better. Let's make it easy on your dad. We'll keep it short—three pulses."

"Three?"

"That's all. The first at the weakest you can manage while still producing something. Then at half power. Then give me all you've got."

"Can my dad hear us?" Nike asked.

"Not a word unless I hit the button. Can't see us either."

At Nike's nod, Santana leaned on the intercom again. "Ready."

On the table next to her father was a cheap purple lighter. It took Trayling three snaps of the flint to light what remained of his stumpy hand.

"Hold it steady, Trayling," Santana said. "I want a no-draw reading on the pilot to get a baseline."

On Santana's screens, a series of graphs and readings popped up. Nike didn't understand any of it, but the lines tracked at the bottom of the graphs, moving whenever she so much as thought about her hand. Her palm glimmered, and the fate lines crossing it warmed.

"Don't worry about my readings. I need your focus on the target," Santana said, waving off Nike's curiosity. "Go."

"Low level," Nike said. She wasn't sure if she could manage her powers at that fine a scale, but she was glad for the chance to practice.

"Lowest you can manage."

Nike straightened, drew a deep breath, and concentrated on her hand, trying to make the marble as small as possible—a mere speck. Glow turned to fire, and she visualized the energy condensing into a bead no bigger than a BB pellet.

"Good," Santana whispered. "Now send it."

Nike flicked the pellet down the gallery. It struck the target with a sudden crackling sound as the metal absorbed the power.

Santana whistled, watching her readings dance across the screens. "Something went wrong there, I think. I said lowest."

"Sorry, I still don't have much control," Nike said. "But I tried. Want me to do it again?"

Beyond the one-way mirror, her dad's hand had resumed the blue flames of a pilot light.

Santana studied the screens and made some adjustments. The scales on the charts changed.

"Halfway," Santana said.

Nike urged a golf ball-sized sun into her palm. The glare lit the room. Was this half? It was as large as anything she'd produced in the field, but she knew she could create more. Maybe things really were improving between her and her father.

The glass reflected the blaze in her palm and the thrill in her face, obscuring her view of her dad. This time she twisted like he'd taught her and hurled the ball. It cracked into the target, fire splashing from it in a pulse of heat that curled back. Santana flinched away, then dove back to the monitors to read the data. She was moving from screen-to-screen, each click eliciting a louder gasp.

"Nike, that couldn't have been half." Santana gestured at the peaked-out charts.

"I think it was. I'm sorry."

Santana pressed the intercom. "Most powerful Burner on record. Trayling, how are you doing?" But Santana hadn't seen what was left of Ambrose's boat.

After a deep breath, Trayling responded. "Doing good. One more?"

"One more, Dad. Tell me if you want to stop."

"Nah, this is easy."

Santana glanced at Nike. "Your dad's good. Better than good. These are excellent ratios—I can tell you're getting along. It shows in the amazing conversion ratio."

"The what?"

"The rate at which energy from the source converts to energy produced by the Burner. In the closest teams, a Burner can wield their full powers without any lasting damage to the source."

At the end of the gallery, the target still glowed with heat.

"You think that's really possible?"

"We're human. We hurt each other. But there can be exceptions for those without secrets. Without grudges."

Nike thought back to earlier, to that moment at the long-term care unit. "There's something you might know that could help. One secret that might make the difference."

At Santana's kind smile, Nike continued. "Do you know how I became infected?"

Santana's smile thinned, her focus returning to the screens. "Maybe your father should be the one to explain."

The avoidance chilled Nike. Something cold trickled down her spine.

"Did he … did he do it?" she whispered. It was a guess—but the only one that made sense. He would have been like Huey, a Burner without a source.

"It would be really rare for a Burner and a source to be discovered at the same moment," Santana said carefully.

"He infected me," Nike said, her voice hollow.

"You must have known," Santana replied. "How else?"

"Sure. Right." Nike tried to bury the anger, the molten anguish of betrayal.

"Last one," Santana said. "All you've got. Don't worry about your dad—he can take a little heat."

Rage balled white-hot in her palm, overflowing. It was large enough that she had to carry it to her shoulder before shot-putting it at the target. Her hand jerked back with the release, and a screech wrenched from her lungs. Fury arced, singing the ceiling. It engulfed the target, collapsing on it like a star.

Santana collided with Nike, bringing her down as fire ricocheted back. The blaze flared, then vanished.

Santana groaned, rolling off Nike.

"Sorry," Nike said.

"Stop." Santana's eyes bored into hers. "Never apologize for being strong."

She wasn't strong. She was angry.

The computer screens were black.

"I ruined your data."

"Don't need a computer to interpret that one." Santana nodded. "I've made a decision." She pulled herself to her feet, pausing to touch the back of her neck as if sunburned. "Fumo hasn't destroyed the nest, despite several days and warnings. I need you to do it. You have the power. Whatever spines you collect, you can keep."

Nike released a breath she didn't realize she'd been holding. They had no data suggesting additional nests. Destroying this one could mean an end to all of it. She could have control of her life again.

"The Italians beat up my dad. Burned our house. They're using victims as bait—or fodder. Whatever's happening, they're hiding something."

"They're part of a crime family," Santana said. "Take out their nest, and it will eliminate their source of income. Weaken their status."

"Can't you do something? Arrest them?" After learning her father had infected her, she really didn't want more to do with him.

"We're not a police force, Nike. The police can handle arson charges, but an alien nest? That's something we have to do."

Nike suspected Santana feared reprisal too.

"I'll handle any attention you draw. You were on three cameras at the auto garage."

Santana hit a few keys on the keyboards, but the screens remained blank.

Nike stared beyond her. With the intercom off, she couldn't hear her dad but, by his gaping mouth and twisted features, he was still screaming.

CHAPTER TWENTY-SEVEN

Trayling leaned against the wall of Joula's workshop, letting gravity do the work as he staggered down the stairwell to the polished floor of the basement.

"Drugs," he begged the short, muscular girl at the desk, keeping his head as still as possible to avoid aggravating the pain.

Nike had rushed inside ahead of him, leaving him to deal with the ride-share door and the stairs. If she was angry, he didn't know why. Something had changed, but she wasn't explaining, and right now, he didn't care. He needed oblivion.

Joula handed him two pills, and he dry-swallowed them before accepting her help in lowering himself onto the Murphy bed. In minutes, the pain grew distanced. Despite the haze and the lingering shriek of agony at the back of his head, he could at least concentrate.

Had he sent Nike to school like this?

Trayling tried to focus on Joula's large screen from where he sat at the edge of the mattress. Blue and red dots of varying sizes dotted a map of the city.

"This first data set is care of Dr. Polanski," Joula said. "Locations of victims are the blue dots."

"She gave you all this?" Trayling asked, wincing as speaking sent bolts of pain through his skull.

"'Gave' isn't quite the right verb," Joula replied.

"But—"

"I wouldn't ask any more questions unless you want to be involved in a felony."

"Just shut up, Dad," Nike said.

At least, that's what he thought she said. A sudden pain lanced through his forehead, and it took him a moment to refocus. When he could listen again, Joula was explaining the map.

"Victims are in blue; spines harvested are in red."

Trayling recognized parts of the red pattern, like a familiar constellation—hunts, time spent with his daughter, and the celebratory desserts that followed—but other red dots weren't his. They were outside his territory.

"This is Ambrose's data?" The clustering of locations reminded him of the maps that had been lost in the house fire.

"No. Ambrose's data is too old. I'll get to it later. Some of this came from the boat, but it wasn't his."

"Those are Sylvain and Chuck's districts," Trayling whispered.

"Must be Sylvain's data on the memory key."

Ambrose hadn't told Trayling about that. "Then where'd Chuck's data come from?"

"Felony, remember?"

He glanced at Nike, who shrugged without meeting his eyes. Ambrose having Sylvain's data meant she was an ally. At least, she had been.

"Are we okay?" he asked Nike. "That last burn was rough."

"I know the feeling." Nike waved to Joula, who continued.

"The data suggests a series of trails between districts and the major nest in the Italians' territory. But …" She pointed to a large blue bubble in Chuck's district near St. Jamestown. "This makes no sense."

"Victims with no raitgur," Nike said.

"Maybe we're missing data," Trayling replied.

"There's not even a trail to this cluster of victims. Not from your district, Chuck's, or Sylvain's. If there's a cluster of victims, we should see a nest or a trail—something."

"Okay, so Chuck didn't harvest there. What else do we know about the victims?"

"Mostly low-income or unhoused. That's true across all districts." Joula leaned forward, hands clasped and eyes shining. "What I think is that they're being targeted."

"The raitgur go after people who are alone at night. What if victims just worked in these zones and were infected while commuting?"

"Weak, Dad. All of them?" Nike asked. "Who's walking to and from work in back alleys?"

Trayling scowled. "You're right. I'm just trying to figure this out." He looked back at the map. "But we've confirmed the main nest. One nest. All of these raitgur trails lead into the Italians' district."

"No question," Joula said.

"And Santana has given us the go-ahead to raze it to the ground," Nike added. "Let's get this over with."

Trayling stiffened as he heard footsteps coming from the entrance. A man scuffed down the steps and straightened at the bottom, holding a white plastic bag. Sahle. Trayling's head hurt enough already.

"What's he doing here?"

"I called him," Nike said, though her expression suggested she regretted it.

Sahle lifted the bag. "Nike said you needed steak." He glanced away. "And could pay for it."

Soon, Trayling's lap was warmed by a slab of steak on a paper tray. Ignoring the utensils with his damaged hand, he chewed greedily.

"So, I'm going to be your fight coach?" Sahle asked.

Trayling swallowed a too-big bite. "My what?"

"You know, mentor figure," Joula said.

Nike laughed.

"He's not my—"

"You can't depend on me to be there to save you," Nike interrupted. "Last time you got the stuffing knocked out of you."

Judging by the pounding in what was left of his hand, Trayling wasn't sure her presence would save him either.

"Your job is to burn. My job is to light up." The real question was whether he'd live long enough to finish the job. He didn't need a coach. Trayling glared at Sahle. "I've been fighting these things since Nike was in pigtails, and you two are just learning aliens even exist. What can you teach me?"

Sahle smiled. "He who fights with monsters might take care lest he thereby become a—"

"Save the Nietzsche for high-school girls." Trayling turned to Nike. "And who's going to protect you if something happens to me?"

"I have a line on a weapon more practical than fists or fire. Joula, how's the prosthetic coming?"

Trayling didn't like the sound of that.

"Sorry," Joula said. "Gathering all this data took legwork. The prosthetic won't be ready. But ..." She slipped a headset over her scalp, and a drone rose from her desk. "I'll have eyes on you. This baby's equipped with different light spectrums to see if I can identify these fuckers too."

Nike stood between the three of them. To Trayling, she suddenly looked like Analia before her infection—tall, strong, powerful. Nike had said Sabra looked like her mom, but Nike acted like her. He was simultaneously proud and jealous of everything that lay ahead for her.

"You sure you want to do this?" Nike asked, looking at Joula and Sahle. "It's not art or philosophy. And I don't know what will happen. Two people have already gone missing—one dead in a fire." She cast her father a quick, disparaging glance. "This has to be your choice."

"You kidding me?" Sahle said. "This is the fight of the century."

"No," Trayling said. He was losing control and didn't like it.

"What about you, Joula?" Nike continued.

"Well, I could be prototyping talking toilets and shit, but this will have to do for now."

"But you said to follow my dreams. To be an artist."

"I said that before I knew you were a witch. Paint the town, bitch—but paint it with fire."

Nike hugged them both. "And then be done." At the word *done*, Nike's eyes once again flicked to Trayling before jerking away. Within a minute, she had packed her backpack and was heading toward the stairs.

Sahle blocked Trayling's view, and he didn't have the strength to move.

"You well enough to practice a few techniques?" Sahle asked, his expression doubtful. "I can't help with aliens, but I might know something about stopping humans."

"I used to box a little."

"I'm a fifth-degree black belt."

"Guess you're qualified, then. But first, I've got a favour."

Sahle nodded.

"Follow her."

Sahle glanced back in the direction Nike had gone.

"Our girl can handle herself," Joula muttered, inputting data into a spreadsheet.

"I've known Nike for seventeen years, and I've never seen her look so angry," Trayling said.

"I'd say she has plenty to be angry about," Joula replied.

"She also took my baseball bat with her."

Sahle and Joula exchanged a look.

"I'll go catch up," Sahle said, hustling after Nike.

"You know what you just did?" Joula asked Trayling after Sahle had left.

"I asked a twenty-one-year-old man I don't trust to do my job?"

"It's the first thing you've done that I agree with."

***

Nike watched the Billy Club Boys' alley from behind a delivery truck. A gang member stood at the corner as a lookout, slapping a baton into his palm every time someone passed. The alley itself was draped with tarps, catching the misty rain that now coated her shoulders. Her father's bat was slick in her hand, black like the baton the boy wielded. Twice, someone had laughed at the kid. Nike knew better than to laugh. Somewhere down that alley were the boys who had beaten her. Somewhere down there was a gun.

Nike wasn't here for retribution. After the testing, she realized she needed that gun. She had to do everything possible to burn her father as little as she could. If she had a gun, she wouldn't have to burn him when they faced Fumo. Without it, her father was going to go up like a flare and burn to nothing just as fast. If that happened, she wouldn't be able to clear out the nest.

She strode out from behind the truck, crossed the street, and kept her eyes on the lookout as she approached. Beneath her oilskin was the short dress she'd changed into after leaving Joula's workshop—a dress patterned like fireworks. The loose fabric swept carefree, a dress for summer nights, dancing, and catching boys' attention.

Her coat billowed open a few yards from the alley, revealing legs and a plunging neckline. The sentinel's expression twisted from suspicion to embarrassment.

"Ho-ho," he blustered, trying to cover it, making it abundantly clear what he thought of her.

Cracking his head would be premature. Instead, she winked, did her best imitation of Sophie, and ducked under the tarp.

"Incoming, special delivery!" the boy yelled.

Nike sensed movement in the darkness as her eyes adjusted. A second tarp, pitched higher than the first, gave her enough room to stand. Beneath it moldered several couches, occupied by figures whose cigarettes glowed in the dimness. The air was rank with sweat, sweet smoke, and humidity.

"You boys shouldn't be stunting your growth." She'd pocketed her father's palm light and now used it, strapped to her stump.

"Fuck off with the light," snapped one of the figures. But he wasn't the one she was looking for.

She scanned with the light. Then she saw him, the only face she remembered from the confrontation: sandy, boy-band-swept hair, a cleft chin, and green, hateful eyes. She unleashed a shriek, swinging the bat with all her might. It struck his skull with a hollow crack, and she dropped the bat, leaping on him. She sensed, rather than saw, the others scrambling to help their leader. Her hand jerked down his side, reaching his waistband and tracing it to the steel of the gun at the base of his spine, warm from his skin's heat.

A phone flashlight captured her with the gun now out, aimed at another boy's chest.

"Shit." The boy with the light staggered back.

Nike waved the weapon, trying to track the gang members, but she'd lost her father's light to the couch cushions, leaving her in semi-darkness.

The boy she'd hit lay splayed on the couch, unmoving.

"Touch me, and I'll kill every one of you."

"Nike!" someone screamed from the street.

She froze.

"Nike!" And then he was closer. She felt relief when she saw Sahle, but also annoyance.

A shadow advanced, and she jerked the gun toward it. "Don't give me a reason." The boy stepped back. "Today's not the day, if you hadn't noticed."

"Don't," Sahle said, standing by one of the boys as if to protect him rather than her.

"I don't need saving," she said.

"These guys aren't the problem. Look at them."

He picked up her father's bat and light, searching their faces. Terrified. One boy had pissed his pants.

"They beat me."

"They're boys. Kids with shit families and shit prospects."

"They *beat me*. They don't deserve your help, and I don't want it."

"Is help so bad?" he asked. "It's hard to ask for help when you've never been shown how."

"I'm not one of your cases," she screamed, the gun barrel shaking, making the boys shrink back.

"Cases are people," Sahle said. "Brothers, sisters, mothers—people."

"I don't want to be that kind of people … to you."

"You're not," he replied. "But this is wrong. Someone else is manipulating them."

"They. Beat. Me."

"But why? Why did they pick you? You don't have money. No drugs."

She turned to the boys. "Who runs you?"

When the boy hesitated, Sahle grabbed his hand and had him kneeling in a flash, whining, his wrist bent to the breaking point. "Tell her, or I'll leave you with her."

"Okay, okay, okay!" the boy shouted, and Sahle relaxed his grip.

"Old Money," the boy gasped.

The barrel of the gun lowered. "Chuck," Nike whispered.

"Who?" Sahle asked.

"Burner. This is his district. The beating was a warning to stay out." The boy had even said it: *No one paints in this district …*

Sahle checked the pulse on the comatose boy. "One of you call an ambulance," he ordered, then to Nike added, "Let's go."

She turned back to the gang. "Go home to your moms, your sisters, your aunts, and your grandmas. Tell them you're sorry. Tell them you're going to try harder than this shit."

The boys didn't move.

"Do it!" she shouted.

They nodded fiercely.

"And don't think I won't be checking."

"Yes, ma'am."

She glared at them as she walked past. "Want to know what makes a man?" she said. "Don't be an asshole. It's not that high a bar."

She strode out of the alley, Sahle following. They walked in silence for a minute as she tucked the gun into her coat and collected herself. Finally, she turned to face him.

"Thank you," she said, holding back everything else she wanted to say—about her father, about her shame for really hurting that boy. "I …"

He pulled her into a hug.

"You didn't."

"But I did."

"Those boys have a chance not to become monsters."

She nodded into his shirt, then lifted her head. His face was close. Warm. Musky.

He'd stopped her from punching holes in adolescents—kids like her with absent or sick parents, kids with nothing to look forward to.

She grabbed the front of his shirt. His arms folded around her. She gave him a sharp jab of a kiss.

"I've wanted to do that for a while," she said.

Then their lips met, hard and long.

*****

Trayling woke to the sound of Nike and Sahle in conversation, his mind still gratefully groggy from the drugs but not so fuzzy that he missed how they were holding hands. His injured hand thundered like a distant explosion. Joula was at her desk, working on her maps, using AI to process the data. He was impressed; the woman was brilliant, and he couldn't help but feel a little behind. They were a team now, and he was the odd one out. The switch had happened so quickly—after years of secrecy, it left him off balance.

Nike noticed he was awake and nudged Sahle.

"You ready?" Sahle asked, crouching to tighten his shoelaces.

"What can you teach me in only a couple of hours?" Trayling asked.

"You're right, it's not much time, but I can show you a few things."

Within minutes, Trayling was sweating. He'd shown Sahle what he already knew—most of it from a couple of years of boxing and a short stint in a dojo.

"You have a good punch, but you're telegraphing it. Try this," Sahle said.

"I'm telegraphing because I don't want to make quick movements with my injury."

"This will help. Don't use your shoulder." Sahle demonstrated how to lash out with quick punches that lacked power but were so fast they were almost impossible to evade. Then he pulled out a knife.

"If someone pulls one of these—"

"I run," Trayling said, waving the offered weapon away. "Seriously, they're useful for collecting samples, but I don't want to kill anything except aliens."

Sahle twirled the hunting knife with its wicked point. "What are you planning to do if Nike is incapacitated and someone's shooting a fireball at you?"

"The oilskin is a decent fire shield because the blasts aren't continuous—usually." He thought back to the night he'd burned Nike's hand and remembered the fire flowing uncontrollably from him. "But I'll be knocking heads with that." He pointed to the baseball bat Nike had returned.

"Family weapon?"

"So I gather."

"I'll bring the knife," Sahle said, sheathing it.

"I have my own and you're not invited," Trayling replied, motioning to Joula. "Neither of you are."

"No problem with that," Joula said with a wink. "More of a lover."

Sahle straightened to his full height.

Nike was preparing a burn kit near one of the humming printer beds. "My dad's right."

"I can defend both of you while you focus on the nest," Sahle said.

"You can't fight what you can't see," Nike replied. "If all goes well, we won't need bats or anything else."

Nike and Sahle exchanged a glance Trayling couldn't interpret, but at least Nike seemed to be supporting him on this.

"What am I supposed to do?" Sahle asked.

Nike walked over, caressing Sahle's chin with her hand. "So pretty."

"I'm serious."

"So am I," she replied. "I don't need a karate expert. I need a geek."

Disappointment flashed in Sahle's eyes, quickly replaced by determination. "I'll have to figure out a way to be useful."

Joula snickered, the only one amused. "Gather round, children," she said.

When they did, Joula smiled. "You know this is the scene, right?"

"What scene?" Nike asked.

"The one in the movies. After the techie lays out the battle plan. The quiet scene where they take what they've learned and get ready to face the big bad."

Trayling glanced at Nike but couldn't catch her eye.

Sahle sulked toward his toes.

Nike swallowed. "It should be," she said, turning to the large screen.

The satellite image of the neighbourhood overlaid with raitgur trails filled the display.

"I want you to advance on the nest from here," Joula said, pointing to a spot far from the main trails, which branched and intersected in places. "It'll let you penetrate deep into enemy territory without getting near a trail—and hopefully without being spotted until you start burning."

"Not the sewers?" Trayling asked.

"I'd be covering the exits if I were them," Joula replied.

"You're assuming these things can think?" Sahle asked.

"We have to be prepared for that," Nike said.

"They've shown the ability to organize and entrap," Trayling added.

"Fumo saw us drop into the sewers. He'll be watching," Nike said.

"Even squirrels will announce to the neighbourhood there's someone around," Joula said. "All social creatures look out for each other. That chittering Nike described sounds like communication."

"And if they alert each other, they'll move the breeders if there's a threat," Trayling warned.

Joula nodded. "Most trails converge here. Your breeders should be there."

They all stared at the point of convergence, dead center in the rowhouse complex. It was farther than Trayling had penetrated last time.

"How many can you expect?" Sahle asked.

"Hundreds?" Nike suggested.

"That's a lot of burning," Joula said. "Trayling already looks a bit punch-drunk. No offense."

"No offense, but I can handle it. We're doing good." He grinned at Nike, who cracked her neck and turned away. She wasn't giving him an inch. "And she's the most powerful Burner on record."

"We don't need to burn everything tonight," Nike said. "Just get in, kill the breeders, get out. We only need to keep the breeders from escaping and keep Trayling alive until they're dead."

Trayling flinched at Nike's deliberate use of his name—and at the implication there might not be an *after*.

"Ouch," Sahle said quietly, shutting up when Nike glared.

"It would be good to have someone covering the flank," Joula said.

"I can do that," Sahle offered.

"Someone who can see them. Remember the alley?" Nike replied.

"Are you done mocking me?" Sahle asked. "Because I can watch for the human element too. In case you forgot, you're entering another Burner's territory."

"No," Trayling and Nike said together.

"I'll have eyes on them, Sahle," Joula said, tapping her first-person-view goggles.

"Ready?" Nike asked. Again, she barely glanced at Trayling. His fingers clenched.

"For you, a gift," Joula said, handing Trayling some more pills.

"Time to burn," Trayling said.

"Time to burn," Nike agreed.

Chapter Twenty-Eight

Nike welcomed the silence. She led the march to the Promise Complex, never looking back, never slowing to ensure her father kept up or reached a streetlight before it turned red, never giving him the chance to break the quiet. She'd caught his reflection in store windows along Queen, staggering and wan among the mannequins. This man, who had decided for her at nine years of age that her life would be one of pain and disability, who had led her to an alien and let it drain the life from her—she didn't know that man. All the sundaes and kittens were bullshit. A real father would have done everything in his power to protect her from the raitgur, not sacrificed her to them for his own gain.

By the end of the night, the rucksack over her shoulder would be full. Santana had said Nike could keep the take, and she would—tens of thousands of dollars' worth of spines. Enough to rent her own apartment. Enough to take a break and focus on her art. The future she'd always thought was out of reach now seemed within her grasp. A final burn. It would cost her father, but he'd have the rest of his life to recover. After tonight, she wouldn't need him at all.

They threaded through her territory, Nike scouring the shadows for tendrils of purple light. Jittery energy buzzed through her, but she forced herself to focus on the logistics of her future. Even if they destroyed the breeding pair, she'd still need to keep her district clear. That wouldn't require much additional work—Santana had warned her that eliminating the nest would reduce the hunt. That suited Nike just fine. Maybe she could get a place outside the city entirely, somewhere beyond the Burner districts.

For once in her life, Nike wasn't useless. Her mind flashed back to Santana's target gallery. She still couldn't believe she'd done that—or swung a bat at a boy. Had she really done that too? Cold guilt prickled up her spine. Had becoming a Burner changed her personality? What would have happened if Sahle hadn't shown up?

She would have fired the gun.

Shit.

She'd been so lost in thought that she hadn't noticed where they were headed. She'd overshot Joula's recommended approach, and her dad had fallen behind. No, he was still there—just hobbling along, hand at his hip. He looked old. Done in.

"Thanks," he gasped, catching up. "But I thought—"

"I want to take the long way around," Nike cut him off, not waiting for a reply. His face was an abyss of lost time.

"Are you sure you're okay?" he asked. "That we're okay?"

Nike pulled out her phone and whispered to Joula. "We're almost there."

"Let me know when you're a block away," Joula replied. "I'm in the air, a few minutes out."

Nike pictured Joula with her headset on, Sahle hovering at her shoulder. As if summoned by the thought, Sahle said, "Good luck, Nike. I'm with you."

She slid the phone into her oilskin pocket and nodded to her father.

It was past midnight when they reached the checkpoint. They huddled near an outdoor city pool and a street vendor packing up their Tex-Mex stand. Lampposts, set too far apart to light the path properly, marked the trail toward the rowhouses.

"Ready, Trayling?" she asked.

"I'm glad we're doing this," he said. "You're amazing, you know. This will protect so many people."

She bore the weight of his hand on her shoulder but couldn't reply without betraying how furious she was. If she let herself go there, she knew she'd spiral too deep to climb back out. The deeper and darker she went, the worse the burn would be.

He pressed on. "If anything happens—"

"You've got life insurance?" she snapped.

"Not a dime of it."

Nike addressed Joula. "We're here."

"Good. This is also the retreat line," Joula explained. "There should be a sewer manhole nearby. Use it if you run into trouble."

A manhole in the middle of the street rattled as car tires rolled over it. Hopefully, it wouldn't come to that.

"Trayling has the tool."

He lifted a length of iron with a loop at one end and a hook at the other.

"Any company?" Sahle's voice cut in.

"I spotted a couple squid in the distance," Nike said.

Her dad pulled a cheap Bic lighter from his pocket—the same one from the test. Nike found her Zippo and tossed it to him.

"Here. Keep it."

"You sure?" His face softened.

"Yeah, may it light your way." By his expression, she could tell he'd missed the sarcasm. "I'll say when."

"I'm overhead," Joula said. "I've got eyes on you. Tell me when you spot another, and I'll shift spectrums to try and see it too."

"I doubt Joula's experiments with light are going to work," Trayling said. "Santana has scientists at her disposal. If spectrums worked, she'd have figured it out."

Nike scanned the sky but couldn't find the drone. "Let's go."

The park was nearly silent, partly due to the late hour, but also because the moisture-laden air smothered sound. Dew glistened on the shorn grass, and halos of moisture ringed the lights. At the last lamppost and the initial outlying tents, Nike stopped and turned back to her dad. Sweat dripped from his brow, and he swiped his forearm across it. Just ahead of them, a gate led into the complex and to the main road connecting blocks of homes, a dozen units apiece.

"Light up. We go in hot and fast," she said.

From his neck, he pulled the bite guard, the leather imprinted with her teeth, infused with her screams. Nike swallowed at the memory of its taste. Her father's hand was already free of gauze, and he ran a tongue of flame across it, kindling half a fingerless hand. The flesh down his arm was riven with oily fistulae.

"Going ahead for an aerial view," Joula said.

Nike loped toward the gate.

A raitgur squidged between two blocks of rowhouse units.

"I have another on my right," she whispered. "Thirty yards in."

But Nike didn't have time for Joula's experiments. She entered the main street at a jog, her father close behind. He peered up at the houses like a tourist, despite being unable to see anything. A foot-high raitgur flung out from a second-floor window, nearly striking Nike before she engulfed it in flame. Her fingers clamped off the fire as the beast rolled on the ground, smoking until nothing remained but spine. Her dad moved to wrap it, but she held him back.

"We'll clean up on the way out."

He hesitated, then seemed to think better of it.

Raitgur crept from house to house. They seemed to guess their goal; those that didn't attack blocked their way, forming a shimmering wall of aliens. Nike settled into a rhythm, molding a pellet of power in her palm and hurling it. Each raitgur she struck seized before disintegrating in a flare of light. On they came—too many. She didn't have time to target them individually. Wrenching her arm back and forth, she scattered fire like paint, ball after exploding ball lighting up the night. The pellets grew from marbles to baseballs, each taking out several aliens at a time. Her lungs competed for air between her grunts.

"I can see movement!" Joula screeched excitedly. "Wait a second … heat signatures?"

Nike ran deeper, heading toward the point where Joula had determined the trails would converge. She heaved ball lightning left and right, screaming, while her dad hauled himself after her, each throw causing him to moan as the flame at the tip of his arm jetted and guttered before flaring again.

The last rowhouse looked different. Its windows and door weren't boarded or broken. It wasn't freshly painted or landscaped, but it looked livable. If anything, the raitgur near it were smaller. Nike didn't have time to consider the details. She needed more firepower. Pulling the sleeve from her stump, she willed energy to gather at its tip. Fire hosed from it, a twisting stream that buried the raitgur.

"I'm in infrared." Joula swore. "Those aren't raitgur—they're people!"

"What are you talking about?" Nike demanded through clenched teeth. "The aliens are everywhere."

"It's a trap. Get out! There are people coming."

Figures rounded buildings, emerged from alcoves, and burst from the doors of neighbouring rowhouses. With them came the heavy mechanical sound of weapons cocking.

"What the hell is happening?" Nike demanded. Soldiers. Military. They should be on their side. "What do we do?"

"Run," Joula shouted.

But it was too late. Laser dots jittered on their chests.

"Put down your weapons," a voice rang out.

Trayling lifted his arms, stump still burning. Nike did the same, but her hand and the tip of her stump glowed.

"We're here on military authority," Nike said, feeling ridiculous. She had no platoon name. No code name. Just Santana and Tyler operating out of a massage parlour.

"Put them down!" the soldier threatened.

"Put what down?" she shouted back.

The raitgur gathered. Those blocking the way to the final house advanced.

"They're coming, Dad," Nike said.

"On the ground," the soldier repeated.

"Soldier, you have ten seconds before your people start collapsing. Listen to me," Trayling said, his voice heavy with fear. Nike didn't understand how he could feel anything for these people.

"On the ground!"

"All around us are the creatures causing people to jitterbug. Aliens that only my daughter's fire can kill. My daughter and I are trying to help the city. Let her burn them, or you will be infected."

While he spoke, the raitgur moved in. Nike watched one climb the pant leg of a soldier.

"There's one on that man's leg," she said, trying to motion with her chin.

The soldier collapsed, and shouting erupted.

"That wasn't us!" her father screamed. "Call Major Santana!"

But even as he said it, Nike realized Santana wouldn't help them. "Santana set us up."

Soldiers slid up behind them, grabbing them roughly, jerking them to the pavement, knees on their backs. Gravel clogged Nike's nostrils.

A raitgur hopped onto her father's cheek, and Nike gasped. A tentacle whipped across her neck. She screamed, her back arching.

"Sir, she—" The soldier beside her said nothing more. With a raitgur crawling down his throat, his eyes rolled back, and he slopped to the ground.

Another lash ripped across Nike's nose, but the weight on her back was gone. She was free.

Her father was suddenly up, wrestling with a soldier. A short jab dropped him, leaving Trayling standing there with a semiautomatic weapon, useless in his one-handed grip. Around them, soldiers screamed at their fallen friends, unaware of the real danger.

"Run!" Trayling screamed, tossing the gun away.

"We have to finish this now!" Nike yelled back. They'd never get this close again. The nest would be moved, or soldiers would enforce a perimeter. Where were the breeders? Nike recalled the map, the satellite overlay, the tended rowhouse—it could just as easily have been occupied, but her father had done reconnaissance.

"I need targets, Joula," Nike said.

"More soldiers coming. You're out of time."

"Find us a route out of here."

"Sewer manhole at your six."

Nike blasted open the sewer cover. Her father choked at the sudden pain and dropped to a knee. A soldier lying beside the sewer rolled over and rubbed his eyes before fumbling for his weapon. Her dad was twenty yards away, oblivious to the raitgur flooding over him. But the aliens protected him from the soldiers. Beyond them came headlights, the jostle of flashlights, and the laser sights of advancing troops.

"Burn it all!" her dad screamed.

It wasn't something you shouted with panicked soldiers around, but the fear in his eyes galvanized her. She urged power into her hand, and rapture surged through her chest and mind. Her dad folded over, his arm a flamethrower directed at the sky. With a roar, she heaved energy at a bank of rowhouses. They exploded. The shockwave threw soldiers to the ground, but she stood against the wind of it. On the ground, her father whimpered. His hand was gone.

Was this what she wanted? For him to fully understand her pain? To know what she felt? No, even if vengeance had been her goal, what he had done to her was far worse than this.

She glanced back at the dark sewer, then at her dad clawing toward her on the ground. How little she felt for him. How little it would have taken for him to say something—anything—for her to leave him to the soldiers. A dozen rowhouses were wrecks of burning rock and molten steel, but she couldn't know if their job was done. Santana had betrayed them.

She ran to him, looping his arm over her shoulder and neck so she could slide him to and through the sewer manhole.

He dropped into the darkness.

Fresh soldiers arrived—soldiers who hadn't been attacked by the raitgur—and they spotted her. Bullets chipped the pavement as she followed her father into the sewer.

A sharp expulsion of breath, followed by a groan, identified what had softened her landing.

"We have to keep moving."

She helped him to his feet, and together they slogged down the tunnel.

"Joula, you still with us?"

"I've got something ahead of you, a hundred yards," Joula said, and Nike clung to the sound of her voice.

"Soldiers?" Nike gasped. If they were already in the sewers, there'd be no hope. The exits would be cut off.

"Wrong light spectrum. This is something different. Weird. It's tiny, but it's moving. Two people with it. Sahle's on …" Whatever Joula said next broke into static as Nike moved deeper underground.

Her dad's wheezing filled the tunnel. In slow, short, whistling breaths, he asked, "What. Is. Wrong. Something. Is."

"Not now."

"Not now? Burning …" He lifted his matching stump, unlit and sodden from sewage. Even in the near-lightless sewer, his eyes flashed with desperate, feverish anger.

Heavy boots sloshed behind them. Headlamps flashed. Raitgur too. Dozens of them followed. Nike heard the cries of soldiers being struck down.

She pulled her father along an adjoining tunnel, keeping her back against the cold, damp concrete. A distant light came into view. It wavered. A flame.

"Dad!" she exclaimed, but his pilot was out.

"Fumo," Trayling whispered.

Flame flickered from Fuoco's finger, her face twisted in its glow. Nike pulled the handgun from her coat. The metal was cold and heavy. As Fumo's hands flared, Nike fired three shots. The gun bucked, sending bullets wide and high. Something slumped to the ground.

The light at the end of the tunnel dimmed, and then a scream rose—a young girl's. Nike recognized it. She'd screamed that same scream in her head for years.

The gun slipped from Nike's fingers, and she barely registered her father picking it up.

"What have you done?" he whispered.

"As if there's a difference between a bullet and a fireball," she said, though she quaked.

Nike staggered down the tunnel. Fuoco stared up from where she crouched over her father, eyes feral, teeth bared like a protective wolf cub.

"I'm sorry, I'm sorry," Nike repeated, but even as she said it, she realized that this meant the girl wouldn't be burned anymore. She could live without this. Nike wished someone had shot her father when she was young, rather than leaving her to carry the burden of killing him slowly.

Joula's staticky voice cut in and out, "… right … top … target … right there."

Her father slogged to stand behind her.

"He'll never burn you again," she told Fuoco.

Black hatred rolled from the girl.

The wavering lights of soldiers tracked the gunshots. Raitgur began to converge—some hunting the soldiers, others sliding down the tunnel Fuoco and Fumo had come from. Nike's cheek and nose still burned with acid.

"We have to go," her dad said, waking her from the memory of the gun jolting in her grip.

A tiny raitgur, smaller than anything she'd ever seen, no bigger than a thumbnail, floundered through Fumo's chest hair. While she watched, another dropped beside the first. Nike traced its path to the girl.

"Dad. Get her." At his confusion, she added, "She's the breeder."

Trayling grabbed Fuoco by the arm, but she twisted, pulled, and bit at him as he wrestled her, revealing Fumo's face in the scuffle. Blood bloomed from the shot he'd taken in the forehead. Tiny raitgur crawled on him like lice, leaving red tendrils as they burned paths across his skin.

Nike grabbed Fuoco by the hair and held her for inspection. She whined but didn't cry out, her eyes rolling, mouth spitting. Around her neck hung a chain with a medallion—a piece of black metal, twisted and bubbled like hardened magma. As Nike watched, a speck of light began to grow.

"The meteor," she whispered. "The meteor is birthing them. She has the meteor!"

Nike released Fuoco, caught the chain, and yanked it, snapping the clasp.

Fuoco broke free from Trayling's grip and sprinted toward the soldiers. He lunged after her, but Nike held him back. If the soldiers didn't shoot her, she'd at least force them to hold their fire.

"Let her go," Nike said. "We have the meteor."

"If it's birthing them, let me hold it so it doesn't burn you," Trayling said.

He was right. Nike juggled it until she held it by the chain. Of course, it made sense that a source would be the only person who could handle such a burden.

"Burn it now." His mouth was torn down at the sides, and deep bags were etched beneath his eyes, hazy with pain or drugs—or both.

"You're too injured; you'd die," Nike said. "We still have to get out of here—miles to run." She pulled his arm across her shoulder, and he limped a few steps.

"But the meteor would be gone. Nike, tell me why you're so angry. Maybe we can fix this. You can't hide your anger from your source."

Nike broke from his gaze at the march of soldiers bearing down. Why they hadn't caught up confused her—were they cutting off exits, putting on hazmat gear, or overwhelmed by raitgur?

"You infected me," she said. Angry tears stung her eyes, and she hated herself for feeling anything. That the way her mouth tugged down at the sides was a betrayal. She refused to look at him, to show her face, but his next words were heavy with sadness and understanding.

"Santana told you."

"Does it matter?"

"She wanted this. Don't you see? This whole setup. She planned the ambush and wanted to make me pay."

"We've both paid." Her words echoed as they sloshed deeper into the tunnel.

"No, she wanted you to hate me, so you'd destroy me, so we'd no longer be a threat."

Nike paused for a second before continuing down another side tunnel. He wasn't listening to her—maybe he couldn't bear to hear that he'd made the wrong choices.

"Is it true? Did you infect me? I want to hear it from you."

She stopped to meet his gaze. Light filtered through a nearby sewer grate and refracted in his eyes.

"Did you?"

"Santana told me I was a source and that Sabra would be a Burner," Trayling responded.

"Sabra? Not me?" Nike straightened, no longer supporting his arm. She didn't understand.

Her father started up the ladder toward the exit.

"No, it's too soon. Crawling with raitgur and soldiers." A tiny raitgur wormed over her hand, stinging. "What about Sabra?" She sensed his hesitation and let the sound of encroaching soldiers encourage him.

"They tested you both," he explained. "I thought it was just a test. But it was an infection."

She choked. "You did this to Sabra, too?"

He said nothing.

"You killed my sister." Her voice broke.

"I …" He didn't deny it.

"Oh, Dad, I really do hate you."

The soldiers were calling out, shouts of discovery. Another man hollered. If she didn't know better, she would've sworn it sounded like Sahle.

"We can't take this back out of here," Trayling said, pointing to the meteorite. "We can't spread the infection. Let me finish this."

"Not now." They both knew why. If it didn't kill him, it would seriously maim him.

"Do what you have to do. I'm ready. It's my fault." He struck the lighter and held up his arm like a medieval torch, the flame lit not only at its tip but several inches below. At the sound of noise farther down the tunnel, Trayling hid the flame inside his jacket. The soldiers passed the junction, moving fast beyond them. Lured away.

As she watched, another soldier dropped listless into the sludge. The ephemeral glow plastered to his face turned its attention toward them.

"Do it," Trayling said.

Nike nodded and dangled the pendant between them.

Her phone flashed, killing her night vision. A text read: *Sahle has your back. He's drawing the soldiers away. Go now. Be safe, love.*

The guy couldn't follow orders. She didn't have it in her to smile.

"Look," Trayling said, pointing at the meteor. "Look, it's sheered."

In the light of his guttering arm, a tiny raitgur toppled from the meteorite into the sludge. Nike flipped the pendant up to catch it in her palm. It burst into flame. Alien larvae baked, tiny flares even her father could see. She stared at the area beneath the rock. It was sheered flat—not a meteorite, but a chip of one.

"How big was the meteor, Dad?"

"I don't know."

"Where's the rest of it?"

She missed his response as a raitgur launched from the tunnel toward her head. She ducked.

Nothing remained to be done but burn—burn the attackers, burn the meteor shard, burn her dad. Trayling must have sensed it, because he stepped back. She dropped the pendant onto the ground where it hissed. Acid sizzled across the back of her cloak. She whirled, gripping the offending raitgur in her hand. Her fingers closed around its spine. Tentacles flailed, and she screamed as she fried the creature.

With the spine dead in her hand, she turned back to the pendant. Raitgur raced down the tunnel.

Light swelled in her palm. She drew more from her father, whose jaw bulged as he bit and frothed like a horse at the end of a race. She lowered both arms, letting fire drool over the pendant, burying it. A full minute of near-constant fire, only interrupted to torch a few fledgling aliens, finally melted the stone.

"Snuff it," she said, waiting in the darkness and his huffing breath until she was certain no sinuous light crept from the slag. "Let's go."

She let him swing his arm across her shoulders. So much power flowed through her, she could've swung him onto her back.

It wasn't until they climbed out of the sewer that she realized her dad's arm was missing past the elbow.

"Fifty grand, lucky you," she said.

But everything was wrong. There would be no payday from Santana, not for the spines and not for the limb.

Fire trucks and police sirens fragmented the darkness.

Chapter Twenty-Nine

Joula helped Trayling down the stairs of the makespace to the bed, where he collapsed.

Nike scanned the room.

"No word from Sahle," Joula said.

Nike sighed and began gathering her things, periodically checking her phone for any sign that he'd made it out safely.

"So what happened?" Joula asked. "You were amazing, all witchy with your fire."

"It was a trap," Nike replied. "Without Sahle …"

"He'll get out. He's going to make it."

Nike gave little nods and carried the package of medical supplies to her father, who lay unmoving.

"What happened in the sewer?" Joula asked. "I lost you."

Nike hesitated, her shoulders tensing. "Something bad."

"Like my—"

"Like your felony times ten," she said through clenched teeth.

"Okay." Joula, sitting in the chair at her drafting desk and its computers, pointed to the wall screen where a blue dot was visible on a road. "I saw this, and then it disappeared. I think I might've caught a piece of one of your aliens."

The return to the mechanics of fighting aliens eased the knot in Nike's throat. "The raitgur were all over the place. What did it look like?"

"That's it—just that blue dot, but under a really weird combination of spectrums."

"And then it vanished?" Nike paused in her laying out of the ointments her father would need if he wanted to survive the day.

Joula snapped her fingers.

"The meteor," Trayling croaked.

Joula glanced over. "He needs help."

"Meteor," he repeated.

"Trayling's right," Nike said. "If it was the meteor, then your signal would have disappeared after I burned it. The meteor is the key—there never was a breeding pair. That's not how these creatures work. They're produced by the stone, dropping off like ants."

"You got it then?" Joula asked. "No more aliens!"

Nike finished packing her stuff and zipped the rucksack, wondering what would happen now. Where would she go? Did she really have to take her dad with her? "It was only a small piece. The meteor was bigger."

"Where's the rest of it, then? Where do you keep a meteor that keeps shitting out aliens?"

Nike shook her head. "This explains the victim clusters."

Her father propped himself up on one arm, listing heavily. "I don't understand. How can the meteor be causing the clusters?"

"When we were down there, the raitgur seemed to be following us. But what if the raitgur weren't following us? What if they were following the meteor?"

"Like a lodestone," Joula said.

"Right. If the raitgur follow the meteor, it explains why they stuck mostly to Fumo's territory," Nike replied.

"And why they need to ship victims around to spread out signs of their nest," her father added.

"Shouldn't we be able to find the rest of the meteor by using the trails and clusters?" Joula brought the map back up on the screen. They all stared at it, searching for a pattern that might indicate the location of other pieces.

Nike shook her head. The only big cluster was Fumo's district.

"Wait." Joula's fingers rattled on the keyboard, and the data shifted. A huge, obvious cluster now appeared centrally on the map.

"What's that?" Nike asked.

"Ambrose's data."

"Before the districts," Trayling said.

Nike's mind raced. "Ambrose said the government moved to a district model because Burners were tripping over one another, right? It wouldn't have taken Burners long to figure out where all the raitgur were coming from if the government didn't separate them—didn't keep them competitive."

"Yeah, but that doesn't explain why the raitgur decided to spread out," Joula said, flipping back to the district model with its relatively scattered spines and victims.

"They didn't. They followed the meteor," Nike said.

Her father swore. "They aren't only moving victims." Nike nodded at him.

"What are you saying, sister?" Joula asked.

"What if the meteor moves? And the districts are like fields."

"Pastures," her father suggested.

"Right. And the raitgur are sheep being led to fresh places to feed."

"So sick," Joula said. "They're taking them to the poorest areas and letting them feed because they don't think anyone cares."

Nike swallowed hard. Had she cared? Had she attended a protest? Cared about Dan? Stood guard?

"We have to get out of here," Trayling said.

Nike understood. This was worse than she could have imagined. Last night, dozens of armed soldiers had been sent out just to protect a tiny fragment of the meteor. What would Santana do to protect the rest?

"They have to keep it moving," Nike said. "It can't be protected all the time, or it would infect whoever was guarding it."

"Which means we can still destroy it," Trayling said. But he didn't look ready to get out of bed, much less burn again.

"I'd give your dad a couple of days to heal," Joula said, shaking some pills into her hand and offering them to Trayling.

He waved them off. "No. No more drugs. I need to be awake."

"He needs fluids and protein," Nike said.

Joula opened another drawer and pulled out a Ziploc from the back. "These are different. They won't dull the pain—they'll keep you upright. For a bit."

"You're giving my dad … Is that molly? Dad, don't." But why should she care? She only needed him to burn.

He took the pills greedily and asked Joula, "Can you find the meteor?"

"I can try running a grid search of the city using the drone."

"How long?"

"About a day. The drone needs to charge. And we're not sure what I saw, right?"

He nodded. "In the meantime, we have to disappear."

"Joula, will you find Sahle?" Nike asked, trying to calm the fear twisting in her stomach. For Joula's sake, she had to take her dad away.

"On it."

"No phones. No internet. No credit cards," Trayling warned. "We'll find you when we're ready."

"Where are you going to go?"

"Somewhere they've already looked."

***

In the cool morning, ropes creaked, rubbing against wooden docks and straining at cleats. Resting his arm on his daughter for support, Trayling crept across the gravel lot, through the marina gates and onto Ambrose's shell of a home. The police tape was gone.

Once inside, Nike brushed off her father's arm as if it were an alley rat on her shoulder and dropped her rucksack on the melted fibreglass.

"Two days. Sleep here, eat here, we figure this out," he said. The drugs Joula had given him had propelled him this far, but he knew his injuries would catch up soon. He needed help to apply the ointments, but Nike clearly wasn't interested.

She slumped on a charred bench. "It was supposed to be the end, Dad. I was going to burn the nest, take a hundred spines back to Santana, and start my life." She buried her face in her hands. "Everyone's a fucking liar."

Trayling swallowed. He had nothing left to offer her. His life had been a sham. He wasn't a hero, just another wolf the government had brought in to control the breeding populations of the aliens they'd never intended to exterminate. The same stray aliens that had infected his wife and daughter. No, he corrected himself, they hadn't infected Sabra. He had. Nike was right: it was his fault.

Santana had pulled him from a psychiatric ward, where he'd been committed for so-called psychotic delusions. He was lucky it hadn't been a prison cell. He'd been incoherent, drinking, chasing raitgur, attacking the aliens. Many of his worst acid scars were from that time. He'd been a danger to himself and others. The doctors had restrained him, dosed him with drugs. But even then, he'd known what he was doing—what Santana was saying when she visited him with her offer. If anything, he had been primed to believe it.

The meteor, the aliens, his duty as part of a Burner team. He'd accepted it with a kind of magical thinking, almost reverence. He only needed to find his other half, his Burner—that's what he'd been told—and they could burn. Not him. He could have vengeance on the freakish things. He could prove his sanity, if only to himself and the young Santana before him. A community of Burners was a dream, and their task of protection was a religion.

So he'd allowed Santana to test his daughters. He'd pulled them from warm beds, out from under *Dora the Explorer* comforters and mountains of teddy bears, to face aliens. He hadn't been present for the testing—he'd been left in the psych ward, presumably because that was the right place for him if no Burner was obtained. But there was no doubt now that his daughters had visited the meteor eight years ago.

Trayling knelt to inspect the one area of the boat untouched by fire. "A Burner burns. The source giveth—"

"I'm sleeping up here." Nike pulled a ruined mattress off a bunk and checked under the hatch beneath, finding only moldy lifejackets.

"A Burner didn't do this," Trayling said. The degree of damage surprised him, as did the hint of sulfur in the residue smell. He sniffed along the ground. "Arson of some kind."

"So Santana sent soldiers, not Fumo," Nike said. "Does it matter?"

"Not really," he replied. His stump brushed lightly against the ground, and he bit back pain. "The source giveth."

"Shut up."

He breathed, holding her stare. In her eyes, he saw contempt. He felt it too—impatience for this to be over, to move on, to be gone. There would be nothing left of him.

He eased back on the bumpy mess of fibreglass, covered himself with his coat, and tried to sleep, quaking with chills. But sleep wouldn't come. His mind tumbled with raitgur, fire, and meteors. After half an hour, he wrestled with the pain until he was upright. Nike slept—or feigned sleep—curled on her bunk. He left a note for her on the ground, saying he was heading out for supplies. He didn't bother explaining. Her arm now lay across her face. When she woke, she'd need to eat. He had one more job to do, and then his fatherly duties would be over.

And he could go.

***

Nurse Chui whistled as he twirled a set of keys and IDs on a lanyard, walking through the underground parking garage. Trayling stepped out from behind a concrete column, and the whistling died, the keys snapping into Chui's palm.

"Trayling?" Chui asked, his shoulders sagging. "Crap, man, you frightened me there. Didn't recognize you off the ward … and all. I've been worried about you. Eight years, you never missed a day, and then you stop coming. Everyone gone. No goodbye."

"I have a favour to ask," Trayling said, dropping a backpack at his feet.

Chui's expression turned cautious. "Okay?"

"I need you to take care of Analia and Sabra. I need you to pass along payment for their ongoing care." Trayling unzipped the bag, revealing bricks of cash. His first stop before the garage had been a safety deposit box. Trayling kicked the bag, so it rolled to Chui's feet. "Five years' worth."

"What's going on, Trayling? This doesn't make sense."

"It's a big favour."

Chui glanced over his shoulder, then scratched his head. "You're bringing them back?"

"What—" Trayling's mind struggled through the fog of pain and drugs.

"They were transferred last night. I thought you—"

Trayling was on him in seconds, hand twisted in Chui's cotton smock. "Where are they?" He barely had the words out before his strength gave way, and he slumped against the hood of a car.

Chui smoothed his spattered smock. "Buddy, I didn't do anything. I wasn't even there."

"Where?" Trayling whispered.

"I didn't see the discharge papers. I was really surprised when I heard."

Papers wouldn't matter. Whatever the transfer orders said would be fake. Chui placed a hand on Trayling's back.

"You don't look so hot. Oh my god, what's happened to your arm, Trayling? I need to take you to the emerge."

Laughter chugged from Trayling as he bent over the bag of money. "No, I'm not so hot." He picked up the money and pressed it into Chui's arms. "Will you hold on to this for me? If not for Analia and Sabra, then for Nike?"

Trayling staggered again and fell back across the car hood. He woke in the backseat. Chui hovered over him, syringe in hand, a fresh bandage on his arm.

"You're lucky I carry an emergency kit. Help is on its way."

"No, no," Trayling said weakly. "No time. Please." He couldn't fight past Chui's light touch. "Please."

"You could die."

"I know. I need to find my family." Trayling had watched Chui care for his wife and daughter every day for the last eight years. Chui was one of the few people he trusted.

"I'll find out where they are," Chui said, removing his restraining hand.

"Thank you." Trayling pushed himself up and paused. "You're a good person." But he already knew where the rest of his family was. The bullets in the gun at his waistband would be for Santana.

Before he left, Chui handed Trayling his emergency kit satchel. Inside were caffeine pills, energy bars, and a half dozen needles.

"Epinephrine," Chui said, his tone sending a chill through Trayling. "For when there's nothing left to give."

CHAPTER THIRTY

Trayling popped four caffeine pills and chewed through a rubbery energy bar while tucked into the alley across from headquarters. The caffeine made him twitchy as he shambled toward Healing Touch's plate-glass windows. He expected to need the gun at the base of his spine, but Tyler waved him inside and locked the door behind him.

When the lock snapped home, Tyler grabbed his burned bicep. Pain dropped him to his knees. She reached down and plucked the gun from his waistband.

"Come on, Trayling, we've known each other too long for this."

"Please, Tyler. Let me through. You know your commander is using people as fodder. The poor, the homeless."

Tyler said nothing. She pulled him up by his good arm and nudged him toward the back.

"Room number four."

He knew the drill.

"Where are my wife and daughter?" he demanded.

If Tyler knew, she didn't say. She shoved him through the door and along the corridor to its end.

The door still unlocked with his retinal scan. He hesitated, waiting for Tyler to nudge him forward. When she did, he swayed, using his injured arm to press up against her. He moaned as agony shot black spots through his vision. She shoved him upright, and when she did, he snagged the pistol from her holster, sliding it out of her sight.

In the laboratory, Santana was dressed in the same body armour the soldiers had worn. Mascara smudged her lower eyelids, and her lips were a tight line. A full black body bag lay behind her.

"You were there," he said. "At the nest."

She didn't respond, only nodded for Tyler to leave. The door shut.

"Where's my family?" Trayling demanded.

"I can't tell you that right now," she said.

"I trusted you."

"And I you," she said. "I entrusted you with our greatest resource. Do you know the damage you've caused?"

"Damage? They're disease-carrying aliens."

"These spines are forwarding materials research by a century. Investigations into raitgur invisibility could upend particle physics, biotech, nanotech. Who knows what molecules we can extract from them? Not a resource? Don't be so naïve."

"What about the thousands you've infected over the years?"

"I think of them every day—and every night when I'm trying to sleep. The nest was another modification to reduce infection rates, and it was working."

"You were working with Fumo." His gaze flicked to the body bag.

"Working with another Burner to reduce infections? That's the crime you're accusing me of?"

"It is when the meteor could be destroyed."

"Tell me, Trayling, how are we supposed to find a cure for your wife and daughter if we eradicate the raitgur entirely?"

Always with the false hope. It no longer played.

"You're using people like animal feed."

"Every one of those infected gave us more information, more time. Every person contributes to the greater work. Those losses mean many more will live in improved circumstances. What's important is that we do our best—we minimize infections. Raitgur cannot be contained, so they must be managed. These crimes you suggest are nothing compared to the millions who will benefit. This is a once-in-a-generation opportunity, and we are at the center of it."

"We? Who is *we*? Not the infected. They aren't part of this organization." He swept his arm at the boxes and crates around them. "The victims aren't volunteering for duty. *Who is we?*"

The sound of someone running down the hallway toward the room made him smile. They slammed into the door, and he jumped clear of it.

"My gun," Tyler called, banging on the door. "He has my gun."

Trayling pointed the barrel at Santana's head. She didn't flinch, though her eyes flared.

"That won't give you vengeance."

"I never wanted—"

"You worked on this project for years. You infected your children. You gave Nike's hand to make the world better. Shoot me, and it was all for nothing."

He flicked the safety off the weapon.

"You won't, because if you do, your family will never be cured. They'll never see the light of day again."

His arm shook. He leaned a shoulder against the wall, struggling to remain upright.

"What about the cure you gave me? What was that?"

"Saline. Harmless. You needed hope." She lifted her arm for him to hand over the gun. "Turn yourself in, and you can see your family."

"I don't believe you. I have nothing. You have nothing."

"You're right. You have nothing to lose, but ..." She took several steps toward him. "... we have footage of your daughter torching a garage where three people died. We have an eyewitness to Nike shooting Fumo. That makes her a serial killer. And I have your family. They'll die of dehydration if you kill me. Their lips will crack. Their eyes will sink into their skulls. Their brain cells will dry, making them vomit and seize. Turn yourself in, and they'll go back to their cushy nursing home until I cure them—and I promise to cure them. Nike will be able to live a normal life. All you have to do is give me the gun."

The gun barrel wobbled.

"Or are you going to waste Nike's life like you did Sabra's?"

"I thought you were testing them," he said, fighting tears. "You know that."

"You were too much a coward to ask. But you knew." She shook her head.

And then the tears came—but tears cured nothing. They were followed by anger. Santana was right—he might not have known for certain, but he'd suspected. He'd needed vengeance, whatever the cost.

"This is easier than burning through your arm, Trayling. We can't have you running around out there with Nike, trying to be heroes. Either she needs to be dead, or you need to be in prison. It's your choice."

If he shot Santana, Nike would always be on the run, and his family would be kept imprisoned—or worse, kept as lab rats. Or they'd die. He thought of Analia and Sabra, helpless, waiting for him.

"You'll cure Analia and Sabra?"

"The cure is known and simple but not guaranteed."

He fought the desire to empty the gun cartridge into her. "I want to say goodbye to Nike first." Before Santana could object, he added, "I can shoot my way out of here, or I can walk out. That's your choice."

"You have one hour."

"Show me my family."

Santana walked across the room to the large mirrored window. She hit a switch, and suddenly he could see into a long, narrow room with soot-blackened concrete walls and floor. Sabra and Analia lay on gurneys, staring back at him with eerie accusation. But they were alive.

The source giveth ...

***

Her dad was acting weird, even for him. He kept smiling. The scars from his acid burns twisted his mouth in a way that was hard to look at. Twice he'd tried to hug her. The sushi he'd bought was from Nike's favourite takeout place. She'd woken to find him at the side of the bed, his jacket draped over her, despite his quaking. While she ate, he picked at soggy tempura, staring at her as if trying to memorize her face. Her own face itched from burns, and she wanted to rip it off with her fingernails.

"What's your problem?" she said.

"Nothing."

Trayling was lucky he'd brought the food. With what was to come next, he really didn't want her burning him while she was both hungry and angry. Full of sushi, she set down the chopsticks and assessed their stores. Two large knives, several lighters, a small bundle of cash, and enough food for a couple of days. In this heat, the fish wouldn't keep long. An iced cappuccino would've gone down well right about then. Most of all, she wanted it over. To be free of the meteor and of this man. "We've given Joula a day to find the meteor," she said. "A few more hours and we check in. Risk a text."

The sun was already high, the cool morning lost to steadily rising humidity.

"I can't let you do this," Trayling said.

She snorted, fingering the edge of a blade and checking if the matches were waterproof—they were. "Bit late."

"It's not. I'm sorry. I see what I did now. To me, the right direction was so obvious I didn't think about what *you* wanted. Now I want you to be an artist. Fulfill your dreams. You're brilliant."

The edge of the knife was honed razor-thin.

"There's a meteor birthing alien predators," she said. "Not to mention a platoon of soldiers chasing us and possibly holding Sahle hostage. It's too late for this talk."

"There's a way out. Santana has you on Fumo's shooting, the garage. They'll probably frame you for Ambrose too—" She narrowed her eyes, but he kept rambling. "They want to bring you in. But they'll consider a trade. A deal."

The pad of her thumb split under the knife, and she dropped it. So *that's* where he'd been.

"You," she said.

"They can't leave us together. Together we're a threat to Santana."

She didn't reply, and he pressed on.

"I've been saving for you. Hidden cash. But you'll need to take care of Sabra and Analia. Find their nurse, Chui—he'll give you money. Enough to get you started."

She shook her head. It was too late for any of this.

"Turning yourself in won't stop the aliens. You can't stop now. It's already cost you a wife, a daughter, your arm, my hand, a career, friends, lives." Banked anger flared in her gut. She was surprised her hand wasn't aflame. She knew what was right, even if he didn't—or didn't have the will to face it any longer. "We destroy the meteor, find Sahle, then we run."

Her father kept looking at her like he knew something she didn't. He opened his arms. "Can I?"

"Fuck no." She backed away.

Car and truck engines roared into the yacht club parking lot.

Her father went to the window and checked his watch. "Shit."

She went for the knife.

"Leave it. They're here for me."

"Light up," she ordered, shoving matches into his hand.

"No." The matchbox tumbled to the ground, matches spilling.

"We can stop them!" she said. Boots thudded on the dock boards.

His eyes held hers—so sure, so at peace. "You go be awesome. Be amazing. I know you will be."

He might as well have stabbed her in the neck. He was dooming Sahle. Possibly allowing them to track everything back to Joula.

"You do not get to choose this for me. You do *not*! Light up!"

Windows bristled with gun barrels.

"On the ground!" soldiers screamed. A gun emerged through the doorway, and then the tiny houseboat rocked under the weight of a dozen men and women. No raitgur roamed here to save the day. No Sahle to lure soldiers away.

"Light up," she repeated, desperate now. Just when she'd come to terms with her role, her powers, her job—he *fucking* cut the legs out from under her as surely as if he'd burned them.

"You traitor!"

"It's for the best, Nike. They're here for me."

Her dad dropped to his knees, his hand going to the back of his skull.

A soldier shoved him to the floor, trying to cuff him.

"He's injured on that arm!" Nike yelled, but soldiers grabbed her, lifting her bodily until the room spun.

"Not her," her dad called. "Leave her! That's the deal."

A cuff clamped tight on her wrist, the soldier swearing as he struggled to find her other one. She willed everything into her hand, but there was nothing. A soldier pressed her face to the cold, melted floor.

They pulled her father from the boat first, screaming, and waited for a truck to drive away before hauling her up like a trussed deer.

Nike felt eyes on her—shadows behind the tinted windows of yachts and sailboats. She imagined the people beyond, watching like peasants had watched witches on the way to the stake. She hadn't thought it possible to be angrier at her father, but he'd figured out a way. He'd infected her and her sister, spent his life blindly following the orders of a psychopath and dragging Nike into the mess while cooking her. And now he'd turned himself over to the same government that betrayed him and expected them to adhere to some deal? He was an idiot.

An optimistic, overly trusting idiot.

Soldiers tossed her in the back of a van. In lieu of handcuffs, six soldiers on benches pointed their guns at her spine.

Without windows, she couldn't tell where they were going, but soon the van entered the stop-and-go of traffic of the city. After ten minutes, it halted. The rear doors opened, and she was carried by her limbs into a brightly lit hall, face down, staring at linoleum tiles, through a barred gate, and into a room.

Her chin grazed the concrete floor. She caught a whiff of coconut oil.

"I want a lawyer!" she shouted, then chuckled a little crazily.

No one replied. The door slammed shut.

She rolled to her side, noting a distinct lack of windows in the cell. Caged lights buzzed overhead. The door was nearly seamless.

After hauling herself up into a sitting position, she slumped against the wall. It was so cold—even colder than the floor. She rapped her knuckles against it. Metal. This was like Chuck's vault, specially created to defeat sources and Burners.

It meant her father could still be close by.

"Dad!" she shouted, then leaned her head back against the wall.

She might have imagined it, but in the distance came a muffled gonging.

She slammed the meat of her fist against the wall. Pounded. Tears splashed onto the concrete floor, darkening it.

"Dad … idiot …"

Her hand itched.

Slowly, she opened her fingers.

There. In the creases of her palm, a whisper of light.

"How?"

She remembered the dropped matches spilling onto the houseboat floor, where soldiers had pressed her and her father's heads.

"No," she said. "It's too far."

It was too far, through too much metal, and nowhere near enough power to be useful. She hated him. This would kill him.

But somewhere, somehow, her father was burning.

Light filled the grooves in her hand. Life line, heart line, fate line.

Somewhere, he was burning bright.

Chapter Thirty-One

Nike stood, swept her leg back to brace herself, and tried—*really* tried—to shove the hate she felt for her father down. Far down.

Then she burned.

Her neck corded, and veins swelled on her forearm, glowing as they thrust fire into her hand. She imagined her father's anguish and fought harder to burn faster. She tried to love him. She tried to think he was amazing. She tried to remember the things he'd done right—hot caramel sundaes after a burn, the way he made sure she knew all her mom's favourite books and movies, the way he'd tried to fill the place of two parents.

But she couldn't trust him. It had all been pretend. A means to control her, not love. And he'd never filled the place of a sister, let alone a mom.

Power came slowly, but it came, whatever the cost. She pressed her hand against the door, feeling the heat sweltering from it. But it wasn't enough. She searched her heart. His love for her mother was clear—he'd never taken a girlfriend, visited his wife every day, kept her memory alive, held hope. Could Nike love him for that? It was untainted. Could she at least *not* hate him for that?

The metal around her hand glowed red, warping, blistering, and finally melting. She kept going, probing for the lock mechanism until her fingers caught on bolts of hardened steel. Sparks fireworked. The mechanism melted to nothing.

Breathing hard, sweating from the heat, she kicked the door, and it bounced open. Her hand flared as if suddenly granted oxygen, and she realized it meant she was one wall closer to her father.

The hall was empty, save for a barred gate and another door with only a keypad for entry. Behind it would be her dad.

Pressing her hand against the steel door, she focused her power, willing it into two fingers that flared like plasma torches. Sparks bounced against the floor as metal oozed before her fingertips. A chunk of door crashed to the concrete. She toed what remained of it open.

Heat and the reek of burnt flesh billowed out. Her dad was cooking.

The rest of his arm, up to his shoulder, blazed.

She snuffed her hand then used her coat to dampen the embers of what little remained of his upper arm, but left the tip of his stump flickering. She'd need it to escape.

Sweat poured down his face. Burns slid up his neck and over his chest—a quarter of his body. He was pale, shaking, the rest of his skin ice-cold. With his good arm, he tried to push himself up and crumpled.

"Sorry," he slurred.

"Come on, Dad," she said.

"Tried. Always …"

"Save it."

She pulled him up, relieved he could bear his own weight as she dragged him from the oven. The gate's metal bars softened under the sharp tooth of her finger's flame. Her father had a thin smile on his face witnessing it.

Shoving the gate open, they hobbled toward another door. Nike readied a marble of energy to throw at whatever was on the other side.

The door was unlocked.

With her dad leaning against the wall, she eased it open, revealing Santana's lab.

Nike's eyes stung, and her skin prickled. The stench was overwhelming, and her father started coughing. Among the tables of samples, steel slabs, and boxes was a large metal tub. Tendrils of vapor rose from it.

With the crook of her arm over her mouth and nose, Nike inched closer. She gagged. Inside, a headless, naked corpse burbled in a stew of melting flesh. A gold chain hung around the severed neck. She retched again, unable to stop, and vomited on the floor.

"What the hell?" Nike croaked, coughing raggedly.

"Fumo … his bones," Trayling said, then waggled his smouldering stump toward a mirrored window. "Sabra, Mom …"

She staggered toward the window, collecting her and her father's phones from a steel table along the way. Hands against the glass, she couldn't see beyond.

Desperate to escape the stinging vapors, she pressed her shoulder to the door. It swung open.

As always, she rolled her marble of power in her palm.

The room stank of urine and feces, but it was better than the lye. She turned on a light and stifled a scream.

In the shooting gallery, her mother and sister lay on gurneys, pallid and slack-jawed. She ran to them, finding them warm and alive.

"What are we going to do?" she asked.

Her father could barely walk. They couldn't start wheeling people out of here, yet they couldn't leave them behind.

Her father slumped against the doorframe to the lab, wheezing. He jabbed his leg with a needle, then shut the door behind him, locking them in together.

"Back up requested," a voice came from beyond the adjoining doorway to the hall. "Escape in progress."

Before Nike could jump to secure the second entrance, Tyler burst into the gallery, gun drawn, her mom and sister between.

Nike dove, throwing the marble as Tyler fired. Her hair sizzled as explosive heat billowed over the room. She slapped out the sparks, jumped up, and coiled new energy into her palm—but Tyler had been thrown back into the corner, her gun punched up against the sidewall. She screamed and writhed, burning.

Nike's father groaned. Rushing to his side, Nike rolled him until he was out, but once again left his stump lit—just the shoulder now, with a stick of blackened bone like a wick measuring the life that remained.

Soldiers were coming.

"We have to get out of here!" she shouted.

Smoke bounced along the ceiling. Sabra's bed had caught fire. Nike swore and ran to it. She smothered the burning sheets with the thin woolen blanket, halting when Sabra winced.

That was all—a wince.

Nike slapped Sabra's cheek. Nothing.

"Dad?"

He moaned.

"Sabra's face moved," Nike said.

It might have been the only thing that could stir her father. He crawled on his knees toward the bed, his face twisted in pain, but in his eyes, an ember rekindled.

"The soldier," Nike thought aloud. "At the nest. The sewer. One of them got up."

At the time, she hadn't known if the soldier had been knocked over by the blast or whether he'd been infected and then somehow woken. But she'd wondered.

"Dad, you said that in some people, the fire burned them out. Others, it ignited something inside. Maybe we can jump-start it. What if the burn is the cure?"

She was talking about frying her family.

"Where evil goes, the flames shall shine …" he murmured, staring at her. "And the broken will rise again, cleansed by fire."

Her dad's head sagged. Smoke curled from his stump toward the ceiling, joining currents of brown tarry haze that pumped from pot lights.

"What does it mean?"

His eyes rolled. "Ambrose. Santana taught Ambrose the prayer. She knew the cure." He drew a deep, raspy breath. "Do it."

They couldn't leave her mom and sister here to die, but soldiers were coming.

About the only thing alive in her father was his rolling eyes. The skin of his shoulder and neck had split like a cooked sausage. His coat clung to his flesh, baked into it. One leg of his jeans was burned away, exposing skin that was red and raw beneath. His lungs rattled. But his eyes—they shone.

"It'll kill you, Dad."

"You don't need me. You saw what was left of Fumo. When I die, take a piece of me with you. And burn."

She knew it to be true, and she also knew it was what he wanted.

"Do it!" he said, and his eyes flared—not just with anger, but fear. Fear, perhaps, that if she waited any longer, he wouldn't live to see his wife and daughter one last time. Fear that the soldiers would arrive and take the choice from them. Or maybe, he was just afraid to die.

"We have to talk first," she said.

"Now?" he gasped.

Somewhere, a ram slammed against a door. And then again.

"Listen to me, for once," she said. "I'm not going to kill you."

The Chatelaine article had missed something. An important part.

"I want you to know what this meant to me." She held up her ruined stump. "Not only infecting me and Sabra. Not only the flesh and bone and pain—but everything."

The ram splintered doorframes. Plate-glass windows shattered. The noises faded into the background as her father grew calm, his tearing eyes focusing on her.

"The times you made me lie to my teachers and friends. The way you called me Kitten. I *hate* that nickname. It's so … diminishing. No friends at our place—I couldn't let them get close. I couldn't go to their homes either. You were afraid of people asking questions. 'Where did you get your burns, Nike?' 'Oh, from my father, the psycho hunting aliens!' If I had too many friends, I'd lose track of the lies. But it was me I lost. Me."

Fire stole oxygen from the room, tugging tears from her eyes too. The building burned.

She continued, "The way you dismissed my dreams. *Hobby,* you called my graffiti. I was fuel. Out all night. I could barely keep my eyes open at school. You watched me eat drugs—pill after fucking pill. And even after I wasn't fuel anymore, it was still only *your* dream that mattered.

"With me, you burned. With them—" She pointed to Sabra. "You loved. You loved them more than you ever loved me.

"Dad, I wanted … I wanted them to die. To die so I could have you back. That's what you did to me."

As if no longer able to support its weight, her father laid his head on the bed, his face turned to her. He reached up with his good hand and clasped hers. "Close," he whispered. "Come close."

Boots pounded down the hall. They were coming, but she didn't care. It was too late for escape. They would be captured, separated, killed. But for now, this moment was all that mattered.

She laid her cheek on the bed so that they were inches apart.

"I love you," he said. "I am sorry. I made so many mistakes. Loving-mistakes—that's fatherhood." He gathered himself. "Now finish this."

Watching the light fade in his eyes through tears in her own, she saw there was nothing left of him to offer. Nothing would change the pain or undo what he'd done.

The same setup that made him obsessively chase aliens, that oppressed her, had told him to be strong, to protect, to sacrifice himself. It had let him down too.

There was no such thing as a normal life.

The only thing that remained was for her to accept him—a weak man who had made many mistakes—or not. All that remained were tears.

"I forgive you," she said.

A heady lightness swept through her. Oxygen returned to the room. It stoked the fire. Unleashed power.

"I understand you."

Cleansing.

"I can love you."
Her mind had never been so sharp. She had never been so dangerous.

Chapter Thirty-Two

The door exploded open.

Nike leaped from the gurneys, standing before Sabra. She swung both arms around and slammed them together.

Soldiers staggered back into the hall as fire climbed from the floor to the ceiling. Nike blocked the doorway, feeding the wall of fire with a steady stream of energy, muffling the soldiers' cries. Shots fired were swallowed by the furnace.

Nike stared at the white blaze, then glanced to her father. A single lick of flame flickered on the stub of bone, flickered like a candle flame. It was as though she wasn't burning him at all.

She hurried around the bed, crouching between her mom and sister. One hand pressed to Sabra's chest, the stump to her mother's. She willed power into her limbs, casting a jolt of energy.

Both suddenly seized—backs and muscles rigid, jaws flexed. Then they sagged, moaned, and fell still.

The flame of her father's stump wavered but didn't flare.

The wall of fire in the doorway held, but the soldiers' voices were gone.

Again, she willed it—a jump of power. More.

Electricity crackled across her shoulders and down her arms. The point of her stump smoked, and her mother cried out. Sabra's eyes snapped open, staring down at the smoking handprint on her chest.

Nike could only gape, her mouth as open and useless as Sabra's had been moments before.

Her father wheezed. "We did it. We did it."

Another ram crashed against a door in the hallway. They were breaking into the lab.

"You burned my boobs," Sabra rasped, her voice raw and crusty from disuse. Then, "I have boobs?"

"Sabra?" Her dad's cry brimmed with joy. He rose to hug Nike, then clambered onto Sabra's bed, tears streaming down his cheeks. Nike caught it then—the sharpening of Sabra's eyes, the flattening of her lips as she tolerated her dad's arm around her neck.

"You did it, Nike! You did it!" he exclaimed, using the bed for support as he sidled to his wife's side.

There, his face collapsed.

"No …"

Nike's mother lay still. Gray.

"Do it again!" he ordered.

Nike knew he meant shock her. And she did. Once more, her mother's back arched, her muscles spasmed, but still, her chest remained flat and unmoving.

"Again."

She tried, but nothing.

"Again, *please.*"

Her mother seized, then stilled.

Again. Nothing.

There came more ramming.

"That's the lab," Nike said. "I don't think I can maintain two firewalls at the same time. We need to leave. Now."

"Analia! Wake up!" Her dad shook his wife, pressing his hand on her chest like he was still a Burner.

By the defeat on his face, Nike knew he didn't want to leave.

She called Joula. "Joula—where are you?"

"Finally! About time you checked in. I expected you hours ago. I'm presently tracking a big, mother-fucking, blue dot."

Joula's voice brought tears to Nike's eyes. "What?"

"Your meteor—it's on the move."

"Can you pick us up at the Healing Touch massage parlour?"

"Do I want to ask?"

Nike didn't have time for humour. "There's going to be a lot of heat."

"On my way."

"Bring some kind of climbing harness, something to strap someone to my back."

"I'm not leaving Analia," her dad said. "Leave me Tyler's sidearm. I'll cover."

"I can't get out of here without you," Nike replied. "How are we going to find that meteor and destroy it?"

He swallowed, shaking his head.

"She's gone," Nike told him. "Don't let her die for nothing. And don't you dare take us down with you."

"Daddy?"

He looked up. Sabra's fingers touched his shoulder and then recoiled as if she'd touched a hot pan. He threw himself over Analia, body chugging with anguish, his fingers threading through her hair.

Another crash. The soldiers were through.

Sabra shifted on the bed, trying to sit up. Nike was grateful for all the time their dad had spent on the ward, keeping her muscles toned, but there was no way she could bear her own weight after eight years in bed.

Trayling kissed his wife on the lips, hesitating as though deciding whether to crawl into bed with her and steal the last of her fleeting warmth.

"This isn't over, Dad. Not until that meteor is destroyed."

Nike ran to Tyler. A burn ravaged Tyler's face and arm, and Nike choked back rising nausea. "Tyler's dead."

She'd done this.

The guilt of Fumo's death. Of Tyler's. No matter the justifications, Nike would have to carry it just as her father had carried the guilt of infecting his daughters. These thoughts carved more space into her heart, cutting the distance between her and her father. Veins of power threaded through her hand, and her forearm throbbed with the effort. She took Tyler's gun. She knew the soldiers coming for them weren't evil, but she'd have to do what it took to escape, then find a way to live with the consequences.

At the door, face aglow with flames, her dad lit his still-whole hand.

The window between the gallery and the lab shattered.

"Down!" soldiers shouted.

Nike sent fire surging forward, forcing the soldiers to retreat. She spooled power until it swelled to a boulder in her palm. All the while, her father's bone smouldered on.

Nike stepped to where the soldiers could see her, lifting the ball of lightning high. "You shoot me—or any one of us—and I will drop this. All of us will die."

The firewall blocking the soldiers in the hall collapsed, leaving behind a charred arch.

On the other side, the soldiers looked past Nike to a soldier in the lab. The leader spoke into an earpiece.

"We have a bomb. Fall back. Clear the area and all unnecessary personnel. We have a bomb."

As half the soldiers withdrew, Nike addressed the leader. "We're going to move toward the exit, and you'll let us go—or I'll blow this place and everyone in it."

"Yeah, my sister's name is one letter away from 'Nuke,'" Sabra said. "What is in your hand?"

Hearing Sabra's voice, raspy from disuse, brought an unexpected smile to Nike's lips. Suddenly, she fought for more. She had a new member for the team.

The leader nodded, and the soldiers backed away from the blackened doorframe without lowering their weapons.

In Nike's palm, energy crackled and buzzed. She decreased her draw, worried she might lose control. Her father's shoulder flame burned red with heat, his hand smoking.

Sabra was too weak to walk, but she was also tiny and light. Between Nike and her father, they supported her.

They shuffled into the hall, soldiers trailing them. Boots crunched over fragments of door and shards of glass. Beyond the broken front door, the road was bordered by several black Suburbans but otherwise empty. Everyone looked to Nike for what to do next.

The boulder of power balanced in her palm rolled with her panic.

Once on the street, the soldiers would have a clear shot.

Nike focused her energy, sending a stream of fire to the ground before the soldiers. They edged back, shouting as the floor melted away, revealing gaps into the basement below. She didn't stop until it was a blazing pit. A wooden beam gave way, and a soldier dangled, gripped by the others.

"Go, go!" Nike cried, hoping the fiery gap would hold the soldiers.

They hobbled for the street, only stopping once out of sight.

"Sabra, in my pocket is a phone," Nike said.

"You have your own phone?"

"Get it, check the texts."

Sabra pulled out the phone, her arms trembling with the effort. "This is amazing. Dad, I want a phone."

"Not the time, big sister. Is there a message from Joula?"

"I can't get in."

"Hold it up to my face."

"It opens to your face!" Sabra was in, wide-eyed, catching up on nearly a decade of technology. "Oh! She says she's a block south. Can't get through. Bomb threat. Surprise for you."

Nike nodded. "Change of plan."

They shuffled over to her father's favourite skateboard shop. Nike didn't need to say anything more to her dad. A window broke, and two boards were slapped down.

"I kind of get the skateboarding thing," Nike said.

Her arms cramped from holding Sabra, light as she was. She'd need to piggyback her now. Nike had no choice—her dad barely looked able to balance himself. Even so, she used his shoulder for stability as she wobbled onto the board and burned his bone for strength.

Around the corner came men in black fatigues.

Nike willed a firebomb into her hand, lifting it as high as she dared.

"Follow us and this blows," she warned, knowing they wouldn't listen.

Her father sped away. Nike and Sabra shot after him. Boots slapped as the soldiers struggled to keep up.

One soldier yelled, "Out of my way!"

A third electric motor whirred before being overwhelmed by the rumbling of truck engines.

Their only chance was to shake their pursuers before reaching Joula. The combined weight of Nike and Sabra taxed the board's speed.

She didn't recognize the sound of gunfire until bullets chipped the sidewalk. The surprise nearly threw her off, and the energy she'd been holding rolled from her hand. She lunged for it, dodging a lamppost, before the sidewalk behind her erupted in chunks of concrete and dirt. A wave of heat shoved them forward.

The gunfire stopped.

"Shit," Sabra said. "You have to teach me that."

"How'd you get a mouth on you asleep?" Nike asked, laughing.

"Sister," Sabra whispered into Nike's ear. "I heard *everything*."

The response sent shudders through her.

They turned onto Adelaide. Her father had found Joula's van and was holding the sliding door open. Nike and Sabra tumbled inside in a tangle of limbs.

Joula wasted no time crossing the road, turning south, and disappearing from the soldiers' view.

"Well, hello there," Sabra said, pushing out her newly discovered chest.

Nike turned to see Sahle in the passenger seat.

"Surprise," Joula said.

"Sahle!" Nike cried, relief flooding her as she folded over him.

"Your sister?"

"Sabra, meet Sahle. My …"

"Boyfriend?" Sahle asked, a note of hope in his voice.

"Boyfriend," she confirmed, giving him a last squeeze.

Sabra's expression suggested disappointment.

"This what you wanted?" Sahle asked, holding out a climbing harness.

"It's for my dad."

"What? Why me?" Trayling asked.

"For when you pass out."

He seemed to understand. Their new understanding of one another didn't mean burning no longer carried a cost. The bone sticking out of his shoulder had shrunk further, eating into muscle and sinew. Smoke streamed from it. His eyes held back screams. Grimly, he began removing his shoe and sock. Nike knew what was coming—his foot would be next to burn.

"Is anyone going to explain anything to me?" Sabra wondered.

"What about your mom?" Sahle asked. Nike shook her head, and Sahle's face fell. "Sorry."

"Can I have one?" Sabra tugged at her dad's sleeve, eyeing the pills in his palm.

"Not candy," he replied.

"Your dad's popping ecstasy?" Sahle asked.

"Ecstasy sounds amazing," Sabra said.

Trayling added another syringe to the mix and injected himself. His lidded eyes flew open. "This doesn't last long."

Nike caught Joula grinning in the rearview mirror. "What are you smiling about?"

"This. This is the team."

Joula was right. Nike allowed herself a small smile in reply. She and her dad were going to be all right. She'd gotten her older sister back. She felt powerful.

On the dash, Joula's phone tracked something.

"Is that what I think it is?" Nike asked.

"My drone is tracking the meteor, and we're following the drone. It's half an hour out."

"Anybody following us?"

"Not that I can tell," Joula said, laughing. "You just escaped from a platoon of armored vehicles."

"On skateboards!" Sabra said.

"I'll never be embarrassed by you again," Nike told her dad.

"You were embarrassed by me?" he asked.

"You're a forty-five-year-old man who does magic tricks and rides a skateboard."

"Drone stopped moving," Joula said.

"Where is it?"

"C. L. Industries, looks like a rock quarry."

"Why would Santana go to a rock quarry?" Nike asked.

"Makes sense if you want to break a meteor into pieces," her dad replied.

"We'll never find all the fragments if they do that," Nike said. The nightmare would never end.

Joula hammered the accelerator, and the van roared forward.

Chapter Thirty-Three

The gate to the gravel pit was open, revealing a switchback road leading deeper into the quarry. At the bottom, a large hopper stood empty, awaiting stone to crush and drop onto a conveyor, which carried the debris to a pile capped by a white tarp. Nike could just make out two figures hauling something out of a Humvee parked in the machinery's shadow.

Pockmarks fractured the van windshield. A side window shattered.

It took Nike a second to realize what was happening. "Gunfire!"

"Shit, shit." Joula jerked the wheel, sending the van skidding to the edge of the road and out of sight of the shooter below. The van fishtailed before regaining traction. Sahle knocked out the side window's remaining glass with an ice scraper. Dust and heat rolled in. At the next turn, they'd be back in the shooter's line of sight.

"Dad," Nike said, holding up the harness she'd fashioned into backpack straps. Trayling looked tired and gray-skinned, almost as pale as her mother had been.

He followed orders, slipping the harness over his legs and tightening the straps at his waist and thighs.

"Let me carry him. I'll stay close," Sahle offered.

"Nope. My dad and I are a team," she replied. "You watch my sister."

Trayling handed Tyler's gun to Sahle. "You ever fire one, son?"

Son? Nike blinked.

"No, sir."

"Well, try not to hit the good guys." Trayling leaned over to flick off the safety.

They made the next turn, and the side of the van caught more bullets. Shot from below, the rounds pierced the roof. Joula accelerated, and everyone ducked. The van skidded on the loose gravel as they made the final turn, ending at the bottom of the pit.

"Put the engine block between us and the shooter," Trayling ordered.

Sabra had not taken her eyes off Nike's phone. "Can I try that?"

Nike ignored her.

"Santana's got the meteor out," Joula said.

The van slewed to a stop. Joula ducked beneath the steering wheel as the grill took the brunt of gunfire. A cloud of dust enveloped the van, filtering through the missing windows.

"Your turn, kid," Joula said.

Sahle lurched upward and fired the handgun. The gunfire paused. Nike yanked open the door, secured the straps around her shoulders, and pulled to a stand.

"Light up," she said. Her hand blazed. With a glance at her stump, she willed fire. "You okay?"

"Steady as she goes," Trayling wheezed at her back.

Nike balanced herself, the straps biting into her shoulders. Despite his injuries, Trayling managed to bear some of his own weight, hopping to keep up. His left foot burned along with his hand.

"Why is Dad's hand and foot on fire?" Sabra asked, her tone more curious than concerned.

"So your sister can go witch on that bitch," Joula called after them.

Another bullet kicked from Sahle's sidearm. "That's the last. Muzzle flashes are coming from behind the conveyor controls."

Nike whirled, hurling a softball-sized grenade to where Sahle indicated. Flames splashed over the controls, and someone screamed. A man ran ablaze before toppling and guttering on the ground. Nike's flame faltered. She'd killed another man.

"Santana," her father managed, his words garbled by pain and the leather bite guard.

Nike knew what he meant. Santana would be at the crusher beyond the Humvee. She took a step forward.

A fireball arced from the top of the gravel pile, hitting the ground at Nike's feet and spilling flames in all directions. Nike staggered through the blaze, legs searing. Behind her, Trayling moaned and chanted, "The Burner burns. The source giveth. The Burner burns …"

Halfway up the gravel pile, wearing a lacy dress, stood a small figure. In one hand was a burning skull, a fireball in the other.

"Fuoco," Nike said, understanding now. Her father's death must have accelerated Fuoco's switch from source to Burner. The skull completed the headless corpse in the lab.

"Fuoco, we can help each other," Nike called out.

The skull flared, and Nike dove aside as an explosion rocked the ground. A crater smoked where she'd stood moments before.

"I don't want to hurt you," Nike said. But in Fuoco's hand burned her father's head. Her eyes blazed with vengeance, unshakable and all too familiar.

Sahle rolled out from the van, sprinting to Nike and helping her upright. Then he ran for Fuoco. She turned her attention to him, collecting fury in her palm.

Nike didn't want to kill the girl, and Fuoco was too far for a direct hit. She focused her fireball into a smaller, denser marble and whipped it at the base of the gravel pile. The explosion sent up a plume of gravel the size of a truck bed. The side of the hill rushed to fill the void, churning the stone beneath Fuoco's feet, and she tumbled down, her fireball vanishing as the skull bounced away.

Sahle reached the base of the pile and started climbing.

"If Fuoco's here," Trayling warned, "others …"

Nike stepped around Santana's Humvee and spotted Chuck's unmistakable slick hair and Santana's dark figure, both just yards from the hopper. Raitgur, no taller than a foot, scrambled over the meteor, their acid whips leaving lesions on Santana's and Chuck's flesh.

"Stop!" Nike shouted. "Or fry."

From behind the conveyor, Chuck's little girl, Charlotte, emerged, fear in her eyes. A pinky flame flickered in the wind. Nike hesitated.

Santana turned to Nike, taking in the unspoken exchange between the girls.

"You going to burn a little girl?" Santana asked. At her chest smouldered a medallion.

"You're a Burner," Nike said, and then in rushed her nightmare. "You were there when I was infected. It was you."

Santana brushed back her hair, revealing an angry scar on her forehead. Nike recognized it—an acid burn.

"Meet my father," Santana said, her hand touching the medallion. Fire collected—not in her palm, but in her eyes.

"If that's all that's left of your daddy, then you must have hated the fuck out of him," Nike shot back.

Santana's smile disappeared. Lightning erupted from her eye sockets.

Nike half dove, half fell, her father breaking her fall and taking the brunt of their combined weight. Her stump jolted with electrical energy, sending waves of pain, leaving it numb.

"Didn't know we could do that," she said to the gravel.

"You know nothing," Santana replied.

Nike struggled to her feet. "One thing I don't understand. You can still be hurt by acid, so you can't be the one who kept the meteor. For that, you'd need someone immune … a source."

Ambrose stepped out of the Humvee behind Santana, wobbling on prosthetic legs.

Her dad's cry was of a different sort of pain. Nike thought it sounded like the crushing of his heart.

"I just wanted to be a part of it, Trayling. You, of all people, can understand that." His sleek, white carbon arm was capped with what looked like a cannon. Strapped to his back was a large pack, and, with the snap of a trigger, a flame ignited in the cannon's hollow. "And a chance to burn."

"I trusted you," Trayling said.

"This stuff costs a mint," Ambrose replied. "Sacrifices needed to be made."

"Why the Burner meeting?"

"Needed to see who the traitors were."

"Sylvain …"

"No longer a problem."

"And the boat?"

"Did that myself. Fire cleanses—you know that." He lifted the cannon.

Between the noise of the conveyor and the grating teeth of the crusher, Nike hadn't noticed the rumble of the van's engine. It smoked as it chugged around the Humvee. Ambrose turned just as fire exploded from the cannon tip. Joula's determined grimace disappeared when flames swept the hood. Still, the van bore down.

Ambrose tottered on his prosthetic legs but couldn't clear the van. Its grill slammed into him, sending his body flying. The engine popped, sputtered, and went still.

Santana screamed as lightning crackled over the van and through the windshield. Joula dove through her door, but Sabra was still inside, weak and helpless against Santana's power.

"Sabra!" Nike shouted. "Get out!"

She turned back to see Santana and Chuck rolling the meteor into the crusher. The teeth rumbled and screeched, shearing metal and stone into fragments.

"Now, Nike," her father said.

"Out of the way!" Nike yelled. But Charlotte stood her ground, inches from her father.

"He's made her bed," Nike's father added.

And that was the problem—too many adults making their children's beds for them.

Weirdly gleeful laughter trilled behind her. For a moment, Nike feared Ambrose had survived, but the sound was coming from the van.

Her father screamed. Nike felt the heat of his burning. "What's happening?" she shouted, glancing at her hand. But it wasn't her.

A bolt of fire sizzled over her shoulder, blistering the air as it passed. It struck Chuck in the chest, knocking him backward into the crusher. His daughter stumbled, teetering at the hopper's rim. Chuck clawed for her, his hands scrabbling for purchase, but Nike extended her fingers and sent a jet of fire that severed his reaching wrist just as his fingers caught Charlotte's hand.

"No!" Nike screamed.

Chuck fell back, screaming, his cries cut short by the rock crusher's teeth on his skull. Charlotte sagged over the hopper rim, staring at the grisly mess below.

Nike shrugged off the harness, dropping her father, and dove to grab Charlotte's ankle, pulling her back from the rim and into a hug. Chuck's severed hand dangled limply in the girl's grip.

Nike's dad's limbs flared again as he seized on the ground. Nike released Charlotte and checked her own hand again. She wasn't burning. And yet, her father was cooking.

"Nike!" Joula and Sahle screamed in unison.

Santana was half inside the Humvee, making her escape. Nike threw what little fire she had, but the armored car shrugged it off. Then it was too late. The engine roared, and the truck sped out of her range.

"No, no, no!" she screeched.

From the van came a guttural, devastating sound. Another firebolt shot through the shattered side window, streaking like an arrow to punch into the gravel pit's cliff.

Her father's breathing rasped, and understanding hit.

"Stop it, Sabra!" Nike shouted, scrambling toward the van and throwing open the door. Sabra's hand was aflame. "You're hurting Dad!"

"I'm hurting Dad," Sabra repeated, her eyes glowing with an echo of Santana's flames. "I heard what you said. I heard his confession. He put me in a coma for eight years. Eight years! You got to stay normal, have a phone, best friends. Me?"

Nike studied the fire in her sister's hand. "Put it out."

"Why?"

"Because …" Nike faltered. "Because he's our dad. He helped me grow up, fed and clothed me. I'm a better person because of him. I know that. Yes, he cost me a hand. Yes, he put you in a coma. These are terrible things, but they are complicated things. Dad doesn't have to die."

"All we need are his bones," Sabra replied with a weak shrug. "You've had your turn, sister. Now it's mine! And it feels amazing."

Sabra seemed to reach to her extended radiant palm and pull the fire back like a sizzling bowstring with her fingers. With it, she drew a scream from their father's lungs. She released—fire darted across the plateau. It angled up the switchback road to where the Humvee climbed. Fire smashed into the front tire of the truck, sending it spinning and rolling back into the pit, half-crushed and smoking.

Their dad's scream cut off.

Nike started toward Sahle, who bent over her father, but Joula grabbed her shoulder.

"Nike," Joula said, her voice soft but firm, somehow enough to hold her.

"He's all I had," Nike said, collapsing to her knees as tears splashed onto her thighs.

Her father's limbs smoked. Sahle checked his neck and shook his head. Gone.

"Now you have me," Sabra said.

Nike shrieked and lunged at her sister in the van, clubbing her with her fist. "You. Didn't. Have. To. Do. This!" Her blows weakened, and they both fell into sobbing.

Sahle approached, dropping a white tarp slung over his shoulder. It unfolded to reveal the crushed meteor, pieces ranging in size from a marble to mangled metal the size of her head.

Nike drew a ragged breath. Her sister had woken from an eight-year coma to face the man who had caused it. How would Nike have reacted? No, their father had this coming—but it didn't ease the hurt.

Burying her anger, she stood. "Sabra, help me. Help me finish this."

Sabra's red-rimmed eyes landed on the tarp. Sahle unfolded it further, revealing the shards of metal and stone frothing with tiny raitgur.

"They're beautiful," Sabra whispered.

"They killed Mom. They put you in a coma," Nike replied.

Sabra's face twisted, and together they hobbled closer. With a terrifying jerk of her hand, projectiles shot from her palm to strike the meteor fragments. The tarp ignited, and Nike added her own flame. Fire engulfed their father too, climbing his leg and arm, climbing toward his waist and chest. This would be his pyre.

Flame had burned so much of Nike, and now it hollowed her, cleaved from her anger and sorrow. Flames licked dozens of feet into the air, molten rock and metals pooling. Nike howled—not only for her father, but for her mother, for Fumo, Tyler, and for both her own and Sabra's stolen childhoods.

And then it was over.

Magma burbled where the meteor had been. Their father's flesh was gone, leaving only charred bones.

Chuck's little girl stood nearby, gripping Fuoco's fingertips in one hand and her father's severed hand by the thumb in the other. Fuoco held her father's skull like a bowling ball. Both girls stared at Nike and Sabra while Trayling's corpse smoked.

"Those kids are going to be messed up," Sabra said.

Her laughter echoed in the cavity of the quarry.

EPILOGUE

Nike tracked the raitgur—a big one. In the void left by Santana's demise, with no system of payment or quotas, it was up to Nike to find and destroy the remaining aliens in the city. Up to Nike and Sabra, that is—when Sabra decided to join in.

The chink of Sabra's cane on the pavement echoed in the graffitied alley. Every day she grew stronger. Every day she grew a little more annoying.

"Tonight, we've got a rare chance to see Nuke in action," Sabra said into her phone.

Nike glared at her sister, hating the nickname. "Turn that off."

"Nuke's a little shy about public displays of power."

"I'm shy about livestreaming and dragging your cult of followers into harm's way," Nike replied.

Sabra paused the stream. "I'm not here to clean up your and Dad's mess. I'm here because this is going to pay for a condo."

She pulled out a short black bar and attached it to a harness on her arm.

"Is that a selfie stick?" Nike asked.

Sabra answered by affixing the phone to the tip.

"If someone recognizes where we are, comes here, and gets sick, what then? What happens if people think they could be Burners and try to get sick on purpose?"

"Who am I to deny a dream?"

"That's not cool," Nike said, reminding herself that, though Sabra looked twenty, inside she was still twelve.

"Isn't that what hottie's for?" Sabra jerked her thumb at Sahle, who stood with his arms crossed behind them. "Keep the normies out of the way?"

"I'm right here, and my name is Sahle," he said.

"We'll come up with a better name," Sabra replied.

"Um, dudes?" Joula's voice came through their earpieces. "There's a warm body about a hundred feet ahead, tucked into an adjoining alley." Joula was overhead, scouting with her drone for potential victims and incoming people who might end up as collateral damage.

"Sahle," Nike ordered, extrapolating the raitgur's path as it climbed. "The target's headed right for him. I'll change its course—you pull the victim out of there."

Sahle nodded.

"Watch. This is savage," Sabra said, positioning her phone to get a full view of Nike's prosthesis.

With a flick of her mechanical finger, Nike ignited a flame. The prosthetic, crafted to incorporate half of her father's skull, lit from the inside out, flames licking out of the nasal cavity and eye sockets. Paint spatter covered the visible portion of the skullcap—residue from her work on the mural in this very alley.

The canvas was a gift her dad had given her. She'd arrived only to discover the huge swathe painted over by her father, who'd tagged it "For HT2B." Calming the graffiti community had been almost as complicated as explaining to Canadian intelligence how one of their soldiers had gone rogue. Just how rogue was still unclear—they had records of dozens of spines, not thousands.

In place of the gray canvas, Nike had painted herself standing strong, arms out, one foot braced, the skull ablaze on her prosthetic, and a fireball in her other hand. At her back, her sister wielded their father's humerus like a wand, the two of them facing a monster in the shadows. She'd finished it a week ago and was already wondering if it was a naïve dream. Sabra and Nike had clashed ever since.

"Ready, Dad?" she asked, ignoring her sister's antics with the thigh-bone wand.

Lighting up, she imagined him replying.

She willed a pebble of energy into her hand and flicked it near the wall, wincing as the blast took out some of the graffiti and brickwork. The burn forced the raitgur against the far wall, clearing a path. She nodded for Sahle to move. Within seconds, he was hustling a young man out of the alley and away from danger.

"Clear," Joula confirmed in her ear.

The raitgur rose, tentacles stretching to the roof, its gaping maw revealing a pulsing beak.

"Oh, I wish you all could see this nightmare," Sabra whispered to her followers.

Sabra's wand lit, flooding the alley with a white glare. Tendrils of light shot up her other arm as she pulled back like an archer.

"On three," Nike said. "One—"

Sabra released her bolt of energy before Nike could finish. It struck the raitgur, ricocheting it toward Sahle. Exactly what Nike had hoped to avoid.

The marble in her grip swelled to the size of a golf ball, and she pitched it. The concussive shock knocked Sahle back, and the alley fell into sizzling darkness.

"That's what I'm talking about!" Sabra whooped.

Nike stared into the cooling cavities of her father's skull. "Don't know how you did it, Dad." She brushed herself off. "Everyone okay?"

"All good," Sahle coughed, leaning against the wall he'd been thrown against.

Across the alley, Sabra played with fire, a flame dancing from fingertip to fingertip. With each movement of the flame, she sang a note, creating a melody that rang sweetly in the alley. But Nike recognized the death metal song, and its lyrics were anything but sweet. The light from Sabra's play made Nike's mural dance. The caption gleamed gold, her tag written in full: Her Turn 2 Burn.

Sabra showed it to her followers. "See that?" she shouted into her phone. "It's our turn, girlies. Our turn!"

"We're not done yet, Dad," Nike promised to the skull. "I'll finish this."

The glow in its sockets flickered. Out.

Acknowledgments

First, I need to thank Renaissance Press for bringing this book into the world. Marjolaine, Kiri, Jen, Nathan, Callia, Hannah, and Samira—thank you for your ushering, editing, cover, and patience. You are fire.

I'd also like to acknowledge the financial support of the City of Ottawa Cultural Funding Program, which awarded me a grant to continue writing this book. It was the kindling I needed.

Turn to Burn was a long time in coming. I started this project in 2020, originally conceiving it as a limited television series. At the time, my elder daughters were soon to be turning eighteen and, of course, there was the pandemic. Dark times.

I set out to write a father-daughter story in which the magic system acted as a metaphor for their relationship. As a father, I have hopes and dreams for my daughters, and I'm willing to be burned, used up, and emptied if that's what it takes for them to shine. But I also live vicariously through them—I draw something from their successes. So, who burns? When? How much? What do we do when mistakes are made? How can we reconcile?

All this to say: I need to thank my daughters—all four of them—in a very big way, for sharing their experiences as young women, and for the real privilege of being their dad. Love you.

Then there's the early shaping and moulding of this book. To Andrea (my heart), my daughters (again), Catherine Michele Adams, and Joshua Johnson—thank you for all your notes, guidance, encouragement, and time. Sunnyside Writers Group helped with pieces of this—thank you.

And finally, to Bill, for the use of more than just your name. I feel you here, buddy. Still burning.

About the Author

Michael F. Stewart has authored over two dozen books for kids and young adults. From interactive digital epics and graphic novels to humorous middle grade and surreal young adult novels, Michael enjoys stretching the limits on his storytelling and working with other authors young and old to tell their stories. He has an mfa from the Vermont College of Fine Arts and lives in Ottawa with his partner, four daughters, a cat, and a dog.

About Renaissance

Renaissance was founded in May 2013 by a group of authors and designers who wanted to publish and market those stories which don't always fit neatly in a genre, or a niche, or a demographic. Like the happy panbibliophiles we are, we opened our submissions, with no other guideline than finding a Canadian book we would fall in love with.

Today, this is still very true; however, we've also noticed an interesting trend in what we like to publish. It turns out that we are naturally drawn to the voices of those who are members of a marginalized group, and these are the voices we want to continue to uplift.

At Renaissance, we do things differently. We are passionate about books, and we care as much about our authors enjoying the publishing process as we do about our readers enjoying a great Canadian read on the platform they prefer.

pressesrenaissancepress.ca

pressesrenaissancepress@gmail.com

PART TIME GIRL

How much longer can Michael hide his sex-switches?

After making it through the second year of high-school, he knows it's only a matter of time until someone notices and freaks out. Then his family will have to run and lose everything, again, or risk being found by the shadowy group that hunts people like him.

He should go, just vanish and stop putting his family at risk, but his oldest friend Angela is in trouble and he can't leave until they figure out why her troubles with catatonia and hallucinations have reappeared.

To help her, Michael has to trust in Ian—the hottest, richest guy in school who definitely has a hidden agenda—and a mystery woman with a traumatic past who is the only one to know him as a girl.

With people to protect and mysteries to unravel, Michael will need to unlock the full truth behind his identity…something he's been running from his entire life.

A wedding and a summer camp that Tommy and Carter are never going to forget.

Tommy discovers magic exists, his boyfriend is a rock giant, and his sister is marrying one of the leaders of a supernatural community called Aetherborn.

Carter learns to navigate an in-person relationship, introducing Tommy to the magical world, and being involved in his Ariki's wedding.

Both boys need to build their confidence in each other, themselves, and their relationship. The Door Tech summer camp seems to be the perfect way to do that, until they get magically transported to the not-so-fictional world of Everdome. In this realm of Domed continents floating in space, winged beasts, and new cultures, the boys will have to overcome challenges beyond anything they've seen before.

The only way they, and their relationship, can survive is if they start Winging It!

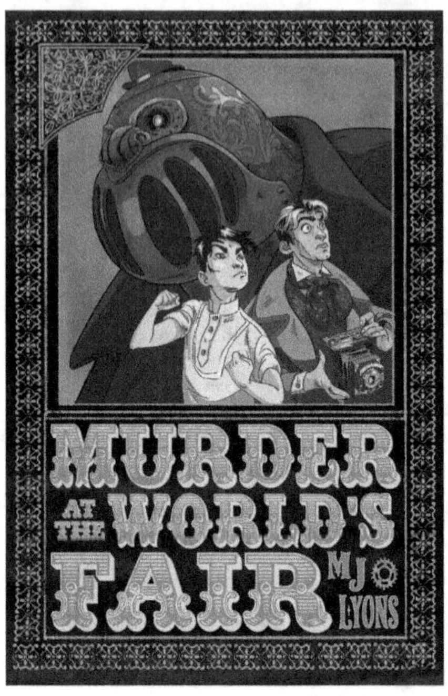

The year is 1893, and airships cloud the skies over the bustling metropolis of Toronto. The city is set to host the world's fair thanks in no small part to the work of two fantastical inventors. The New World Exhibition is to be a celebration of cultural and technological marvels; roving automatons, clockwork contraptions, the world's biggest steam-powered paddle boat, all to be fully lit by the wonder of electricity!

On the day of the grand opening, young Norwood Quigley, aspiring journalist, photographer and scion of a world-famous airship magnate, stumbles onto the scene of a murder; the victim: a Prussian Ambassador; the perpetrator: a Chinese assassin, or so the powers-that-be say. In truth, the suspect is Jing, a roguish but amiable youthful delinquent.

Concerned by Jing's claim of innocence and his assumed guilt by higher powers, including the British Empire's military, Norwood is thrown into a grand intrigue that hinges on Toronto's world fair. As chaos consumes the celebrations, he fears that his influential family is being manipulated in a plot to create an international incident that will lead to a war that spans the world.

Penner had always considered his life ordinary-but when his lover Chess receives a divine revelation that can't be explained, he finds himself on the run from mysterious forces. Upending their idyllic life in a small town, Chess propels them on a journey to find answers to deep questions that plague his thoughts and his sanity.

Partnering with Fred, a boisterous sky pirate with an enigmatic past, they head out to find the answers they need on her airship. But the closer they get to their mysterious destination, the more danger they find themselves in. Facing betrayals, battles and a malevolent being that seems to be hunting them, soon they find themselves deep into conspiracies that threaten the very fabric of their reality. With their wits, their ship and a spot of tea, their quest for answers will make them confront the forces that created the universe. With only each other, will their love be enough to save them?

Mighty: An Anthology of Disabled Superheroes

With great powerchair comes great responsibility...
It's a bird, it's a plane, it's... accessibility!
You wouldn't like me when I'm out of spoons...

All too often, superhero media depicts disability as something to overcome on the journey to becoming a hero, or as a sign of villainy. It's time to make heroism accessible for everyone.

In these 15 stories, you'll meet winged wheelchair users, supernatural spoonies, guardians with glaucoma, and many more. These disabled superheroes fight villains as well as outdated ableist stereotypes, and show that anyone can be Mighty.